J'ADOUBE

Andy Graham

MINERVA PRESS
LONDON
MIAMI   RIO DE JANEIRO   DELHI

First Published 2001 by
MINERVA PRESS
315–317 Regent Street
London W1R 7YB

Printed in Great Britain for Minerva Press

J'ADOUBE

To Cecilia

Acknowledgements

Rarely is anything done without the help or inspirational ideas of others, especially friends.

Thanks to everyone I know (and knew) in Bournemouth and Poole and in Italy, without whom this book would not exist.

My warmest enthusiasm to Paul (with respect) O'Brien for his spell-check and enthusiasm.

And, finally, to Gary Kasparov, with awesome appreciation for his heroic representation of mankind against machine.

Author's Note

In the chess world, *J'adoube* is the official phrase a player should use if he wants to make a minor adjustment to a piece on its square during a tournament game.

As private parts to the gods are we, they play with us for their sport.

Blackadder II, Episode 6 (Lord Melchett's dungeon speech)

The Whole Damn Dynasty 1485–1917, Michael Joseph, 1998
Copyright © Richard Curtis and Ben Elton, 1985

Prologue

'Your move!'

Demonic eyes rolled in an expression of pure exasperation at the snoring, blubbery mass slumped in its chair opposite him. Upon the table sat an ornate chessboard with hand-carved pieces. It was obvious from their positions that the game had not progressed much; in fact, the creature's adversary had evidently nodded off very soon after the first two opening moves. Peevishly, Prince Belfagor kicked out at his dozing opponent's chair from under the huge stone table which separated them, and, despite his fat companion's obvious weightiness, its force was sufficient to topple him backwards, waking him rudely as his head hit the cold stone floor of the otherwise luxuriously furnished castle.

'Whaa...?' wheezed Morpheus as he sat upright, nursing the back of his head, which had already begun to throb a little.

'C'mon!' snorted his assailant, 'It's not on, you know. I mean, you invite me here for, and I quote, "An evening of intellectual stimulus, a chance to wile away some otherwise long, interminable, eternal moments in the company of an old comrade in arms," and all you do is fall asleep on me.'

Morpheus yawned, rubbed his baggy eyes with a pair of chubby hands, climbed to his feet with some obvious effort and, sighing heavily, picked up his chair, repositioned it, and plonked himself down once more at the table, obviously fatigued from all the sudden and unwarranted exertion.

'After all, Murphy, old boy,' continued his opponent, flicking his tail at an insistent mosquito, 'it's not as if all this "beauty sleep" seems to be having any beneficial effect on you.'

'I know, I know,' sighed Morpheus again resignedly, not in the least affected by his friend's taunting attack on his appearance – after a certain number of centuries one learns to accept the defects and realities of one's physical aspect. 'It's just that of late I've been feeling so lethargic.' He stopped talking and leant forward in a mighty attempt to concentrate on the game.

'Do you think I'm getting old?' he asked after a full two seconds of intense concentration.

'Well, if we are talking in years, I'm afraid the answer has got to be a definite yes. But we're immortals, remember. If you ask me, it's just that your work has made you somewhat apathetic and you've let yourself go a bit in recent centuries.'

'You're probably right, Belfagor, old man. Guess it just goes with the job though – being god of sleep and dreams and all that stuff. I mean, it's not that I exactly dislike my work or anything…'

'That's apparent enough,' retorted his friend somewhat dryly.

'But perhaps I should follow your example, get out and about a little more.' Although even the thought of physical activity left him feeling exhausted and, it had to be said, just a little nauseous, its benefits were obvious. Morpheus cast an envying eye over his friend's fine form and chiselled features. 'I bet there's still not a woman around that's capable of resisting your Latin charms.'

Belfagor rose from his seat, evidently pleased by the compliment he had just received. 'Well, goes with the job, old boy,' he said, quoting the other. 'Can't be a god of mischief, wine and seduction without looking the part.' He drained his goblet of its contents and slammed it vigorously down on the table. 'More wine!' he shouted heartily.

But nobody came.

'More wine!' he repeated.

And still nobody came.

Belfagor swished his tail in irritation and glanced about him. All around the huge banqueting hall nothing stirred. A telltale snoring was coming from over the other side where the servants' quarters were. By the great doors, on the other side, two guards snoozed peacefully in exactly the same positions as when he had first let himself in about an hour or so before.

'The service here stinks,' he announced and, swishing his tail around some more, added, 'and these rotten little bloodsucking mosquitoes are driving me crazy. Why on earth did you agree to buy a castle so completely surrounded by marshlands, Murphy?'

Alas, however, his grievances had once more fallen upon deaf ears. Morpheus, bishop still in hand, had managed to doze off again halfway through his move.

Might not be such a bad idea, after all, Belfagor thought, yawning and feeling the strain of being the only one in the castle who was making an effort to move. He glanced at his wristwatch (even a god has to keep track of time one way or another in this day and age), and what he saw next brought him back from the land of nod with a start. His watch distinctly read Saturday, but he was sure he'd arrived on Wednesday.

'By... err... all the... err... heavens!' – a deity should always be extremely careful about who he swears by – he'd been there for just over three months.

Well, that clinched it. Wrenching himself free of the seductive embrace of the high-backed, leather armchair where he'd apparently just spent the last ninety days or so in somnolent oblivion, he clicked his fingers and rapidly transformed what had been loose and extremely comfortable house garments into a chic, but casual, beige Armani suit. The devilish appearance of a moment before took on the much more human aspect of a man in his middle or late thirties at the peak of his physical powers. He brushed the lapels of his jacket down briefly, straightened his tie and ran his fingers through his slick, dark hair.

'I'm out of here,' he declared to no one in particular. 'It's time to stir things up again and try my hand at a serious game once more.' Then, leaning over the chessboard, he adjusted some of the pieces, leaving his opponent to wake up – if he ever did again – to a checkmated position.

'*J'adoube!*' he added brightly, and turned towards the great hall doors.

It would, of course, have been totally contrary to his nature if he had been able to resist a kick at one of the sleeping guards as he was leaving.

'Ah, bugger off and leave us alone, will ya!' grumbled the disgruntled guard in a distinct Yorkshire accent and, rolling on to his other side, instantly drifted off again.

'Humph!' snorted Belfagor contemptuously, not just a little disappointed at the lack of response he'd been able to provoke.

Then, stopping only to take another swipe at a particularly persistent and suicidally hungry mosquito, he left the castle walls and promptly buggered off.

Chapter One

KILL! KILL!
   WACK! WACK!

Missed again. This one was really swift. He hated the little bloodsuckers. It is only the female mosquito that bites, and Massimo Cugini – Max to his friends – despised the bitches and revelled in their termination.

The flat, marshy lands of the Emilia-Romagna region where he lived were a perfect breeding ground for them. In the early thirties, Mussolini publicly declared war on them (a decision that was indubitably a lot more popular with the people than a certain other decision he was to take a short time later) and had many of the marshlands drained, wiping out malaria in the country once and for all. Sadly, however, for both the Italian populous and tourists alike, the little devils proved themselves a lot hardier than expected and, although the malaria mosquito was successfully dealt with, a surprisingly large number of different varieties survived. It happened to be a rather nasty version, the tiger mosquito, that Max found himself stalking, rolled newspaper in hand, around his room that particular evening.

Splat!

As satisfying as the successful conclusion to his hunt was, he knew that the numerous red marks over his bedroom and living room walls would have to be accounted for, by way of whitewash, later in the year.

For the information of the inexperienced northern hemisphere dweller, the traditional 'splat' technique (which Max had honed, over his thirty-one years of experience, to a fine art) is not the only effective measure you can take against the beastie. Other methods include a tablet that, when burned, is as deadly as mustard gas to the little critters, paralysing and finally poisoning. The time-honoured and rather romantic net over the bed is another way – great until one gets trapped inside – and then, there's a rub- or spray-on liquid, repulsive to the sensitive sniffer of the female insect, but if you get it on your fingers it can absolutely ruin the taste of your pizza.

The problem with the mosquito is not just that it can spread disease and leave a nasty itchy lump on your skin for days afterwards, but also (and behavioural psychologists, please note) the noise the insect makes when she swoops in for the attack. It's all part of Pavlov's 'Stimulus–Response' conditioning theory (he's the guy who used to make dogs dribble by ringing a bell, and pass electric current through Easter bunnies to demonstrate that, after a short while, their eyes would begin to glow and they didn't like it much).

Neeeoww.

Slap!

Hear the noise and involuntarily slap an exposed part of your own body. Nine times out of ten you miss the pest, leaving only a self-inflicted, smarting mark in addition to the multitude of red itchy bites already there. This conditioned response is particularly painful in bed at night when you wake yourself up with a clout around the ear (being often the most exposed and vulnerable part of your body) and then, as a consequence, lie awake, unable to sleep, on guard for the next inevitable attack, thus greeting the new day with bruises and bites, and bags under your eyes.

Still, in spite of man's ingenuity and impressive technological progress in this area, the most practised method seems to be among the most antique and effective. When woken by the infernal buzzing and your own inevitable buffeting around the ear, get up, go to the bathroom, and spend sufficient time there to allow it to banquet to its full on your partner. Ah, the wisdom of the ancients! Effective, however, only if you are lucky enough to have a partner.

Max, although still officially a bachelor, was expecting his better half that evening. They'd been engaged for over three years now, which was more or less the same amount of time he'd been living in Piacenza since his job transfer from Turin. He remembered the morning he'd first entered her family's snack bar in the centre of town to drink a cappuccino before starting work, and had decided to return that evening...

It was August, and Maria's parents had gone away to the mountains for the traditional Italian holiday of 'Ferragosto', leaving her in charge of the bar and allowing her to stay nights in his apartment, no questions asked. She usually closed the bar up around half past nine, which meant she'd be around before ten.

Everything was ready: sparkling, Trebbianino white wine on the table, pasta measured out and awaiting the pot, the pesto sauce prepared. Like a lot of Italians, he was particularly proud of the culinary skills his mother had taught him and enjoyed the opportunity of putting them into practice. When he dined alone, however, he never bothered to cook anything special and usually just ate in the canteen at work.

He finished watching the evening news on TV and then went out to the balcony to smell the night. It was typically hot and humid for that time of year. In fact, most people found the humidity of the inland cities during August unbearable, which explained the en-masse migration to the mountains or sea.

Both he and Maria, on the other hand, liked the city during this period. It was so deserted and quiet compared to all the other months of the year. He gazed at the buildings before him. The view of the city from his third-floor studio flat was somewhat restricted by the tall, red and white, pyjama-striped factory stacks which during the day filled the sky with artificial cloud, and at night cheerfully flashed and winked their neons at him.

Neeoww.

Slap!

Max's thigh glowed red in the darkness while his thoughts drifted off to the oncoming chess tournament at Salsomaggiore the following weekend, as they had done at least twenty times that day and, for that matter, every day since he'd first started preparing for and worrying about it.

He wasn't the best player in the world, he knew that, but he wasn't the worst either – when prepared. That was one of the advantages of being a programmer for a big computer company. There was always time for a quick game on one of the better chess programs at opportune moments throughout the day. It was surprising the amount of preparation you could get in on a normal working day, and, if the boss passed by, a quick flick of the mouse discreetly hid everything. Well, who knows, maybe this time round he'd even finally get to move up from the category of 'candidate master' to the hallowed status of 'master' itself.

Fat chance.

He'd probably have one of his classic brain blasters, find himself in a winning position, and then go doolally and place his queen directly in the path of a hungry enemy rook or bishop. The only thing that had prevented him from losing horrendously in a previous tournament had been an equally confused opponent. After concentrating on a particularly vital move for over a quarter of an hour, Max had reached over and taken his own queen off the board with his opponent's king. Not to be outdone by such cunning tactics, his Spanish adversary had, displaying an equally bewildering and formidable spirit of initiative, mated his own king with Max's rook. 'Hasta la vista, baby!' or so they say.

Rapid flicks across the sky brought his thoughts back to the present. Small furry bats squeaked and dodged at breakneck speed around the buildings, enjoying the abundant nocturnal feast of mosquitoes. He considered them wonderful little creatures and wholeheartedly applauded their choice of nutrition.

Inexplicably, he was filled with a peculiarly paranoid sensation of being watched. He'd been feeling a little out of sorts recently due to a lot of wacky, but disturbingly realistic, flying dreams every time he'd put his head down. And he could remember them all so clearly the next morning – well, enough to be able to describe in detail the places he'd been to and the people he'd seen. Maria said that he was probably 'astral travelling', but then she had been brought up by hippy parents and these concepts were easier for her to accept.

He looked around him. Nothing seemed out of place. Most of his neighbours were away on holiday, their houses all closed up for the month. Only he and Mr Tagliaferri were left in his block, and he was probably with his friends at some bar right now knocking back the grappa and playing briscola.

No, there was something else that he couldn't quite put his finger on.

He looked down at himself, framed and unmoving in the soft electric glow of the balcony light. And it was then that he realised what was amiss. He was looking down at his own body! He was watching himself! He was his own voyeur! Not only that, but he was, in fact, commanding quite a spectacular aerial view of the whole apartment block. Somehow he had become suspended in mid-air and his body was down there below him.

So, after a brief but fully understandable sense of totally mystified helplessness had passed him by, Max indulged himself in the luxury of some screamingly serious panic.

Chapter Two

'C'mon, man, get your arse in gear and skin up, will ya?'

'Hey, Chris! Yow, hippy! Wake up!'

'Yeah, man? What's wrong, guys?'

'Roll us a spliff, man!'

'Oh yeah, sorry, man. I just drifted off there for a minute – forgot the job at hand, you know.'

Chris sat himself up straight and crossed his blue jeans, reached over and opened the magic tobacco tin. With an upward flick of his head he casually tossed the dangling, shoulder-length, blonde hair from his eyes and commenced solemnly with what had, by now, become almost a religious experience: the creation and crafting of the perfect joint.

'I've been having these wild dreams lately, guys,' he began, carefully placing the tobacco from a freshly gutted cigarette down the middle of a crisp, white rolling paper, 'about this beautiful chick…'

'Wahey!' chorused the other three T-shirts who were sprawled untidily over a surprisingly large and varied area of Chris's bedroom.

Chris Hasi had been on and off the dole now for nearly ten years. Sure, he helped out in his father's Burgy Bar every now and again when he needed the dosh, but it didn't figure big in his plans. No, in fact, the grandeur of a dream could be ruined quite easily when forced to continually ask: 'Is that with or without cheese?'; 'No onions?'; 'Help yourself to the sauce'; and then watch some spotty kid hover indecisively between the brown and red plastic squeezy bottles, finally to decide upon the one with the least suspicious-looking sauce remnants around its edge. Anyway, he'd concluded, working with all that dead meat had to be bad for your karma.

'Hey, man, you're hoggin' the joint, pass it over here.'

He had dreams and visions like everyone else, only his were a lot less ambitious than most, and therefore much easier to make good, he soundly reasoned. The big dream, the one he'd been nursing along with his mates for a few years now, was to somehow earn a modest but sufficient amount – enough to buy a small piece of land, maybe in India, and farm their beloved marijuana there, living off the interest of the rest of the money placed in a high interest account. Everybody knew that the cost of living in India was extremely low, and with only £500 you could live reasonably well for a year.

Once, he and two other friends had got it together enough to go there and 'check out the scene'. Unfortunately, they'd had to return within a week due to all three contracting rather severe cases of 'Gandhi's revenge'.

'Well,' Chris had said optimistically, as the intrepid trio were on the Air India flight back home. 'Next time we'll just eat tinned food until our stomachs are used to it,' and had then proceeded once again to rush off to the back of the plane in a very agitated manner.

Much to Ira Hasi's despair, his thirty-two year old son was more than just a disappointment; he was a university dropout, a dope-head, and now the latest was that he'd turned vegetarian. Having escaped from Persia just before the fall of the Shah, the British government had accepted him, his family and cousins with open arms (due mostly to the long friendly numbers that lived in their bank accounts – he knew that) and red tape reduced to a minimum. It hadn't even been a problem to get the money out of the country – a trickle here, a trickle there – they'd known of something in the pipeline for a few years and had had ample time in which to prepare; after all, he had been under-secretary to the Shah himself. When they'd arrived in Britain, he'd bought a house in a nice suburban area between Bournemouth and Poole, and had established a thriving little burger chain.

That had been a cinch, as they said in this country. But had he known the effect this permissive western lifestyle would have had on his family, he would never have left. His beautiful, blonde, half-Swiss, half-Persian wife, the woman who had made him the envy of all his friends in the old country, now spent most of her time sipping exotic cocktails at her bridge club or simply watching television. She didn't seem to have time for him any more.

But what caused him the most pain were his children. They wouldn't leave home. His lovely daughter, Sharlì, backed up by his wife, had recently refused to marry her third cousin and pre-chosen husband, Mustafer, saying that she didn't even know him; this had caused no small rift between the families. And Chris, well... Ira sighed softly to himself.

Ah, how he missed the old country! Perhaps the Ayatollah had been right, perhaps it was time to return to the old values before they were lost for ever.

He chopped some extra onions and warmed a few buns. Some more customers were about to enter, but then they changed their minds. Maybe they'd seen the sauce bottles. Maybe he should have opened a kebab house like his cousins had advised. He was tired and not just a little fed up. Perhaps it would be a good idea to close up and go home. The burgers, still sizzling on the stove, would do for a family snack later that evening.

What Ira Hasi could not have known, however, was that his decision to close early that day would, as a consequence, inadvertently land his wayward son in much warmer climes, where he would dine on curry at the table of a goddess.

Ah, yes, the ceaseless wonder of cause and effect.

Chapter Three

Sir Giles Winston OBE snorted angrily across his great oak desk at the little weasel of a man who was facing him. He could certainly not be classed as a happy MP right at this moment. Ever since he'd accepted the position as Minister for Food and Hygiene, he'd had nothing but niggling worries. Hippy housewife groups opposing food-preserving irradiation techniques, coming to terms with the damnably awkward EEC food regulations, the Farmers' Union putting on economic pressure to ensure the sale of livestock abroad and animal protection groups protesting over the shipment conditions, and, of course, that mother of all mothers, mad cow disease. How he missed his old position as Minister of Roads and Transport – all he'd ever had to do there was cut public transport funding on an annual basis and attend dinner functions.

'Well, just how much of this bloody contaminated meat has leaked out on the market?' he blasted.

'Not much, Sir Giles. Most of it was stopped at the processing plant as soon as they discovered it.' Nigel Wilcox couldn't quite meet Sir Giles's penetrating glare and continued, instead, to stare at the red report file in his hand. 'But it's always possible that some boxes have managed to slip through, despite all the measures taken.'

'Boxes? Boxes of what?'

'Frozen beefburgers.'

Sir Giles gave a little inward sigh – he and his family never ate the junk.

'Mad cow?'

'No, Sir Giles. Salmonella.'

'Oh, thank God!' He sighed and relaxed back in his seat. Then suddenly, a new and horrifying thought occurred to him. 'Abroad?' he choked.

'No, Sir Giles. Of that we're pretty sure. The only deliveries made from the factory in question at that time were in the south of England.'

'Oh, thank heavens!' At least there'd be no chance of another hotheaded, European boycott of good British beef.

'Well,' he said, much relieved, 'the answer is simply to remove the product from shop shelves.'

'Already done. But some stores had already reported sales, not many, and it's far too early to know if those sold were infected or not.'

Sir Giles chewed thoughtfully a while on one or two overhanging whiskers of his otherwise impeccably kept moustache before asking as to the possible effects of the infected meat if consumed. Nigel Wilcox stared even more intensely down at the closed file he was holding, and wondered briefly what the hell a man with a degree in Ancient Greek and Latin was doing as the head of food and hygiene anyway.

'Like I just said, Sir Giles,' he began, trying not to sound in any way patronising, 'it's a strain of salmonella and dangerous only to the very young or the very old (and careless politicians, he thought to himself) if not cured immediately.'

'I see.'

'Should the public be alerted?'

Sir Giles chewed a little more. 'And is there a reason why they shouldn't be?'

'Well, going public means a huge loss of revenue for the company in question. Not to mention, of course, all the inevitable bad publicity that hangs around long after the scare is over, the possibilities of another cattle feed investigation, and the consequent increase in support for those hippy animal rights supporters and vegetarian groups.'

'So? At least we're covered and in the clear – always best to keep your nose clean when possible,' said Sir Giles, tapping the side of his rather red one. 'We'll come out of it smelling of roses, public heroes, so to speak.'

'Yes, sir, but then there's always the little matter of who owns the company in question.'

Sir Giles looked over at Wilcox and frowned. The other handed the file over and, with an index finger, silently pointed upwards at the floor above them. Sir Giles read the name on the file. It was part of a chain owned by... He swallowed hard.

'After all, it's not certain that any of this meat sold is contaminated.' He sounded more than convinced. 'No, under the circumstances I think the best thing we can do is wait. I mean, it's not as if we're talking about a risk of mass infection here. At the worst, just a few isolated cases on which we can screw the lid down tight.'

Chapter Four

Sat with a glass of wine in his hand and a belly full of pasta, Max began to doubt if what he had just told Maria had really happened at all.

'Well, it sounds to me like, either you've just had one of those "out-of-body experiences",' Maria reasoned, 'or it's possible that you just dreamt it. We've both been extremely busy at work recently. Maybe you're just tired, that's all.'

'In that case I've just had one of the most realistic and disturbing nightmares of my life,' he mumbled while draining the contents of his glass. 'But perhaps you're right, and it's just fatigue and a little too much of this humidity.'

Maria got up, walked over to the table where they had just finished dining, took the bottle of mineral water and returned to her place next to Max on the sofa, tucking her smooth, tanned legs under her as she sat. Like many women of her race she was petite and endowed with that particular Latin beauty – full red lips, and cat's eyes framed by long, dark curly hair. She held up the glass of water that she had just poured herself and pouted playfully at his distorted image through it.

'You know, we haven't really seen that much of each other in this last month or so. It's my fault mostly, having to work the bar seven days a week. We've only been able to see each other for a few hours in the evening before…'

'Before you doze off on me,' continued Max, a little sulkily.

She placed her arms around his neck, pulled herself over so that she was sitting on top of him, and then slipped her hand up inside his blue T-shirt.

'Tonight, however, I'm not going to let you pass the time in philosophical contemplation, zombied out in front of the TV,' she joked, and then added, 'or on your chess. A girl could get jealous of all those queens you play with.'

Casually tossing her hair from her shoulders, she began to

unbutton her blouse, and Max soon found himself distracted from the disconcerting event of earlier that evening.

Chapter Five

A door creaked slowly open, insufficiently illuminating the long, dark hall in eerie, red light, and a thick cloud of smoke gushed forth, writhing and twisting in an orgy of newfound liberation. From out of the dimly lit room a shadowy, slouched figure shuffled; a pair of bloodshot eyes and goaty beard peered out into the darkness through long strands of unkempt hair. It stopped suddenly and began gently, searchingly, patting the sides of the wall. After about a minute of devoted exploration it stopped.

'Oh, far out! I've found the light switch, guys, it's munchies time!'

Three other T-shirts appeared, blinking in the bright hall light – all with one insatiable desire, one single unified purpose, and in agitated silence they headed for the only room in the house equipped for it.

'Where're the fuckin' chocolate chip cookies kept, man?'

'Fuck the chocolate chips, we're talkin' serious munchies here.'

Like a crack Japanese car manufacturing team they went into action; bread, frying pan, butter and...

'Oh wow, beefies, man! The old man must have brought 'em back from the shop... and cheese slices too!'

'Excellent!'

'Hey, Chris, I thought you were a veggie-man,' came a voice from inside the fridge.

'Nawww,' responded a Geordie accent from deep within the recesses of a kitchen cupboard, 'that's just what he tells his folks, man, so he don't have ta work in his dad's shop. Bet it pisses him right off like, eh Chris?'

'Yeah,' Chris grinned back in return. 'Hey, check out the top shelf of the fridge, there should be a few tins of beer there.'

Chapter Six

The next day at MEGA Industries everything was the same as ever, and the unusual event of the night before seemed merely a distant dream. Max, rather disinterestedly, finished loading in the last of the backlog which had somehow managed to accumulate on his desk over the last few days, leant back in his impossible-to-get-completely-relaxed-in office chair (rumour had it that they had been specially studied not to be too comfortable – the company didn't want their staff falling asleep, did they?) and considered the possibilities of a quick game before getting to grips with some of the stuff that had arrived that morning. Glancing furtively around the office floor he assured himself of an 'all-clear' and loaded his chess program.

He was a mere fifteen moves into an extremely pretty and involving 'Leningrad-Dutch' defence when it happened again. It was almost unconsciously that he found himself comparing the open-plan office layout to the inside of a computer. Alberto Tangenti's office situated in the middle was the Central Programming Unit. He'd never realised before just how similar the set-up was. This particular CPU, however, needed a good virus check run on it. It was common office opinion that the frequent commands issued forth from its plexiglass, soundproofed isolation were frequently incompatible with the receiving units.

Then, and with no small helping of bewilderment, it dawned on him that his unusual panorama was once again due to the fact that he was hovering – at least, that was what he thought it was – in the air, just a few centimetres from the ceiling.

This time, though, he didn't panic. No, actually, now that he thought about it, the sensation of being suspended effortlessly and weightlessly in the air was rather pleasant, kind of like floating in the Mediterranean on a hot summer's day, but without the waves. He looked down at his colleagues, wondering for an instant if anyone was watching him, but he knew that that was pure folly.

How could they see him? His body was still down there sitting and staring at the computer – albeit rather blankly – but then there was nothing new in that either.

No, nobody was showing the least bit of interest in his newly attained ability to defy the laws of gravity. Robert Caiali was busy with his novel as usual, and Carolina Boldero was struggling over a crossword in one of the national newspapers. The new head of research, the blonde and very attractive Cathy McDonald, came out of Tangenti's CPU clutching a wad of printouts and bustled by unseeingly below him. He was having a real honest-to-goodness 'out-of-body experience', as Maria had put it. Sure, he'd read about these things, but he'd never thought it might one day happen to him, let alone twice in less than twelve hours.

Quite naturally, he discovered he could move about in any direction just by desiring to go there. He floated over to Caiali and read a few lines of his novel – seemed to be a detective story of sorts – and then hovered in front of Tangenti's office, where he was busy signing papers, made a childishly rude gesture and felt instantly ashamed of himself.

He decided to try something else and, reaching up to the ceiling just above his head, he gingerly pushed his hand through it. He felt nothing. He could pass through solid matter. Feeling a little bolder, Max decided to go all the way and allowed himself to rise up through to the next floor above him.

Although he still felt nothing, the sensation of having and seeing a whole floor pass through your head and body is, to say the least, a slightly disconcerting experience. It was all happening in slow motion. He couldn't take his eyes off the solid floor that appeared to be lowering itself down through him, a bit like an escalator – first stop, Max's neck, second stop, the chest and stomach department, third stop... Max decided to check out where he was arriving.

To his bewilderment, he couldn't see anything at all. Total blackness. Strange. His first thought was that perhaps there had been a power cut, but then a crack of light appeared unexpectedly in the darkness, revealing both a gross geographical error on Max's part and something else that had never been destined for his own private viewing. He moved quickly out from under the skirt of Andersson's personal secretary, Miss Lee.

'Sorry,' he blurted out and then grinned broadly. He knew that in reality she was completely oblivious to his presence and to anything he might say, even though he could hear her tapping away on the computer keyboard quite clearly.

The image of her stockinged legs and white panties rested in his mind's eye and Max couldn't help a chuckle. This situation was really beginning to present itself with certain advantages, not to mention the new horizons. It was just like the fantasy films he had seen on TV of ghosts and phantoms and thingies.

A terrible thought suddenly struck him. Maybe he was dead and he had become a wandering soul awaiting his ascension to heaven – or wherever! The overwhelming calm and well-being that had possessed him a moment before fled. All he wanted was to get back inside his body. Instantly he felt himself pulled irresistibly downwards, through the floor and towards his desk. The next thing he saw was his game of chess on the computer screen. He sighed and realised that he was safe back inside his body once more. He ran his hand across his forehead and then checked the pulse in his wrist. Well, at least his heart was still beating.

Max sat back and tried to reason; this was all just too wild, too surreal. On an impulse, he peered over the metre-high walls that compartmentalised his office space from that of his colleagues. Carolina was still doing the crossword, and he could see by the way in which Caiali was staring intently at his computer screen (something he rarely did when he was programming) that he was exploiting his literary skills. There it was then; it had been no dream or how else could he have known of the activities of his colleagues?

He was falling back into deep thought again, contemplating the possible 'whys' and 'hows', when a sharp tap on his shoulder startled him back to reality.

'Good game is it, Cugini?'

Max visibly winced as he recognised the leering vocal tones of his department head, Tangenti.

'You'd better come with me,' the leer continued, 'there's someone upstairs who's taken a serious interest in your activities.'

Max exited the chess program, resignedly got up, and somewhat sheepishly followed Tangenti towards the company lift. He felt like he had done at school when the teacher would reprimand him for talking to a friend during a lesson or something. Damn! It was always he who had got caught at school, picked out among his equally guilty classmates for talking, smoking, whatever. Then, at university, he was the one who had found himself standing in front of the principal's finely polished, oak desk under threat of expulsion simply because he had retaliated in the canteen after being on the receiving end of a deftly flicked scoop of strawberry ice cream – the consequences of which had started possibly one of the greatest ice cream battles in the history of the Italian nation. The damage was said to have amounted to millions of lira. 'Sunday Sticky Sundae' the press had labelled it. And now, even at work, he was still the fall guy. Well, they said that scholastic life was a foretaste of the real thing. Nothing ever changed.

He glanced briefly back at his colleagues, all of whom were now busily and conscientiously programming the day's backlog as if oblivious to his own personal misfortune. For the second time in a few minutes Max grinned, despite his apprehensions. He knew exactly what they were all going to be discussing as soon as that lift door closed.

Chapter Seven

Relatively speaking, the time it took for the lift to pass from the first to the fourth floor was very short indeed, but for Max, enclosed in that small space with a wordless Tangenti, there was time enough to lose your grip on things.

His head was starting to spin as the experience he'd had just moments before began to dawn on him. He'd passed through walls like they weren't really there. He'd flown around the building. He could have gone anywhere he'd wanted without being seen or heard. Or maybe that was why they wanted to see him on the top floor, because he had been seen. The secretary? But no, that was ridiculous – or was it?

When they finally stepped out of the lift and into the corridor, Max was having a very serious problem handling reality. After all, it's not every day that you discover you're a poor man's Peter Pan. Everything was beginning to seem cushioningly surreal as he entered the executive boardroom for the first and probably last time ever.

A clean, revitalising smell of fresh lemons brought him sharply back to the real world. Obviously the type of detergent the cleaners used, he thought, and made a mental note to start using it in his own apartment – if he ever got round to cleaning it.

Max glanced curiously around him. The room was impressively spacious, and the light that flooded in through the ceiling-high venetian blinds gave it a very bright and pleasant feel, exactly the opposite of how he was feeling right at that moment.

Together with Tangenti, he approached the far end of the huge, oval, tinted-glass table that was the centrepiece of the room. Max was trying desperately to clear his thoughts and reason logically as to why he was there – the lemon smell seemed to be helping.

That someone had seen him floating about was ridiculous, and it couldn't be to give him the sack for a small disciplinary matter like the odd chess game on firm time. No, such trivialities would usually be dealt with by lesser executive staff on the first or second floors. He recognised the two people at the far side of the table, to where they were headed. The woman was Cathy McDonald, whom he'd seen when zipping about only moments before. Now she was sat discussing something rather animatedly with – Max's heart sank a little, that was Andersson himself!

Although rarely seen on the lower floors, everybody in the firm knew who Andersson was. A slim, tall, athletic figure, even at sixty-five, he had come to the firm's Italian branch as the new vice-president just over a year ago and had made a point of shaking hands with everyone before becoming pretty much a hermit of the top floors (generally non-executive employees had no right or access above the second). At the annual Christmas party last year, he had made a five-minute guest appearance, when he had recited a quick speech thanking everyone for their dedication and hard work and then had disappeared again – much to the unspoken relief of all present, of course.

Now Max was somewhat puzzled. What on earth did the most important and reclusive figure in the firm want with him? It was easier to get an appointment with the Mayor of Piacenza than to see Herb Andersson. Filled with an overwhelming sense of curiosity (and a not inconsiderable amount of trepidation), he found himself having his hand vigorously shaken by both parties and asked courteously to take a seat.

'I expect you are wondering why you are here, Signor Cugini?' asked Andersson.

'Uh, yes,' replied Max, and bit his lip a little.

Andersson spoke Italian, but with a strong American accent, and Max was trying his best to take the voice seriously. It wasn't Max's fault, or that he was being rude in any way, only that the English or American accents (there is very little or no difference for the native listener) in Italian sound like the voices of the extremely popular comedy duo, Laurel and Hardy. The Italian television producer who decided, so many years ago, that it would be extremely funny if Stan and Ollie spoke Italian with strong English accents, wittingly or unwittingly condemned any earnest, English-speaking language learner (and this is a shame because it has to be admitted that there aren't that many) to a lifetime of unintentional comic portrayal.

Max plonked himself down on one of the same chromed, leather-upholstered chairs that they had on the first floor. So not even executives were allowed to get too relaxed, he thought.

'I hear you're a bit of a chess player,' continued Andersson, sounding a little more like Ollie than Stan.

Max shot a quick, accusing glance over to where Tangenti was seated next to Cathy McDonald, but then retracted it again, realising that Tangenti had not had the time or the opportunity to spill the beans.

'Yes, I play the odd game,' replied Max in a master understatement. He ran his fingers along the hard glassy edge of the table.

Andersson frowned slightly, then cleared his throat with an impatient growl. 'They told me you were pretty good. Are you or not?'

'I'm a candidate master,' Max confessed, suddenly feeling unwarrrantedly nervous about his favourite pastime. 'I guess that puts me in a sufficiently elite category.'

'Excellent.'

Oliver Hardy sounded pleased again, and Max's disquietude began to give way to feelings of elation and amusement. He half expected Andersson to start flicking and rolling his necktie.

'How would you fancy playing a game right now?'

'Err...' Max floundered, but a quick glance over at Cathy, who gave a brief nod, informed him of the question's sincerity. He liked her. On the few occasions they'd had to chat at the coffee machine, he'd found her very honest, open and down to earth.

'I never say no to a challenge,' he declared. 'Where do we play?'

Andersson smiled like a man who had a secret ace up his sleeve in a game of poker. 'Oh, not me, my boy,' he said jovially and buzzed the intercom on the table in front of him.

'Mrs Lee, is Signor Belvois with us?'

'Yes, sir, he's here waiting.'

'Send him through, please.'

A door, adjacent to the one Max and Tangenti had come in by, opened, and a well-dressed, bearded man in his late twenties entered the boardroom, carrying a wooden box, a chessboard and a stopclock.

Chapter Eight

'Eez a no good.'

The expensively suited Mafia type shook his head and then continued in his typically strong, southern Italian English. 'The boss he no want a this a thing a here. No. He want a Sabrina Falchi.' He stopped and took another long and incredulous look at the creature that lay in a drugged stupor in the boot of the blue Ford Fiesta, a hospital blanket wrapped around its otherwise naked form.

'More drugs,' it said deliriously, and turned over, wrapping the blanket a little tighter around itself and giving a contented little sigh as it drifted back to sleep.

The Mafia type turned and said something in Italian to his companion-in-arms, likewise dressed in suit and tie and still wearing sunglasses despite the scarcity of light in the bowels of the ferry boat parking deck. His companion made some kind of witticism and both of them laughed.

'Sabrina Falchi is a molto bella ragazza.' His hands passed down through the air in an appreciative curving motion. 'Very beautiful girl. You Eenglish, you are terrible that you not know the difference from a beautiful girl very sexy and thees... err... how you call it... hippy, yes.'

He closed the car boot and turned to his friend. There was another flurried exchange in Italian and then he spoke again.

'Okay. Our boss he no want a hippy. Nobody need a hippy. Eez your big a fuck-up problem. Now, I and my friend here, we go for a drink. Bye bye, Eengleesh.'

They turned and left, laughing and chatting loudly as they headed up the stairs towards the upper decks. Dave White watched in silence as they went. He wasn't a very happy man, actually he was well pissed off.

'You fuckin' dickhead! How could you grab the wrong one? Not only is it the wrong height, shape, age, name and bloody nationality, but the wrong fuckin' sex to boot, I thought I could at least rely on you to get that one right by yourself.'

This had been the first time the Italians had tried to pull a stunt of this kind in the Brits' backyard. International cooperation, they'd called it, and he, Dave White and Bumblers Incorporated, had completely and utterly blown it. His orders had been relatively straightforward: grab the girl, get her on the Poole–Cherbourg ferry, hand her over to the Italians, spend a nice day in the company of a few French beers and come back home on the early evening boat.

He hadn't really known that much about the girl he was supposed to have taken, only that her family was very well off and that kidnapping had been a big money-spinner in the south of Italy for many years now. In fact, it had become such a popular pastime that even small-time organisations had got in on it and, as a consequence, many of the wealthier southern Italian families now paid annual sums to certain powerful syndicates as a security measure. Woe betide the nobody that made an unauthorised attempt to approach them. But why bother in Italy when every year lots of rich little lovelies were sent to study English in expensive language schools in the south of England?

Even when the young Miss Falchi had been taken ill and rushed to a detoxification unit in a private clinic with suspected food poisoning, apparently contracted in a local fast food restaurant, the situation had not presented itself as being too problematical. Procuring themselves a pair of hospital technician badges and distracting the night duty nurse at reception long enough for the other to look up the young lady's room number on the register list and head off in the right direction had been a cinch. Discovering that she had been put under sedation for the night had facilitated matters no end – that had saved them from having to do it. They had even managed to smuggle the unconscious form, wrapped up in a blanket and hidden in a laundry basket, out of the hospital and into the back of the car, no questions asked.

They had been a little pushed for time to make the midnight ferry, so he had not bothered to check their prize with much attention – a glimpse of the blanketed form and the mass of long, blonde hair as it was transferred to the boot had been enough to convince him at the time. After all, was it his fault if the tall, powerfully built Aryan type who stood facing him, hand-picked by the top boys in London, was a complete and utter imbecile, incapable of distinguishing between the sexes? He didn't see that it was. Absolutely not. He'd done his part and to perfection, right down to the little agreement with Brian, the organisation-bribed Brummy, who'd made sure he was the only officer on customs duty that night at the ferry port.

The blonde giant scratched his head in bewilderment.

'It's not my fault, Dave,' he began, looking extremely downcast. 'It was very difficult. There were no room numbers on the doors and I had to keep looking into all the rooms just to see who was there.' He shook his head sadly and continued. 'I guess when I saw all that pretty hair I just assumed that it was her, and it was dark and all the lights were off.'

'Wanker.'

'I'm sorry, Dave.'

'Fuck-head.'

'I'm sorry, I said. So what we gonna do now?'

'What are *we* gonna do? What am *I* gonna do you mean? I'm takin' the next ferry back, but you'd be better off leaving the country or something. It's all over for you, matey. You've fucked up big time.'

For a moment the huge Aryan said nothing as the implications of his mistake seemed to dawn on him for the first time.

'And what we gonna do about the hippy, Dave?' he asked finally, sounding distraught and rather helpless.

'I don't give a flying fuck,' Dave snapped back. He was pacing up and down by the side of the car. 'It's a your bigga fuck-up problem,' he said, badly imitating the Italian. 'I wash my hands of it.' And then he too stormed upstairs towards the duty-free bar, leaving his ex-partner standing alone with only the hum of the ferry boat engines and a hundred empty passenger cars as company.

Had he glanced back as he was leaving, however, Dave White might have seen something that he would have found more than just a little disconcerting. The blonde man's azure eyes blazed with brilliant astuteness as he stood watching the other's departure – he was also grinning broadly. Reopening the car boot, he looked down into it and shook his head, laughing slightly.

'C'mon, sunshine,' he grinned, picking up the unconscious bundle as if it were weightless. 'It's time we got you sorted.' And then, almost as an afterthought, he leant back into the boot, still holding the blanketed form effortlessly under one arm, and fished out a largish sack that rattled as he lifted it. Indeed, this would have struck Dave White as particularly odd because it contained numerous small plastic squares with hospital ward and room numbers on them. It would have seemed even odder if, ten minutes later, he had seen him fling that same sack over the side of the ferry and into the churning waters of the Channel.

Chapter Nine

Have you seen this man? Of course you have, or at least something very, very similar. Perhaps you exchanged formal salutations while waiting for the train this morning, or politely discussed the weather at the bus stop? Or perhaps (and this is probably more the case) you failed to notice him at all while he shared your taxicab.

If the police put together an identikit of him, the description could well read as follows:

'...aged between thirty and fifty, greying hair, medium build, five feet ten inches, about 175 lbs; considered very dangerous, do not approach under any circumstances etc...'

Suddenly, you might well become suspicious of a lifelong

friend, a business partner, your dog's vet or even a member of your own family.

But this is all, of course, pure conjecture. The 'Beardomorph' (Hairius Facius Similum) is, in fact, a master of social etiquette and conformity. Rarely, if ever, does he find himself in trouble with the law, with the possible exclusion of parking fines and occasional petty cases of tax evasion which, as every emancipated modern businessman knows, should be considered results of macro-social injustice rather than a defamation of moral character.

Yes, his honesty is a strange and yet somewhat fortunate phenomenon for our respected and overworked forces of law and order. Indeed, if a beardomorph ever took it upon himself to commit a serious offence, the police would find themselves hard-pushed to arrest, question all possible suspects and then, ultimately, convict the real guilty party. No mean undertaking if you consider that statistical research reveals one beardomorph for every hundred square metres of inner city living space, rising in residential areas to one in fifty.

In fact, one certainly could not blame any innovative bank robber from seeing the criminal potential in such a disguise. No need to wear an attention-grabbing stocking or Halloween mask; simply invest in some grey hair dye, an equally grey full beard and moustache, a pair of large spectacles, and Bob's your uncle! (The author stops at this point to briefly ponder the origins of that last idiom.) No one notices you in the queue right up until the last minute when you produce the revolver and then, well, there's no more need even for a fast and well-planned getaway. No, when the job's finished, calmly walk out into the high street and merge with the crowd – very slick indeed!

Certainly it would be extremely fatuous of the author to think of himself as the only one to have seen the potential in such a disguise. On the contrary, it is well known that certain Middle-Eastern terrorist groups have also toyed with the idea and have, in fact, made certain attempts at creating their own version of a beardomorph to the scope of facilitating penetration of western security, but, as yet, with only feeble results.

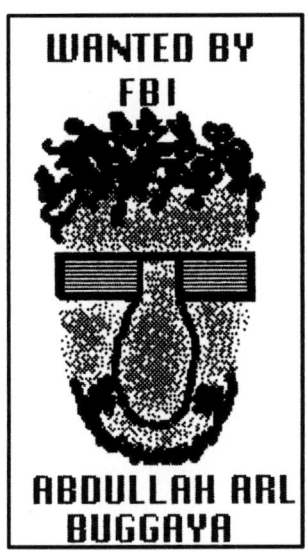

WANTED BY
FBI

ABDULLAH ARL
BUGGAYA

Thus demonstrating a lack of attention to certain essential details.

Ian Armstrong was a beardomorph and had been so for the larger part of his thirty-six years. His friends even knew him as Morph, and he'd grown quite affectionate towards the nickname – after all, it gave him a kind of image with which he could identify and, more importantly, live up to quite easily.

The problem with images, Morph had always reasoned, was that very often they didn't reflect the true personality of the owner. Take, for example, almost any modern political figure. It must be like a living hell for most of those guys (or gals) having to lead such clean-living, puritanical lives when all the time they are fighting an overwhelmingly insatiable urge to bonk the living daylights out of their office secretary or get pissed as farts and sing Tom Jones karaoke numbers down the local.

For him, on the other hand, Morph stood for honest, loyal, dependable and, with the girls, cuddly, although deep down he too had to admit to a certain desire to bonk the living daylights out of his own secretary, Sharon.

As to his honesty, albeit unbeknownst to himself, Morph was about to commit a crime of a very serious nature in leaving the ferry and passing through customs at Cherbourg.

Chapter Ten

With a squeal of delight, Maria skipped into Max's living room. 'I've done it, I've done it!' she repeated excitedly.

Max was wallowing miserably in the deepest recesses of his favourite armchair. His confidence had received a serious battering at the hands of Belvois that morning. All his hopes of making master status, all that time and study, and yet an unrated player with no tournament experience had completely embarrassed him. Done him low. Oh, sure, he had had the excuse (which of course he'd refrained from using) that something very weird had recently begun to happen to him, but all the same, Belvois, a mere novice, had stuck the boot in while he was down and had come out three games to zero.

Still, the whole scene had been a little strange, and not just as a result of his own personal mind-bender. For example, why would Andersson have wanted him to play against Belvois, a competent and likeable, but in no way outstanding, programmer if he hadn't had a special reason for it? And why should Cathy McDonald and Tangenti have wished to be on the scene? After all, for the uninitiated, a chess game is not the greatest spectator sport in existence.

It was obvious that they'd all been interested in Belvois' performance, but the motive still remained a complete mystery. Anyway, he wasn't going to spend too long thinking about it. He was actually beginning to be afraid of concentrating on anything, as it seemed that every time he did so his mind just kind of popped out of his body and went walkabout. Maybe he should see a doctor or a psychologist or something; he certainly couldn't go on like this.

'Max, are you listening to me?' repeated Maria, standing indignantly with her hands on her hips and obviously feeling just a little narked at being ignored. 'I said "I've done it".'

'Huh, what?' said Max, the glazed-over look in his eyes slowly disappearing. 'Er, done what?'

Having assured herself of his complete attention she continued. 'I've finally succeeded in proving one of my most important theories. It could even lead to one of the most stunning scientific advancements since the invention of heat-retaining pizza delivery boxes.'

Max looked suitably impressed even if, to be honest, he had always had to reheat his when it had ultimately arrived.

'Which theory?' asked Max, all too aware that Maria had developed a fair few, mostly rather radical and somewhat too dubious to ever be supported fervently by the scientific community at large.

'Oh, you know,' she went on excitedly, 'the one about the inter-dimensional doorway that exists inside washing machines and sucks in socks, but only one of each pair, so you're always left with odd socks after a wash.'

She vanished into the kitchen and then returned just as quickly.

'Look!' she exclaimed in triumph. It was rather like watching Sir Isaac Newton's face shortly after he'd got over the irritation of being stupid enough to doze off under an apple tree.

She held up three bedraggled odd socks and one complete pair. A dismayed expression shot across Max's face after a closer study of her trophies revealed the full implications of what she was saying.

'Twenty minutes ago,' she continued proudly, oblivious of his increasing anguish, 'I put four pairs of your best socks – and I can assure you that they were perfectly matched before they went in – in the washing machine along with some pants and things.' She stopped for a breath. 'And now three of them have completely vanished.'

For a moment Max just sat and stared, mouth gaping ever so slightly. Bit by bit his incredulity passed to a kind of resigned sadness. It hadn't been the first time that something had gone awry when Maria had tried her hand at being domestic. She said she needed the practice for when they were married and her mother had banned her from doing anything of the sort in her own house. You couldn't argue the logic, but secretly Max feared the possible financial consequences of her domestic education. He knew he'd probably end up doing it all himself as he'd had much more experience, but, in this day and age of the emancipated male, he didn't see why he should. He decided to take a reasoning approach to the situation.

'It would appear,' he began calmly, 'that this inter-dimensional doorway is not only capable of distinguishing between your basic low quality nylon and top-notch cotton, but that it deserves to be complimented on its good taste. The only pair that seems to have survived intact is the cheapest.' He stopped and sighed, his brow furrowing slightly in an injured expression. 'Those were my favourite socks, Maria,' he added miserably. 'Are you sure they're not still in the washing machine, I mean stuck up in some odd angle or something?'

'You don't believe me, do you?' Maria cried excitedly. 'I knew you wouldn't. Go and check for yourself.' She pointed authoritatively towards the kitchen door.

Realising the futility of further discussion, he prised himself free from the soft, womb-like comfort of his armchair and, leaving Maria to take his place in it, went dutifully into the kitchen. Once there, he proceeded to open up the washing machine and peer dubiously inside. What he was about to see next would change his opinion of the wildest of Maria's theories for ever – well, maybe.

At first he saw nothing and rightly reported so to Maria. Then it occurred to him that to see absolutely 'nothing' was very odd indeed. There should have been something in there. Wasn't there supposed to be some kind of silver tub with colander-like holes in it? He looked again and saw nothing, just blackness, void. He frowned and reached inside in an attempt to touch the sides. This wasn't possible – nothing! He couldn't feel anything. He withdrew his hand and, as he did so, something caught his eye. He took a closer look.

There was a light in there and it appeared to be moving, moving towards him. Max stared, dumbstruck, unsure of what to do next. No, wait, it wasn't a light after all, but a face. It was a man's face. He knew that face. It was the guy who used to present the cult 1960s series of the *Twilight Zone*, Rod Serling!

'Dur dee dur dur, dur dee dur dur,' sang the head as it floated merrily towards him. It was the signature tune of the series. 'You're travelling to another dimension, a dimension not only of sight and sound but of mind…'

'Wooaah!' said Max, unable to move. He wanted to jump back and slam the door shut, but he was frozen, captivated, like a rabbit caught in the glare of car headlights.

'Wooaah?' echoed the head in a strangely sardonic tone. 'Is that the best you can think of saying?'

'Wuuuh?' suggested Max.

'Oh dear!' commented the head in a tone of genuine disappointment. He turned from the aghast Max to look behind him into the darkness. 'I must say that from your description I had expected him to be somewhat slightly more literately endowed.'

'Oh, don't be beastly, Blitzy!' came a voice from nowhere. 'And stop teasing him, poor thing, and change that ridiculous head at once.'

The other obeyed, and the chiselled features of Rod Serling were replaced by the equally sharp features of a broadly grinning, blonde-haired, athletic male who seemed to be around his late thirties or early forties.

A woman's face appeared beside him. She was extremely beautiful and although he'd never seen her before, Max couldn't shake the strange sensation that she was in some way very familiar.

'Hello, Max,' she said simply, and smiled comfortingly at him.

'Hello,' said Max, jaw still hanging loosely and unable to think of anything more eloquent.

'I'm very sorry if my friend, Blitzkrieg, here gave you a shock. I can assure you that he was only kidding.'

'Whoo… err… who are you?' Max stammered in a tiny voice. The whole situation was getting just too absurd. His, of late, somewhat tenuous grip on the pole of reality had started greasing its own fingers.

'I'm Caissa,' she answered.

Something clicked in his head. 'The goddess of chess?'

'Yup,' interrupted Blitzkrieg. 'She began as a wood nymph, but in recent centuries she's received a bit of a promotion.'

Despite his obvious mastery of the language, her companion sported a slight trace of a German or possibly Nordic accent.

Caissa continued. 'Please forgive us if we frightened you in any way, but you see I've never been able to resist a dramatic entrance.' She studied Max's guppy-like expression and added, 'Oh, and I assure you that we are both quite real. I believe you have been having a fair few other rather bizarre experiences lately?'

'Uh, yes,' Max managed. 'How? I mean, you…?'

'No, absolutely not,' she said, shaking her long dark mane of hair in denial. 'I've got nothing to do with that. That's to do with you, nature and evolution and all that. Oh, no, you haven't got to worry about something like that,' she said, quite matter-of-factly, 'and I know about what's been happening to you because it's my business as a goddess to take an interest in all of her most ardent admirers.'

'So that's why you seemed so familiar,' said Max, finally beginning to feel he understood something – kind of. He suddenly felt an inexplicable sense of relief. Perhaps it was just because someone seemed to understand and could offer him some sort of an explanation for the recent bizarre events, even if the source of this was coming from a floating head inside a washing machine.

'How do you mean "nature and evolution"?' he asked, his wits blinking and fumbling their way back as he accustomed himself to the unusual circumstances of the conversation. He was sat cross-legged and chatting amiably with the occupants of the inside of a domestic device. This way lies madness…

'The ability to leave one's body', she explained, 'is a very special gift of nature or, if you like, the next step in the chain of evolution.'

'A kind of Homo superior,' grinned Blitzkrieg, with no small amount of irony insinuated in his tone. Suddenly he looked very bored. 'Listen, Caissa, I'm off down the pub. Catch you later,' he added, and promptly vanished with a burp.

'He's got such a short attention span,' Caissa sighed resignedly. 'What's happening to you, Max,' she went on, reassuming the original subject, 'is something very special indeed, and you have to learn to appreciate and use it, as it can and should be used, instead of fighting it. You're not the first and you certainly won't be the last to have the experiences you've been having. Learn to control it and you'll discover just how wonderful a gift Mother Nature has granted you. Which brings me to the point of my visit.' She stopped and continued in a lower and more serious tone. 'I need your help and, in return, I'll help you to do things you've never even dreamed of.'

'My help?' said Max, a little uncertain.

'Yes,' she said, 'I need you to win that tournament in Salsomaggiore next week. It's very important to me.'

He wasn't sure whether to laugh or panic. Caissa, the goddess of chess, really had so much faith in his abilities? 'But there are going to be some really great players there. Why me? I'm not even sure I'll ever even make Master, and I was defeated by a novice today at work.'

'Hmm.' She looked thoughtful and added, 'That was no ordinary novice and you really do have great promise. You just have to learn how to use it, that's all.'

That's all? Wow! Private chess lessons from its deity certainly would be something else.

'No,' she answered, laughing, as if she had read his mind. 'I'm not going to give you personal tuition in the game. That would never be allowed. But I am going to teach you how to take full advantage of your new-found potential.'

Max shifted a little and scratched his chin. 'When do we start?'

'Right now,' she answered, assuming a half-serious teacherish air. 'Lesson numero uno. It's all about concentration. Practise it. Now I have to go, there are a lot of other things I have to see to. I'll see you soon for lesson two.' And, at that, she began to disappear, away into the darkness. 'Remember, Max,' she called back, her voice seeming to fade into eternity, 'concentration is the key.'

Max remained motionless and dumbstruck on the cool tiles of his kitchen floor, staring after her into the void that used to be the inside of a perfectly good and functioning washing machine. As first lessons go, he couldn't shake the feeling that it was just, perhaps, a tad cryptic.

'Max, are you all right?' came a concerned voice from behind him. 'Can you see them?'

'What? See who?'

Maria looked amused. 'Your socks, silly.'

'No,' he responded, 'and you're quite right. There's definitely something very odd about that machine.'

'Yes,' Maria concurred solemnly, 'there really should be some kind of warning in the instruction booklet.'

Chapter Eleven

Having heard only the grumbling lamentations of his stomach for the last two hours, even though his radio had been on almost full blast, Morph decided it was time to replenish both his and the car's fuel supplies. He had been on the road almost fourteen hours and had only made one brief stop for petrol – quite a feat even for him, and certainly something with which to impress friends and colleagues alike when he got back to good old Blighty.

He'd driven from Cherbourg, right across France, over the border into Switzerland and was just about to enter the chaos of Geneva. A very ordered chaos, admittedly, because, in spite of everything, it is in Switzerland. However, if disorder can be found anywhere in the land of banks, cuckoo clocks, chocolate and muesli, then that place is Geneva.

Not being inexperienced in the ways of the European business traveller, he considered it wise to stop for a bite and a wash before embarking upon the hunt for the hotel he'd had Sharon, his secretary, book him. Sure, he knew where it was more or less, but as any hardened globetrotter knows, there is a vast difference between theory and practice. A rest and some directional advice from the locals was what the sage ordered. At the first roadside restaurant he turned off.

It was only when he had switched off both engine and radio that he heard the thumping and muffled moaning. Probably a dog or something locked in a car while the owner gorged himself on a juicy whopper and chips. Oh, well, what did he give a damn?

He got out of his new, armour-plated (or at least that's what the advert had claimed) Volvo, stretched in the cool evening air and gazed at the twilight buildings around him. It felt sooo good. After fourteen hours' driving, your car seat, suit trousers, shirt, back and legs feel like they have all become bonded together at a genetic level. It was then that it dawned on him. The origin of the increasingly frantic pounding was coming from inside his own car. Stiffly, he bent over and flipped the lever on the driver's side which released the catch on the car boot. He walked around to the back and watched warily at a discreet distance. He'd seen enough horror films to have learnt the virtue of caution in such situations. The inhuman moaning and wailing suddenly stopped, and the boot began to slowly rise up. Morph's heart rose along with it and started thumping on his Adam's apple – he hated that. He hated anything that made him feel like the way he was feeling right then. It was different in the movies - he enjoyed scenes like this in movies – his physical being wasn't endangered then. He wanted to call for help, but his heart had by now entirely blocked his vocal passage and was feverishly beating out a lively and entertaining mambo percussion solo on his tonsils.

A thick odour of sweat and stale air steamed forth from the back of his car and, even though he was standing a good two metres away, Morph's eyes watered.

Maintaining his distance he studied intently the darkness inside the boot. Something was moving, something white. He could just make out certain demi-human facial traits, a long blonde mane, a white goat-bearded face and two primordial, pale blue eyes which blinked nervously out at him.

'Uuuh!' it grunted.

Morph took an instinctive step back.

'Heea!'

It seemed to Morph that the beast was making some kind of primitive attempt to communicate. Suddenly the street lights came on and everything became clear.

'Oh, no!' exclaimed Morph in horror.

'Oh, man! Where am I? Who are you? Are you a kidnapper or something? I need a drink. I think a camel's died in my mouth. Hey, dude, can you give me a hand here? I don't seem to be able to move my legs.'

'Oh, no!' cried Morph again with increasing dismay and unconsciously placing a protective hand on his wallet. 'It's a hippy.'

The assistant manager of the burger restaurant stared out over his long acne-ridden nose at the two clients seated in the corner under the stairs.

One was rather unremarkably dressed in a pale blue, short-sleeved shirt and could have been his bank manager; the other, wrapped in a white sheet with long, shoulder-length hair and a small beard, bore a striking resemblance to one of the more saintly figures in the print that his mother kept in the guest room at home – the one by Michelangelo.

His first reaction had been to pick up the phone and call the police, but then, on second thoughts, he decided that even religious nuts had a right to a deep-fried chicken, chips and coke when they got the urge – as long as they had the money, that was.

Chris gulped back his second coke and burped heartily. 'Ahh, I feel better now all that caffeine is finally beginning to kick in. Thanks, man.'

Morph stared at him a little piteously, but mostly in disgust. For him a hippy represented all that was wrong with society. They were lazy, scrounging and crap at nearly everything. He'd never met one that knew how to do anything, apart from imbibe excessive amounts of intoxicating substances, carve oddly-shaped smoking utensils out of bits of wood and milk the social security system for all it was worth. Nevertheless, here he was, paying for a hippy's meal and also guilty of smuggling one halfway across Europe. It was probably just another method these people had cooked up to get from A to B without spending a penny.

Chris looked over the plastic table at his benefactor. 'So, that's all I know, man.'

It was quite uncanny. He was still able to talk even though he had just crammed almost an entire chicken drum in his mouth. Morph wondered if this hippy had ever considered exploiting his natural gift in the field of ventriloquism.

'One minute I was recovering from an evil beefie in a clinic – that's why this time I asked for chicken – the next I was bouncing about in the boot of your car, man.'

'Have you got any documents on you, you know, passport, driving licence, UB40 card, something like that?'

'No, man, nothing. Just this white hospital sheet, and that's beginning to get a little itchy.'

Well, that clinched it then, thought Morph. He had to be telling the truth. Hippies don't go anywhere without their UB40 social security cards, it was a well known fact, like a yuppy without a mobile phone. He was also telling the truth about that blanket if it felt anything like it smelt. Morph began to feel almost genuinely sorry for him and very curious as to why anyone would go to all the trouble to organise a kidnapping of the sad sight that sat before him.

'Are you rich?' he asked bluntly. 'Or is your family?'

'Well, my father's got that burger place I told you about, and we're not poor, but as to "rich rich" no. Not as to be worth kidnapping.'

'You were in a private clinic when they took you.'

'Yes, but my father has a health insurance policy on us all.'

So had Morph, and he wasn't rich either.

'Well, I can't take you to the police here, that's for sure. They'd arrest us immediately and ask questions later. I'd probably be booked for hippy smuggling and you for vagrancy and being generally unhygienic.'

Chris nodded his agreement and almost smiled for the first time since he'd crawled out of Morph's boot. He really wanted a shower and some fresh clothes.

'I have an idea,' he said suddenly. 'Why don't I phone my parents, let them know I'm all right, and see if my father can organise something, maybe send some money via the British Embassy or by post along with my passport?'

Morph couldn't help but be struck by the hippy's spontaneous ingenuity and capacity to maintain a sense of blind optimism. Certainly, to depend on any postal service as a partial solution to your problems was pushing it, even for someone with probably unlimited time at his disposal. He nodded his approval. What was happening to him? Despite a lifetime of healthy prejudice, he actually found himself beginning to feel sympathy for a hippy, a longhair.

'Only thing is,' the hippy went on, 'I'll need to borrow some money for the phone call.'

Chapter Twelve

Having successfully ridden out his relieved mother's tidal wave of emotion, Chris was handed back to his father.

Ira Hasi's reaction, on the other hand, ranged from concern to just downright irritation at his son's inability to explain his predicament. Like most of his countrymen who had managed to escape before the fall of the Shah, he had always considered the possibility of Iran's Secret Service tracking him down for whatever fanatical crackpot excuse the Ayatollah or his successors might see fit to dream up.

This, however, did not seem the work of highly trained assassins. To go to the trouble of abducting his son and then depositing him in a car boot headed for Switzerland did not make much sense from any angle. But you could never be sure. Certainly one of the things he had learnt as under-secretary to the Shah was always to try to avoid official channels. No, much better would be to trust the family, sound things out on the network and check up on the owner of the Volvo that Chris had been taken in.

When Chris finally put the phone down and returned to the table where Morph was sat waiting, he was unable to contain his delight at his own good fortune.

'Good news?'

'Oh, wow, man! I've got a few weeks' holiday in Europe.'

Morph raised his eyebrows slightly, and Chris explained that his father was of the same mind and thought it wiser to leave the authorities out of the matter. Instead he was to go to one of his father's half-brothers who, by lucky chance, actually lived in Geneva, and where his passport and money would arrive by courier express.

'He also suggested that until the matter is a little clearer, I should stay a while in Europe – about two or three weeks to be exact.'

'Well, I'm glad everything has worked out for you. Would you like a lift to this guy's place?' Morph asked, relieved at the prospect of getting rid of the hippy and feeling that his generosity knew no bounds that day. He felt tired and dirty and just wanted to find his hotel room and take a long refreshing shower.

Chris held out his hand and displayed a scrap of paper (obviously torn hastily from a telephone directory) with an address scribbled on it. 'That'd be well cool, man.' He looked down at the address and frowned a little as he tried to read it. 'If you take me there, I can pay you back the nourishment and the expensive shout I just made.'

Despite his natural aversion to hippydom and most other things hippy, Morph had always wanted to be able to speak like that. He considered it very groovy and made a mental note to try and use the two expressions himself from time to time when he was out with the lads.

'But this time I'm travelling up front, right, not in the coffin.'

'If you insist,' said Morph, a little dryly. 'First, we have to find out where this place is, though.'

'No problem.' Chris leant over the table and addressed a young couple who had just sat themselves down and had been eyeing Chris, wondering where the fancy dress party was.

Morph's jaw dropped as he realised that the discussion was being held in fluent German.

They found a note written in Arabic and Blu-Tacked to the building's intercom. Chris read it and then explained that apparently the intercom and bell system didn't work and that they should go up to the second floor and knock at the door of apartment C, and to use the stairs as the lift didn't work either.

'Curious,' panted Morph, looking around him as they climbed the second flight of stairs, 'a nice, seemingly well-kept and modern building like this and yet nothing seems to work.'

When they arrived, Chris tried the doorbell. It emitted a kind of dribbly wet sound at them, so he knocked.

A clumsy fumbling with locks and keys could be heard the other side of the door, and a male voice called out for them to wait a minute. Finally it opened, and a man with thinning white hair in his mid-fifties appeared, dressed in a long, white house gown.

He smiled, waved his hand, and bowed in a typical Arabic greeting. The lines on his face showed an amiable and gentle nature. 'Hello, gentlemen. Good evening and welcome.'

He spoke English with only a slight eastern inflection and the tone was soft and calm. It made Morph think that perhaps this man was incapable of ever losing his temper.

'My name is Ali Abdul Hassan Buzerji-Hasi, but please just call me Ali.'

He looked from Chris to Morph and then back again to Chris who was still wrapped only in a hospital blanket.

'You must be Chris, Ira's firstborn. And you must be Mr Armstrong, Chris's saviour. My family will be eternally grateful to you. Will you both please come in.' He took the fabric of Chris's blanket between his thumb and forefinger and compared it with his own gown. 'How nice it is to see that, despite my years, I am still in fashion.' He smiled again, revealing two rows of pearly white teeth.

Morph hovered at the apartment threshold uncertainly. 'I really just wanted to be sure that the hip... er... Chris, here, was okay,' he said, and then explained that he was badly in need of a shower and still hadn't checked into his hotel.

Five minutes later Morph was outside the building and headed towards his car. He had managed to refuse all financial compensation for his help, but had succeeded in escaping the hospitality and gratitude of Chris's new host only by promising to return and dine with them the following evening.

It was only when he was sat in his car that a strange thought occurred to him. He couldn't remember ever telling Chris his surname and yet that Ali character had used it.

Chapter Thirteen

Splat!

'Gotcha!'

The evening was particularly hot and sweaty. The linen sheet covering the mattress where Maria lay clung to her bare skin as she rolled over on to her belly and propped her head up to observe Max. He was patrolling the bedroom walls, rolled magazine in hand, seeking out rogue mosquitoes that had managed to resist the thick sweet fumes of the pastel smouldering away in the corner. It was a scene she'd lived many times, and she had learnt that it was easier just to let him get on with it rather than insist that he return to bed.

She had heard many tales of people who had had out-of-body experiences. She remembered a magazine article from a short time ago on the subject – Swami something or other, a practitioner of yoga who could do all kinds of weird things to his body, including getting out of it and leaving it all alone for long periods of time. They said it was an ability that took many years to perfect, and at the time Maria had not been able to understand why anyone would want to do such a thing – she had always been very happy in hers.

But she knew Max was feeling very disturbed, and since this afternoon things seemed to have worsened. She decided to confront him with it. Her father had always taught her to face up to her fears: 'Fear is a pH imbalance in the soil,' he always said – he was a passionate gardener – 'it must be faced and rectified immediately, otherwise whatever grows in it will only bear sour fruit.' Max, on the other hand, was bottling his up and waiting for the vintage.

'So, what's it like then, when you leave your body? I mean, what do you see or hear?'

Thwap!

Max glanced over his shoulder at her. He knew that it would

help him to talk about things. It would help to clear the mind, and reason. So, while continuing his inspection of the bedroom wall, he began a complete account of what had happened that day, right up to the washing machine incident.

'Damn!' cried Maria on hearing the last part, 'Now I'm going to have to refine my sock theory.'

'I still seem to have all my senses – except that of touch, obviously – and more: I can fly or float, walk through walls like a ghost and…' He faltered as he realised something else. 'There's an incredible sense of peace, calm, tranquillity, as if you leave behind all your worries. A sense of, I don't know, pure joy. Maria?'

'Yes?'

'Tell me I'm not going mad. It all seems total fantasy to me too – until it happens.'

She sat up straight on the bed and crossed her legs. 'Sounds pretty neat to me. Prove it.'

'Huh?'

'Prove it to me. Leave your body and tell me what's going on out in the street right at this moment.'

Max looked dubious. He wasn't sure if he was capable of performing on cue. 'I think it's a bit like going for a piss, I can never go if someone else is watching.'

Maria jumped off the bed and padded over to him. She draped her arms around his neck and pouted seductively. 'Go on, you can. Do it for me. I promise I'll be very impressed.' She ran her hand down between his naked thighs and lingered there. 'What was it the woman in the washing machine told you, something about concentration, wasn't it?'

'Okay, okay,' said Max, grinning and kissing her on the lips. 'But I can't concentrate like that.'

He tried to embrace her, but she nimbly ducked out of arm's reach.

'Later,' she said, 'if you're a good boy. Right now I want a demonstration of Mr Homo superior.'

There was a kind of testing quality in the way she had said that, Max thought, but then he guessed she had a perfect right to be dubious. He still found it hard to believe himself. Maybe it was all just a figment of his imagination, all part of the earliest symptoms of a brain tumour or something. He shook himself out of the self-doubt he was sliding into. Hell, if he didn't believe in himself, how on earth was he going to convince anyone else, even Maria? He guessed he'd better come up with the goods for both their sakes. Screwing up his face, he tried to float out of his body. Nothing.

He tried a second time, this time trying to recall the sensations he had felt on the other occasions.

Still nothing.

'I don't think I can go when you're watching,' he laughed, trying to joke.

'Well, perhaps there's a special trick to it,' said Maria, not giving up on him. 'I mean, if it was simple concentration, then anyone could do it. It must be something particular in the way you concentrate, like when you play chess.'

Max walked over to his computer, switched it on and accessed his chess database. Maria watched in silence, her mouth was feeling a little tacky and dry.

'How long's this gonna take, lover?'

'Don't know. Don't even know if I can do it when I want to; that's the really crappy thing about it.'

If nothing else, she thought, at least he'll get a good game of chess in. She went out of the bedroom and into the kitchen, opened the fridge and enjoyed the rush of cold air as it hit her hot flesh. She reached in, pulled out a can of pineapple juice and held it against her stomach in a further attempt to cool her blood.

The door to the living room balcony was ajar and she went over to it in the hope of a light breeze. Taking her T-shirt from the side of the sofa where she'd left it earlier in the evening, she put it on and stepped out on to the balcony and into the sounds of the night.

Bugs, bats and nocturnal birds were chorusing together in rhythmic chaos, scratching, screeching, and screaming a joyous, a cappella ode to the night, to the abundantly jewelled heavens above them, to life, its creation and eternal perpetuation.

'What a racket!' she exclaimed out loud, and looked down into the street below.

The streets at that time of year were virtually deserted, both by day and by night. Everyone or nearly everyone was, by now, at the seaside or in the mountains, leaving nature to reclaim that which had once been part of her dominion. 'When the cat's away...' as they say.

Well, now you come to mention it...

A small feline shadow prowled from under a parked car, and another appeared from behind the huge communal rubbish bin further up. Slowly they approached each other, ever cautious, diving and weaving, and touched noses. They began to wail: a slow, eerie, half-human sound that usually wakes everyone up and makes the dogs bark. The two lovers sat and jammed their song of love, playing jazz lead to the heavy insect rhythm section while a canine contrabass was just tuning up.

'Noisy buggers!' cried Maria, beginning to giggle at the ever-increasing row that surrounded her. Still, somehow it made her feel much more alive.

Suddenly the front door to an apartment block further up the street clicked electrically open, and light from the hallway shone out on to the road, illuminating two pairs of amorous, amber eyes that shot off in opposite directions, their moggy courtship abandoned until a more opportune moment.

A man stepped out of the light, speaking into a mobile phone. He was closely followed by a small dog that sprang and yapped excitedly around his feet. When he reached the street corner he stopped and tapped out another number, and began once more to casually bounce his voice off a satellite dish that was orbiting the planet seventy-two thousand miles above; a journey more or less equal to that of travelling around the world four times over, probably just to talk to someone a few blocks away. Proof once again that the quickest way from A to B is not always a straight line or the shortest distance.

The little dog, in the meantime, sniffed out a suitable spot on the pavement and did what doggies have to do. Maria hoped that the distracted pedestrian who slipped in it the next day would be the owner himself. Fat chance, though! The deed done and its obligatory inspection over with, both man and dog re-entered the building, closing the door and leaving the street to be swallowed by darkness once more.

Maria left the balcony and returned to the bedroom. On hearing her footsteps, Max turned and gave her a big grin.

'I bet it's me who steps in that dog shit tomorrow.'

'What...?' Her question trailed off as she realised that he'd been watching the scene with her, and that their experiment had succeeded. A smile lit up her face. 'Oh, goody!' she exclaimed in delight. 'Now you're going to teach me how to do it, right?'

'I don't know if it's possible, but it's a neat idea.' His face suddenly turned serious. He reached over and picked up the telephone which sat beside his computer.

'What are you doing? Who are you calling?' she asked, taken aback.

'The police,' he answered quickly. 'It seems one of our neighbours across the street has got burglars.'

Chapter Fourteen

It's nothing like Scotland, Cathy McDonald, the new head of research at MEGA Industries, found herself thinking as they approached the walled, military-style confines of the Piacenza Carabinieri Training Academy.

Her earliest memories of dawn, regardless of the season, had always led her to believe that it was the dampest, cloudiest, coldest and most forbidding time of day, fit only for the hardy wildlife of the Highland Moors and horror film directors. She, for one, had always preferred the snug of her bed. Sure, life at dawn in Washington DC had not been harsh either, but that was a huge cosmopolitan city where the effects and gloom of the weather were reduced to a minimum. Anyway, Italy in the summer was another matter. The flat Padana plains rolled out under the hazy blue sky and, more than eighty miles distant, the white-crowned Alps majestically surveyed their royal domain. To Cathy, the whole scene was slightly surreal, like a hand-painted theatre backdrop in a musical western. She half expected at any moment to hear disembodied orchestral music and someone burst into a song and dance routine. There were no clouds and absolutely no obligatory early morning drizzle. She'd already seen smiling, happy country folk up and about, busy with their daily chores. Nobody smiled on the Moors at six in the morning.

Two rather tired-looking guards, both with serious cases of five o'clock shadow, saluted the dark blue police Alfa Romeo as it entered the confines of the academy. With a shock Cathy realised that one of them was Belvois. Andersson, who was sitting next to her, caught her expression and explained that they had been up all night on duty and that it was to do with the military testing they had agreed to have Belvois undergo.

'Endurance and stamina, you see,' he said. 'All part of the military man.'

A change of guard was effected immediately and Belvois, along with his companion-in-arms, approached the little group.

'Sergeant Verdi and Acting Officer Belvois reporting, sir,' drawled the burly sergeant, and he tried his best to stifle a yawn. How he hated night duty. All he wanted to do now was go home to his wife and curl up sleepily next to her in bed.

'At ease, gentlemen,' said the chief of police, Ciambella, in a relaxed tone as he climbed raggedly out of the driver's seat. It was not his favourite time of day either. 'I hope you're both ready for the little demonstration we've got planned this morning.'

'Yessir!' snapped Belvois.

Cathy couldn't help a little grin; he certainly was playing his part very well.

Andersson patted Belvois on the back in a fatherly fashion. 'Well done, well done,' he said proudly, and cleared his throat ready for the little speech he had prepared. 'I can assure you, gentlemen,' he began in English, 'that what you are going to see today will change your ideas on soldiering for ever. Before you stands the prototype for the new super soldier of tomorrow, superior both physically and mentally. And the beauty is that it takes almost no time to train him. Mr Belvois here was just an ordinary citizen off the streets until a short time ago, with no special training or previous knowledge of combat or military strategy. Imagine the saving on government resources and the huge political and military advantage of being able to train an army of crack soldiers or policemen in under a week.'

Andersson was prevented from elaborating by a third man who had shared the ride with them in the car. 'You can save the sales pitch for later, Andersson,' he said rather brusquely. It was obvious that the man was used to having even VIPs jump when he spoke. 'For the time being let's get this show on the road. I want to see what I'm buying.'

The accent betrayed nothing of the man who Cathy had been introduced to only as 'the General'; it was strangely neutral. He obviously spoke fluent Italian because she had heard him chatting with the chief of police in the car and, for all her limited knowledge of the language, it could well have been his mother tongue. There was also something very familiar about him. Perhaps it was just that he seemed to have stepped directly out of a Mills and Boon classic. He certainly would have fitted the part of the Byronic hero. He was tall and well built, and there was an ageless quality to the ruggedness of his features, and a Machiavellian cunningness to the eyes.

As the little party walked over the walled grounds towards the combat range, Andersson explained to both Cathy and the General what they were about to see in the test, repeating that, in every sense of the word, Belvois was a complete beginner and, until yesterday, had never even touched a weapon before in his life, having escaped the military draft on the basis of his flat feet. 'In fact,' he concluded, 'the subject's total inexperience in this area was one important factor in his selection for the project.'

The first part was a standard reflex and accuracy performance test in a combat situation. Cathy had seen something similar many times on television. The soldier had to pass through a mock street scene populated by cardboard figures, some innocent bystanders and others, evil gunmen who popped up in different places and at different instants, the idea being to take out as many bad guys as possible without hitting the good citizens.

Sergeant Sergio Verdi went first, while the chief of police explained how this test was much harder than usual because of the fatigue the two men were obviously feeling, as they had been on guard duty for over twenty-four hours and, although the sergeant was part of the highly trained, crack Italian anti-terrorist squad, even his reactions would be slower.

'Tests show that an ordinary soldier under similar conditions demonstrates a drop of ten per cent in reaction time,' the chief elaborated. 'Mr Andersson, however, assures us that this will not happen in the case of Mr Belvois here. Due to the unusual control over his own metabolism, afforded him by the little device that Doctor McDonald has created, he is able to release, at will, regulated and precisely calculated bursts of natural adrenalin required to stay at peak physical performance. I hope I'm not stealing your show, Mr Andersson,' the chief of police said, turning and smiling at the latter.

Andersson politely assured him of the contrary and they watched as the robust form of Sergeant Verdi weaved and dived through the street, shooting wildly at figures that appeared in windows, out of doors and on rooftops.

Cathy glanced round at the almost fragile in comparison, office-conditioned Belvois, and wondered if they hadn't somehow made a grave error.

Belvois, who had been watching the sergeant's performance with intense interest, suddenly became aware of her attentions. He turned, grinned and winked at her.

'My turn, I believe,' he said. 'Piece of cake, watch this.'

He ran off through the street, gambolling and shooting in much the same way as the sergeant had done before him. However, Cathy knew that behind the human facade, a cold, deadly, computer-like accuracy was guiding his movements.

Sergeant Verdi knew nothing really about the experiment he was helping with, just that his performance was being compared to that of the half-French wimp who had bored him for the last twenty-four hours with incessant chatter about everything and anything under the sun, and now, this great pain in the neck had actually outdone him on the first field test.

'One hundred per cent success rate for an absolute beginner whereas your top pro here only managed eighty-nine point five,' Andersson was saying to Chief Ciambella, unable to restrain his enthusiasm.

'The next stage is a hand-to-hand combat situation in which the success of your man will be severely put to the test,' Ciambella said, his professional pride beginning to show. He wasn't sure if it had been such a good idea to agree to this performance testing, but he had to admit that if this thing worked without side effects, it would certainly revolutionise military expectations and thinking.

'I have no fears for my boy here,' Andersson said with certainty. 'He has been program... er... informed with all the latest literature on the subject.' Andersson wasn't sure as to exactly why he had preferred not to use the word programming, as it was certainly a more accurate lexical choice, but somehow it didn't seem quite so sporting.

Ciambella shot his sergeant a sly glance. It certainly was a little brazen to assume that a man who had read a few books on self-defence could get the better of the tough, experienced men that he was about to face. The sergeant smiled secretly back at his chief – the bookworm wouldn't stand a chance against the cream of his ju-jitsu squad.

They headed back to the main building and through a door inscribed 'Ala B' and found themselves in a well-equipped gymnasium.

Cathy looked around in awe at the myriad machines that had been invented to help keep man in top physical condition. Nearly every square foot at the sides of the gym was taken up by a computer-controlled machine that measured efficiency and planned a workout on the basis of the results. In the middle was a huge foam-cushioned mat that brought memories of school life flooding back to her – the smell of stale feet that she'd had to lie and gyrate upon every afternoon as a girl. She wrinkled her nose a little in disgust. Ah yes, she guessed that no matter how modernised these places became, some forms of torture remained immortal.

Three firmly muscled specimens came out of the changing rooms. Cathy raised her eyebrows slightly in approval. She had always had a weakness for the macho sort; her late husband, Robert, had himself once been a triathlon iron-man athlete.

Both Belvois and the sergeant went into the changing rooms and after about five minutes they emerged, showered and dressed in blue tracksuits. Despite the wash and change of clothing though, the sergeant looked little refreshed. Belvois, on the other hand – much to the good sergeant's ever-increasing despair – showed little or no sign of fatigue whatsoever. Cathy eyed the top Belvois was wearing and noted how it sagged over his rounded shoulders. A little padding was perhaps necessary here and there, she mused, but even then, he would still have looked no match for any of the three he-men that awaited him on the mat.

'Do you want me to go first?' the sergeant asked Belvois miserably. To be honest, this was the part he had been dreading the most. It wasn't that any of the boys were better than him – they had all been his students at one time or another – but in his present physical condition, the tiredness that his older bones were beginning to feel, he just couldn't guarantee himself certain victory. And he hadn't had breakfast yet.

'There's no need to be so gallant, Sergeant Verdi,' Belvois replied politely. 'Anyway, I believe it's my turn to initiate procedures.'

'Very well,' said the sergeant. 'Perhaps you'd like to choose your opponent.'

The taller of the three men whispered something to his colleagues and they all laughed. He stepped forward and stood to attention before the sergeant and Belvois.

'Sir?'

'Yes, Lieutenant?'

'Am I right in thinking that the opponent is to be the little one next to you?' He seemed to be struggling to keep a straight face.

'That's right, Lieutenant.'

'Well, sir, that being the case, if he promises to go easy on me, I'd like to offer myself up as victim – my colleagues are just too terrified.'

There was an outbreak of sniggering from behind the valiant martyr, and the sergeant himself was forced to smother a grin. Those guys! He turned back to Belvois expectantly. 'Well?' he asked.

Belvois looked the three men up and down for a second, and then glanced over to the other side of the mat where Andersson, Cathy, Ciambella and the general were standing.

'All three at once,' he answered simply.

A look of surprise and bewildered amusement cut into the lieutenant's grizzled features. He looked at the sergeant for confirmation.

'You heard the man, Lieutenant. All three of you at once.'

The lieutenant saluted smartly. 'Yessir!'

He turned and signalled the other two to come forward. The sergeant saluted all four and left the mat.

'Don't worry,' the lieutenant whispered in mock sympathy to Belvois as he bent over in the obligatory bow. 'We'll make this as quick and painless as possible. That way we all get to go home early.'

When they finally stood facing each other, and the three huge, unarmed combat experts began menacingly encircling their much smaller adversary, Cathy realised just exactly what it was that

Belvois had requested, even though she'd been out of earshot.

'He has requested to take on all three at once,' confirmed the sergeant as matter-of-factly as possible.

Perhaps it was some kind of mother instinct, but she wanted to scream and get it all called off right there and then. He was going to get himself slaughtered. She closed her eyes, unable to watch.

She needn't have worried: two accurate punches, a well-placed karate chop and a surprisingly savage headbutt later, and when she reopened her eyes, Belvois was the only one of the four left standing.

The chief and Sergeant Verdi could only stare in wordless astonishment as the slight and seemingly inoffensive man turned his back on the strewn, groaning and unconscious, and walked calmly over. He wasn't even breathing hard. The whole thing had lasted less than a few seconds.

'Are there any more?' asked Belvois simply. 'Or was that it?'

He turned and saw the concerned sergeant running to check on his fallen comrades and then caught the curious look of mixed horror and relief on Cathy's face at the extremely excessive and unexpected explosion of violence.

'Oh, I can assure you that they are only stunned,' said Belvois calmly. 'Absolutely no permanent damage. I used only the minimum force necessary to neutralise the threat.'

A quick check by the sergeant confirmed the truth of Belvois' statement, and slowly, the three men began to come round, groaning and a little dizzy. It was decided that all three should report themselves to the medical officer immediately, and they staggered out of the gym, nursing various tender body parts.

Due to the sudden and unexpected lack of adversaries, Sergeant Verdi found that his little combat demonstration had to be cancelled. Both he and his tired bones were secretly most grateful. The final part of the test was a mere formality after what they had just seen. This time they had to walk out once more under the blue morning sky and on to the firing range. As they stood waiting for the targets to be set up, Andersson glanced at the sergeant who, by this time, was yawning and beginning to feel very much the worse for wear.

'Been a long day, eh?' he asked. 'Even for a toughened professional like yourself, I imagine.'

Sergeant Verdi didn't understand a word of English, but he understood the tone of the insinuation. He grunted, straightened himself up and smartly removed the rifle from his shoulder which, to tell the truth, had begun to weigh rather heavily over the last five minutes or so. He pointed his weapon at the target, placed a bloodshot eye up next to the sight and squeezed the trigger. Missing wildly its intended target, the bullet rebounded off the scarred wall beyond and buried itself snugly in the dark, warm earth with a self-satisfied 'phut'. It sounded so nice and comforting. He fired off another three shots that landed close to the first. Phut, phut, phut, they went, one after the other. How he envied them, and what he wouldn't do to lie down just for five minutes himself. He was feeling old, and the bags under his eyes seemed to him to wobble with the smallest physical exertion. A few years back he could have managed this trial with maximum efficiency and continued for up to seventy-two hours, no problem, but this academy life had made him lazy, and it was all too easy to get used to regular hours and shifts.

'A somewhat disappointing result,' commented Andersson in a tone that irritated Ciambella no end.

He turned to the sergeant and patted him on the back in jovial consolation. 'Never mind old man, we're only human, aren't we?'

The crack from Belvois' rifle interrupted once more both the tranquillity of the early morning and that of the sergeant.

'Phut!'

The projectile had followed a similar trajectory to those previously fired by the sergeant.

A wordless silence pervaded.

'Well… uh…' Andersson finally managed.

'No problem,' said Belvois, finely adjusting the rifle's position on his shoulder. 'Being my first time, I hadn't calculated for the recoil drag to the left. I believe I have now remedied the situation.'

The soothingly calm tones of Belvois' voice lapped gently over the back of the sergeant's mind and seemed to lull him into a kind of oneness with the rising sun that warmly caressed the back of his shaved neck. Belvois' second shot hardly made his eyelids flutter at all, and the third and fourth became the pop of tennis balls against rackets on a hot summer's afternoon. He could even hear the score being called…

'Fifteen all in the same hole,' Chief Ciambella reported, holding the target out for the others to see. 'I've never seen anything like it.'

It was true, the hole which had been enlarged slightly every time a bullet had passed through was indisputable proof of Belvois' deadly accuracy.

For the first time since the tests had begun, Andersson turned and looked for the General's opinion. Coal-black eyes squinting from under the dark blue military cap met his and rewarded him with a single silent nod.

Andersson looked like he had just won first prize in a national lottery. 'Really not a bad effort for a beginner, eh, Sergeant?'

All faces turned towards the worthy professional, only to find the space that the sturdy fellow had occupied up until a few moments ago now completely vacant. Instead, a slight downward inclination of their necks allowed instant assessment of his new geographical location. Curled up on the ground at their feet, thumb in mouth and rifle embraced, Sergeant Sergio Verdi snored blissfully.

Andersson beamed at Cathy over his huge oak desk. 'Well,' he said, rubbing his hands together in a way that reminded her of a certain character from a Dickens novel, 'I believe congratulations are in order.' He grinned in turn at the tall, skinny figure who was sat next to Cathy with a lap full of reports.

Bruno Menti smiled gratefully back, despite feeling rather hurt at being excluded from the military test on the grounds of there 'not being enough room in the car'. However, it was good to be recognised for the hard work and time he had spent on the project. Even if the project had not been his brainchild, he was glad that his invaluable and untiring contributions as psychologist and technical assistant to the Scottish woman had been appreciated. Menti cleared his throat and began.

'Here is the complete report of the project's achievements,

which not only equal any other previous candidate's physical and mental endurance, but also exceed all expected estimations.' He spoke English with only a slight trace of an Italian accent – four years' study in psychology at Southampton University had seen to that.

Cathy twisted a little in her seat. She could respect Menti for his precise and complete professionalism, but she hated his cold, clinical attitude to a fellow human being, and that he always referred to Belvois as 'the project'.

'In short,' Menti continued, 'the project's physical strength seems to have increased to nearly three times his original capacity and reflex time to almost six. He also shows no apparent reduction in will-power or loss of independent thought capacity as in previous cases.'

Andersson flicked through the pages of the report that he had just been handed. He already knew its contents, but Menti was a stickler for formality.

'So the little gadget seems to work,' he said. 'Still, there's one more trial that our superman has to undergo.' He turned to Cathy. 'Is Belvois showing any signs of adverse side effects?'

'Nothing evident,' she replied, 'nothing we've been able to detect. Some small confusion at the beginning while his mind adapted to the different information impulses. Everything, if you'll forgive the expression, seems to be going like clockwork.'

Chapter Fifteen

Morph was having a fine day. After having slept late, he had been woken by a sleeky, blonde Swiss number called Nuria who, in Morph's personal opinion, had not only been in possession of the sexiest nose he'd ever seen, but had also served him up a very tasty breakfast. That had been great.

When he'd finally raised himself and showered, he had ventured out into the sunshine, found his way to the firm he had wanted to visit, and they had taken him to lunch. A very good lunch and a successfully concluded deal. And that had been great, too.

Now he was sat in the hotel bar with his feet stretched out under a table, awaiting the imminent arrival of a cool beer. He loved Switzerland and doing business with the Swiss – they were so organised and precise, just like their watches. Everywhere else seemed so untidy and unhygienic in comparison, but that was something that only became apparent when you left the country and returned home or crossed the border into France or Italy. The latter would be his next destination.

Smiling to himself, he remembered the first time he had made a similar trip. Crossing the border into Italy had been like leaving a public library and walking straight into a bookmaker's with the Grand National in full swing. The noise, the emotion, the litter, the corrupt politicians! Still, such contrasts only added to its spice, he was looking forward to Italy as well.

Actually, Morph couldn't see why Italian politicians were considered any more dishonest than all the others. Their only fault had been to get caught with their hands in the sack. And it certainly couldn't be said that they were any less astute or cunning than their foreign colleagues. Quite the contrary, in fact, if what had happened at a meeting of the European Commission just a few years back was anything to go by.

All the foreign ministers had been present, and many other

honourable representatives of their countries' needs and requirements, all armed with the most persuasive of speeches to get the best possible deal for their respective homelands. And while these heated and vital negotiations were in progress, the Italians managed to slip in a little request of their own, a request which not only brought proceedings to a halt, but devastated, depressed and demoralised all the other trouser-wearers present. They asked that an extra two centimetres be added to the length of our slippery, rubber friend, the condom!

Well! No need to comment on the understandable and irreparable damage this had on the self-esteem and confidence of the other male delegates present. After all, how can you continue to promote yourself, your countrymen, and your country's interests under such impossible conditions? In the certain knowledge that when it came right down to it, down to the nitty-gritty, when the game was called and the cards were finally exposed on the table, in a trousers-down, man-to-man, true-grit showdown, you weren't going to come even a close second.

Needless to say, the Italians got their own way on everything that day. Little wonder then, that a few years after, during the 'Clean Hands' investigations, most of them were arrested. Foul play, dirty, low-down tactics, but nevertheless, highly effective. The logical answer? More women politicians, perhaps.

Morph thanked the waiter for his beer, took a long thirsty glug, and then fought the urge to burp violently. Yesterday's copy of the *Independent* lay on the chair next to him. He picked it up and gave it the once-over. There was nothing new: another terrorist attack; the US President had agreed to peace talks about some conflict in an unpronounceable Asian country (he wondered briefly what the Americans had got to do with it anyway); the stock market still in chaos; and the British Minister for Food and Hygiene was involved in some salmonella cover-up scandal in the south of England.

He sighed and turned to the cricket results, shook his head sadly, sighed again and, reaching for the pen in his inside jacket pocket, attempted the crossword instead. In an hour or so he would get changed and find out the latest events in the smuggled-hippy saga. His own personal theory on the event was that some of Chris's friends had got together and pulled a practical joke on him. Anyway, no one had been hurt so far, and the whole thing had certainly spiced up what might have otherwise been a routine business trip.

Chris's day was progressing equally well. Having slept until his usual hour of mid-afternoonish (chronological precision held little importance and he had not worn a watch since schooldays), he made himself a fried egg sandwich and found a note on the kitchen table informing him that a parcel had arrived by courier while he had slept and that it was on the hall table. Ali had gone out to buy some provisions for the evening.

'Far out!' cried Chris and ran to open it. Inside was his passport, five hundred pounds in traveller's cheques and a note that read:

Dear Chris,

We're all extremely happy to know you are safe and well, but the incident still leaves us somewhat perplexed. We feel it wiser that you accept Ali's kind invitation to stay with him for a few weeks until this is all cleared up. Two weeks should give me sufficient time to complete investigations into the matter.

Have fun and, more importantly, don't make any waves that will bring attention to your presence. Hope the money I'm sending will last you – I decided to send it by post rather than use a bank as I was informed that it was quicker and probably more reliable. Was I right?

All the best, Dad

PS Your mother wishes to know if you are completely recovered from the food poisoning and also to tell you that you should stick to your vegetarian diet of before.
PPS You should also know that we are considering changing the burger bar into a health food restaurant. What do you think?

'Far out!' said Chris again, looking at the postmark and the courier express stamp on the envelope. 'These guys are really fast.'

Wearing Ali's 'western' clothes didn't bother him at all as it had been a while since he had looked in the mirror and seen himself dressed in anything other than jeans, T-shirt and trainers. Actually it had been a while since he had looked at himself in the mirror, period. Sporting a multicoloured shirt and safari shorts certainly felt better than a hospital blanket. A pair of flip-flops were the only shoes that Ali had in his size, but anything felt better than walking the streets barefoot. He decided to go out and change some of the cheques and then see what took his fancy.

Passport! Yes, he'd need it to prove his identity at the bank. He picked it up and tried to slide it into the back pocket of his shorts.

No way, José.

Why does British officialdom feel that its citizens need such a cumbersome monstrosity to accompany them on their travels? Every other nation in the world has passports or identity cards that fit snugly into any standard shirt or trouser pocket, but the poor British traveller has to either use up precious luggage space or have it protruding rudely from some pocket or other, declaring his or her nationality to all who wish or don't wish to know it. Not that there is anything particular to be ashamed about in being British. It is more a matter of personal privacy and discretion, both of which are reputedly good solid British values. A strange irony.

Chris had actually heard of a smaller passport version and, when he'd applied, had even gone to the trouble of including a small note requesting it, but they had sent him the usual monstrosity regardless. He rammed it down into the breast pocket of his shirt and the top part stuck out half a mile; he tried to force it down a little further, but only succeeded in ripping some stitches. He gave up the struggle, took the spare keys from the dining room table and he and his nationality walked bravely out to meet the Swiss nation.

Five minutes later he was back in the apartment and quite annoyed about it too. Apparently it was some kind of bank holiday and everything was closed. He decided instead to put some sounds on, and went into the living room to look for the sound system.

When Ali returned, Chris was sitting on the sofa twiddling his hair and drinking another cup of coffee.

'Is everything all right?' asked Ali cheerfully as he passed into the kitchen with a brown paper bag full of shopping.

Chris got up and followed him.

'So there is somewhere open then!'

'Of course, this is a major city. And besides, you can always rely on little Asian corner shops to be open in any part of the world.'

'I suppose so.' He was unable to negate Ali's wisdom on that point, thinking back on the numerous occasions he'd had to go out and buy chocolate chip cookies on a late night or Sunday munchies run. 'You don't think they'd be willing to cash a few hundred pounds of traveller's cheques, do you?'

Ali looked doubtful. Chris changed the subject, sagely deciding to spend Ali's instead. So he asked something else that had been bothering him for a good half an hour.

'Why is it that absolutely nothing works in this place, man?'

Silence.

'Well, nothing electric, I mean. The sounds don't work, the TV makes a kind of a weird screaming kind of noise…'

'Oh, does it?' Ali sounded mildly pleased. 'That, at least, is an improvement.'

'Not even the lift outside works, or the doorbell, nothing. Not even the light bulbs – you only have candles!'

'I know. They kept exploding every time I switched them on, so in the end I just gave up.'

'Why? Is there some kind of problem with power surges?'

'No.'

'Well, what is it then?'

'I do not really know.' Ali's tone was getting sulkier and his amiable features took on an unusually sullen air.

'Bit of a bummer, man.' Chris shook his head, bewildered. 'Well, what do you do for kicks?' He was finding it hard to imagine a world without television, video, instant music and computer games.

'Kicks?'

'Relax. Entertainment.'

'Well, I have a rather culturally ancient and traditional approach to that – I go down the Greek bar, drink and play cards. But I am afraid it is closed today.'

Chris wrinkled his nose.

'Monopoly?' Ali suggested, suddenly catching on that his new guest and nephew had probably passed a rather boring bank holiday afternoon.

'Hardly a culturally ancient game. Besides we'd need a third player.'

'Backgammon, then?'

The gauntlet had been dropped. Backgammon was no game to be taken lightly and the challenge had to be accepted. A love of backgammon had been instilled in him by his father from a very early age; it is a love that runs deep in Arabic genes, like football to the Latins, cricket to the English, close harmony singing to the Welsh and porridge to the Scots.

Chris let the dice roll hard against the sides of the wooden board and slammed the counters down into their new positions, revelling in the hollow, woody sounds. Ali played likewise, in the Arabic manner, snapping his fingers together in a frenetic rhythm and thereby maintaining the concentration required to play at a dizzying speed. Played right, backgammon should not be a game with relaxing pauses, but a hectic flurry of counters and dice. And so, amid cries of 'Gammon!', 'Backgammon!', or even simply 'Hah!', they passed a very furious half hour.

'So, have you called a technician or something?' asked Chris finally, his eyes not leaving the board for an instant.

'It does not do any good.' Ali hurled the dice and they rebounded violently off the sides of the board. 'Double, hah!' he shouted triumphantly. 'The problem is me. It seems...' He paused, a counter suspended in the air. '...that everything electronic breaks down as soon as I touch it. It is a real problem.'

Chris looked up at him and laughed in disbelief.

'It is no laughing matter, I am afraid,' said Ali, with an air of being deadly serious. 'Have you heard of people who are allergic to the twentieth century?' He put the counter a little dubiously down on a red column.

'Uh, yeah, but I've never really believed in it. I always thought it was just an excuse to drop out, get back to nature and just hang out, social security financed. I've often considered it myself.' Chris threw the dice, removed two of Ali's pieces from the board, and replaced them with two of his own.

Ali looked accusingly at his position.

'In some cases, maybe. But I can assure you it is a genuine and growing phenomena.'

Chris was having trouble seeing the connection between this and Ali's problem. He started to say as much but was immediately interrupted.

'Well, my problem is exactly the contrary. I am not allergic to the twentieth century – it is allergic to me!' He took a short breath and then added, 'Or at least all the machines seem to be.'

It was true. The first symptoms had begun to show up shortly after his arrival in Switzerland. First his watch, then the car radio; a coffee machine here and a calculator there. But it had been the rather odd television repair man, recently emigrated from Yorkshire, who had first hit the nail on the head. He remembered with clarity the look of anger and frustration on his red, bulldog face after Ali had called him out for the third time in two days.

'Thur's now't wrong with this set or any of these other poor suffrin' maarvuls of modern technolugy,' he had said. 'Ah reckun it's you that's got the ruddy problem, ya bugga. It's you that needs the bloody specialist, so you can sod off if you think arm cumin round 'ere wastin' me time agin wit likes o' you, lad.' And had picked up his tools and stomped out.

However unnecessarily rude the man may have seemed at the time, his words had struck home. After that, Ali had been to see several different types of experts, doctors and specialists in both western and oriental medicine, but no one had been able to find what was wrong.

'And it's getting progressively worse with age. I fear the consequences if I ever have to take a plane or go somewhere by sophisticated transport, or if I happen to come into contact with someone who has a pacemaker. It seems that the more electronically complex something is, the quicker it dies.'

Chris, of course, wanted to see a demonstration, but apart from Ali's understandable reluctance to blow anything else up, the simple fact was that there was nothing left in the apartment that actually still worked.

'I'm sure you could get rich with a gimmick like that.' Chris was fascinated by the idea.

'Doing what?' asked Ali, somewhat surprised. 'It is completely and utterly useless.'

'Industrial sabotage?'

'I am not the terrorist type.'

Chris scratched his head, puzzled. 'Well, why did you decide to stay in a big city? I mean, wouldn't it make more sense to go and live on a farm or something? And how did you get here from Persia?'

Ali sighed softly and shook his head. 'Cumulation of events,' he answered.

Chris sat and listened in silence as Ali began the story of his escape from Persia, how they had known about the Shah's downfall two years in advance and how everything had been dealt with through network agents. This part of the story he knew very well; his father had told it and retold it innumerable times.

'You see, I could not have gone myself, there would have been too many questions asked by state officials. I originally wanted one of those little Swiss chalets, you know, all black and white and made of wood and overlooking a lake.' He stopped and sighed again. 'But they said I would probably have to wait years for something of the sort – highly in demand you know – and I did not have the time.'

Chris recalled the view from Ali's living room window that looked out on to a narrow street and a grey office block.

'Why don't you sell up and move somewhere else now you do have the time?'

'I guess I am used to it now, and I hope one day to find a cure. Besides, I have made a lot of friends here.' He indicated the back wall of the kitchen that joined his apartment to his neighbour's.

'And Madam Depuis next door is one in a million.'

'Oh?'

'For the telephone, I mean. I give everyone her number and she bangs on the wall to let me know when there is a call. I even gave her the money to buy an intercom system, so now I can speak directly with the people who call.' He pointed to a little speaker device mounted on the wall. 'I never even have to touch it,' he added, looking rather pleased with his own ingenuity.

Chris tried to imagine the scene before the introduction of the intercom. His gaze drifted around the kitchen. The microwave looked like it had been dead for years, but the oven seemed functional enough.

'It is gas,' Ali explained, smiling. 'Nothing electrical about it.'

'Gammon!' exclaimed Chris, and removed his last counter from the board.

Chapter Sixteen

Bzzzz.

'Doctor McDonald to see you, sir, on an urgent matter.'

'Thank you, Miss Lee. Have her enter.'

Andersson sat behind his desk and listened to his secretary's voice as she asked McDonald to enter. She was among his most trusted employees, with him for over five years and an excellent linguist who could switch between English, German, Chinese and Italian without batting an Oriental eyelid. Efficient and rather tidy, he thought, but he wasn't the sort to destroy a wonderful business relationship – maybe twenty years ago in his foolhardy youth... His thoughts were interrupted by a black, confidential report file placed under his nose. The words 'Destiny Project' were written on it in bold, blue type. Automatically, he began to thumb through it.

'I think there may be a slight snag,' began Cathy; her left eye narrowed slightly as it always did when she was concerned.

'In what way?' Andersson put the file back down on his desk. Everything had been going so well he couldn't imagine any serious problems, but the tall, pretty blonde who stood before him was in no way to be taken lightly – this was no beach bimbo, despite her appearance.

Cathy McDonald had been with the project since its initial stages, one of its three original creator/designers who had been working in the company's research laboratory in Washington. A top medical scientist whose specialist field had been neurosurgical programmes, she, together with her husband, had come up with a method of directly stimulating and then manipulating the alpha wave patterns of the brain, rendering them compatible with the types of wave transmission that could be generated by an artificial intelligence. In short, direct communication between the human mind and a computer. It had been a small step from wires and electrodes to a tiny surgical implant in the brain itself, a biochemical interface capable of transmitting information directly into the memory.

The original concept had been typically idealistic, Andersson thought. Scientists who wanted to save people time and improve the quality of their lives by doing away with all the need and drudgery of rote learning. The possibility of learning entire languages in a day. Complex mathematical equations assimilated instantly and never forgotten. People could be granted the gift of a photographic memory. Ah, as a schoolboy and then an undergraduate, how he himself had desired such a thing! What vast amounts of time, of precious vital youth, he'd had to waste in memorising large chunks of dusty textbooks never to be needed or thought about again once the exam was over. The efficiency of the computer merged in one harmonious and glorious union with the creativity and passion of the human mind.

An interesting side effect of this union had been the discovery that the interface could also be used to send messages to those parts of the brain responsible for the motor activities of the body. There had been talk of cures for insomnia, certain forms of asthma, epilepsy, and other such psychosomatic-related illnesses.

However, it had taken a businessman to envision the sheer financial potential of such a phenomenon. What country would not pay for the services of such men, such super soldiers, whose muscles, whose entire metabolism could be enhanced by short, regulated bursts of adrenalin, controlled with computer precision from the brain? Tireless and deadly accurate, able to achieve their physical peak on command, and, of course, very well informed. Finding buyers had not been a problem for his little team's invention. The patriotic side of him had put him in contact with the top brass in Washington first of all, and the General had offered them a very handsome sum indeed. He had also facilitated their transfer out of the States and over to their sister company in Italy when certain human rights groups had begun to rally the US government for an official investigation into rumours of experimental human brain surgery. Any official US investigation would then have to pass through the normal chaos of Italian diplomatic channels. This, together with the political and organisational disruption in that country, meant that it would be a long, long time before anything happened, and by then, all too late.

Still, the project's biggest selling point had been the enhanced mental capacity of the subject. As the General himself had pointed out, the Russians and the Chinese had also been working on their own ideas for a super warrior. The difference there was that they were actually substituting parts of human bodies with state-of-the-art technology. Cyborgs! Extremely strong and very effective, but very expensive, and the intellectual capacity of the subjects could not generally be seen as a plus. What was really necessary was the capacity to adapt to and reason well in difficult situations. After all, wasn't it exactly this quality that had made the comparatively feeble-bodied mankind the most successful species on the planet?

The General, however, had been against the usual IQ tests, preferring something more in keeping with the military mind, where the protagonist had to react and adapt in a limited time to the tactical and strategic assaults made on him by the enemy. Chess had been the General's suggestion; well, actually, he had virtually insisted. 'A real test of memory and understanding of complex spatial relationships,' he had said, 'with the unpredictable and often genial nature of the human factor thrown in.'

Andersson had had no qualms as he'd always been a firm believer in the maxim: 'The customer is always right.'

Up until now, the game had always been the stomping ground of a few talented geniuses, with computers coming in a close second because they lacked the creative capacity to recognise and exploit certain positions. But, in Andersson's opinion, this would all soon change. For this reason, the International Open Chess Tournament in Salsomaggiore had been chosen as an ideal test run.

'Well, basically,' Cathy began, 'the problem is Belvois. He's hooked himself into the Internet and is reading everything he can, from mythology and philosophy right through to the latest publications on nuclear fission, and he refuses to stop.' She paused and absent-mindedly scratched her left ear, which had served as part of an evening meal for some hungry mosquito the night before. 'If you can call it reading, that is. Perhaps total assimilation is a better term for someone who is receiving it as direct input. Apparently he's been at it for over five hours.'

'My God!' exclaimed Andersson, taking it in. 'That's a fair old whack of literature.' He paused. 'But I don't really see the problem. I realise he wasn't supposed to become a walking public library, but it's well within the project's capacity, and we do want to find out just what his limits are, no?' A moment of doubt struck him. 'There isn't any risk of an overload, is there?'

Cathy shook her head. 'His theoretical storage capacity is way beyond what he's likely to take in, even if he continued non-stop for over seventy-two hours. However, I am concerned about the psychological damage that might occur. We don't know what long-term effects the constant direct input may have on his mind. Despite everything, he's still only human, and the psyche needs time to adapt the old and come to terms with the new. Doctor Menti says it's possible that Belvois might lose the capacity to differentiate between what he's learnt through personal experience – his natural memories – and what the computer is downloading him. If this happens, the knowledge and memories that originally carved the personality of the man we call Belvois may be lost for ever among the mass of new input.'

The furrow in Andersson's brow deepened, joining his eyebrows together in one long, hairy caterpillar. 'What you're telling me, in layman's terms, is that our man may suffer a severe identity crisis, right?'

'Or worse. I've tried to convince him to rest so that we can have time to study the effects, but he won't listen to me or anyone else. So I thought that perhaps you personally...'

Andersson called Miss Lee and told her to join them in laboratory B and to bring with her a strong sedative. 'I'm not one to take chances,' he said in answer to Cathy's surprised look.

Belvois was sat with his back to the door. A computer screen flashed up information too quick for the eye to read in response to a finger that seemed to be tapping out a fast samba rhythm on the mouse in his hand. His eyes and half his face were covered by a dark, plexiglass visor which served as an intermediary, decoding and passing the digitised information directly into the tiny implant in his head.

Laboratory B was techno buff's heaven. It seemed furnished with almost every electronic gadget under the sun, not to mention a dizzying variety of personal computers and medical equipment. As Belvois had said when he'd first entered the room, the only thing missing was a food blender.

Two men in white overalls sat at their own computers, frenziedly recording and categorising the information that Belvois was accessing.

Andersson approached him tentatively. 'How's it going there? Aren't you even going to stop for coffee?'

Belvois didn't answer, nor did he give any sign of acknowledgement. Andersson turned to Cathy and shrugged. He wasn't used to being ignored and, for an instant, looked unsure as to how he should react.

'When the translator is in operation,' she explained, 'the user is, to a certain extent, isolated from his major senses.'

The translator was what she called the visor around Belvois' head that translated the raw digital data into wave formations compatible with those his biochemical interface could read.

'Well, what do we do now, then?' Andersson asked.

'All things considered,' Cathy replied, glancing over at Menti working on his computer. 'The best thing would be simply to turn the computer off but I'm not sure as to his reaction. He's been totally isolated in the system now for a long time. It might come as a great shock.'

They both glanced over at Menti who nodded his agreement. 'Can't offer a better solution myself. Best do it.'

'Wait!' Belvois' voice suddenly boomed out from under the visor. 'Just... let... mee... arrr, yess.' He removed the translator, placed it carefully on the table beside the keyboard and squinted, his eyes as yet unfocused, in the direction of Cathy and Andersson. He began fumbling in his shirt pocket for his glasses and then laughed good-humouredly. 'I forgot... I don't... need these any more.' It was true, even the short-sightedness that he'd had since childhood had been corrected. 'Old habeets... die hard, I... guess.'

Cathy walked up, took hold of Belvois' wrist and checked his pulse, forehead temperature and the back of his neck where they had made the implant. There was no real need to do it as the translator device had automatically recorded and displayed the user's vital signs on to a computer screen nearby, but it made her feel better anyway.

'There eez no need for that, Doctor,' Belvois said, but left his wrist in her soft hands all the same.

'I know, but I guess old habits die hard with me as well.'

Belvois glanced over and saw Miss Lee discreetly hand Andersson a dart tranquilliser pistol. 'Oh, I assure you that... you won't... be needeeng to take such... drasteek measures. Anyway, I have learnt quite eenarf for one day.'

The words issued forth slowly and awkwardly at first, but with ever-increasing fluidity and precision. 'But really, how could you expect me to be satisfied with just a few pamphlets on chess and martial arts?'

Miss Lee's jaw dropped as she finally cottoned on to what had happened.

'You've learnt English in an afternoon!' she exclaimed, in astonishment.

'Yes, and I've just finished reading the complete works of Shakespeare and Shelley een the original language.'

Andersson placed the gun down on the table beside him and grinned. 'And how are you feeling now?'

'Fine. A leettle tired. I need sleep.'

Shortly after, Belvois left the room chatting merrily away with Miss Lee. Andersson and Cathy stood and watched them go.

'We need to think harder about that language idea,' he said in a light-hearted tone. 'I mean his grammar and syntax are perfect, but the accent and pronunciation certainly need a "leetle" more work.'

'Yes,' agreed Cathy. She shook her head in amazement. 'I wonder if Miss Lee is thinking the same about his Chinese right now.'

Chapter Seventeen

Morph rang the doorbell to Ali's apartment, and it farted wetly at him. He gave it a look of disgust and knocked instead. It was Chris who finally answered.

Five minutes later all three were sat on cushions around a squat, round table in the centre of the living room. In the middle was a large plate full of the huge Persian variety of roasted and salted sunflower seeds. Three piles of empty shells lay on side plates. Morph's pile was particularly small. They tasted good, there could be no denying it, but he was still at a complete loss as to how to shell them, even after the others had patiently demonstrated the technique several times to him.

The rest of the room was sparsely furnished. The cushions and the table were the centrepieces of the room. Off-white lace curtains covered the windows and a picture of a scantily clad black girl carrying pots to a stream hung above the fireplace. A widescreen TV towered protectively over a video recorder nearby and the immense Persian rug which carpeted the room was strewn with books, papers and dirty coffee mugs.

This, thought Morph, was definitely a bachelor's place. His own apartment in Bournemouth would have suffered a similar fate if he hadn't had a cleaner come in once a week to pick up his socks and dust his rubber plant.

'Your helping Chris is deeply appreciated by all our family, Mr Armstrong. And if there is anything we, or I, personally, can do for you, just ask,' Ali was saying sincerely.

'Yeah, man. Thanks a lot. It was really cool of you. I gotta admit that you're one in a million.'

A greater compliment a beardomorph could not receive.

'Aww,' said Morph feeling a little self-conscious, 'it was nothing really. I just found him in the boot, that's all.' He stopped suddenly and a look of concern passed briefly over the visible part of his face – the part that wasn't covered with hair or distorted by his glasses, that is. It had been nagging at him all day and now he seized his opportunity. 'Well, there is a little question that you could answer for me.'

'And that is?' asked Ali.

'You could perhaps tell me how on earth you already knew my name before we'd even met.'

Ali nodded in acknowledgement. 'I see that you are a sharp observer, Mr Armstrong,' he said and laughed. 'Yes, you are right. I knew about you before your arrival at my doorstep yesterday evening. After Chris had contacted his family, his father made some enquiries, and then immediately phoned to advise me of the situation.'

'Through Madame Depuis,' interrupted Chris.

Ali briefly explained about the information network they had set up to protect themselves from the possibility of Iranian reprisals against ex-Shah sympathisers.

'So you probably know all about me?' asked Morph, pretty impressed. He had always liked the cloak-and-dagger stuff.

'Well, no, not exactly,' Ali admitted. 'But we know that you are clean as far as having reasons for kidnapping. I know that you are here on sales rep business, that you occasionally travel over to the continent and that you have your own company in Bournemouth, but as to what exactly it is that you sell, it is rather uncertain.'

Chris eyed Morph, and placed another handful of seeds between his teeth and cracked them open in anticipation.

'Drugs?' he prompted, vainly hopeful.

'It's no mystery,' said Morph, and picked up another seed. It had taken him a good minute to shell one and less than a whole millisecond to devour. It was no good, he would die of hunger first. Out of pure desperation, he rammed a handful in his mouth, chombling the lot, shells and all. His stomach rumbled, discontentedly empty. And to think that he could have been enjoying a delicious fondue back at the hotel right at that moment, with waitress service – maybe even Nuria who had served him breakfast... 'I sell anything legal that comes my way,' he mumbled through his teeth, managing, nevertheless to emphasise the adjective.

Morph looked hungrily over at the hippy happily gorging

himself on nuts. He chombled some more on the now minced and soggy mass of nut and shell in his mouth. He wanted to spit it out but it would have been just too disgusting. So, fighting a violent urge to gag, he swallowed hard, and sharp pieces of shell scratched their way slowly, clingingly, down his throat, as if reluctant to leave his oral cavity.

'No, just joking.' He sounded strangely breathless and had turned decidedly pale. Forcing the sides of his mouth upwards in what he assumed should closely resemble a smile, he continued bravely with his discourse. 'I recently bought a small firm that makes plastic signs, WC signs with pictures of men and women, room numbers, stuff like that.'

There was a silence while the other two crunched voraciously and let the last piece of information sink in. Morph observed their shelling technique, and then reached tentatively for another handful of seeds himself. 'Well, someone has to sell them,' he added, taking the defensive.

'Absolutely.' Ali appeared quite solemn and thoughtful. 'I was thinking just how vital a service it is that you offer.'

Chris sniggered through some seeds. Morph looked offended.

'No, really. I mean we have Mr Armstrong and men like him to thank for our self-improvement both physically, mentally and spiritually.'

'Far out, man!' Chris was beginning to enjoy himself. He hated all this stiff formality business. To hell with it. A bit of ribbing never hurt anyone, he reckoned.

'No, it is true,' insisted Ali, ignoring his nephew's obvious amusement. 'It is exactly these little things that save us so much time in the more mundane areas of our lives.'

Morph was interested. It was the first time he had considered his business from a social service point of view. It could be a good angle to include in his sales jargon. Ali went on.

'Imagine for a minute what life would be like and how much precious time would be wasted if there were no little informative signs of the kind. Every time you wanted to find a certain person in a building you would have to keep stopping to ask people because you wouldn't know the room numbers or floor you were on. How would you find your way across a strange city or simply find the exit in a cinema at closing time? What would you do with the litter in your hand? Where would you take your children to play in a park if you were not sure which area was designated for doggy doos? Down which hole should you pour the water or the engine oil in your car? Think of the lives that have been saved by the thoughtful placing of "Danger" signs, or the explosions and cancers that have never happened due to "No Smoking", not to mention the panic and desperation as to where you should dash to in a city when nature calls.'

'Yeah,' jumped in Chris, 'and not knowing which door was the Ladies and which was the Gents.'

'That could get a little embarrassing,' agreed Ali.

'Not if you're French,' Morph corrected him, remembering an experience in Paris the year before when, upon entering a restaurant, he had hurriedly followed the toilet sign down a flight of steps. After surviving the garlic and onion odours down the dark corridor, he had arrived at his destination only to find a queue of French ladies politely gossiping as they waited outside the only cubicle. On closer inspection he had spotted a men's urinal attached to the wall. Desperation had driven him to ask the ladies to step aside so as to give him access to it. Unfortunately, after bravely unzipping his flies, he had discovered his modesty to be far greater than his need and had had to graciously back out of the situation to whispered giggles of 'Anglais'.

'An embarrassment common to most other nationalities,' Ali proposed in retrospect.

He left the room and came back with plates of couscous and a bottle of Italian red wine. A few glasses and a full stomach later and the three had become the best of friends. Ali and Morph were even on first-name terms. The warming effect on the human soul of shared alcoholic beverage had once again worked its age-old magic, and Morph found himself chatting quite freely about the events of his day.

He had recently clinched deals for a surprisingly wide variety of plastic signs, ranging from the usual toilet sundries like those little signs that inform women not to try to flush tampons down the toilet, the standard 'No Smoking' and 'Silence' signs, to personalised management nameplates and titles for lucky, newly appointed executives to stick on their new office doors.

Morph leant over and refilled their glasses from a second bottle that Ali had produced. A puzzled look came over his face as Ali lifted his glass to his lips.

'I thought Muslims didn't or weren't allowed to drink alcohol,' he said at last.

'Ah, but I never said I was a good Muslim.'

Morph nodded sympathetically. 'Like I am not always a good Catholic, and tomorrow I'm going to a place where there are many more of my kind. I'm leaving for Italy on more business.'

'Far out, man! Where are you going?'

'Oh, a place you've probably never heard of,' answered Morph, noticing that his own speech was beginning to slur a little. 'Piacenza. It's just an industrial city south of Milan.'

Ali suddenly sat upright and leant forward towards Morph, eyes sparkling with intense interest and some astonishment. 'Piacenza, eh?' he said. Reaching over and refilling Morph's glass for him, he asked: 'How would you fancy a couple of paying travel companions, one of whom also speaks a little of the native tongue?'

Another bottle of wine later and the world had become a much finer place.

'But is it contagious?' Morph was asking, looking understandably concerned. He wasn't sure whether it was the effect of the wine or if his two hosts (especially the one dressed in the white gown) were completely wacko. 'Machines are allergic to you, so you want a lift to see some kind of witch doctor who lives in Piacenza who might be able to help you?'

'Yup,' butted in Chris, delighted at Morph's disconcertion.

'And no,' added Ali. 'Allergies are not contagious, and nobody I have met over the years since this... er... thing first manifested itself has ever shown or developed any similar symptoms.'

Morph heaved a silent sigh of relief.

'And yes, I really do believe that this "mago", this Italian witch, can help me.'

'If you're so convinced that this man is the answer to your problem, why haven't you gone to see him before now?' asked Chris reasonably.

Ali reached over to the bowl which a few hours ago had been piled high with sunflower seeds, and scraped out what remained into the palm of his hand. 'It is funny you should ask that.' He selected three choice-looking seeds, placed them in his mouth, cracked them open between his teeth and sucked out the succulent morsels with practised ease. 'Call it coincidence, or destiny even – as some would say that in this world such a thing as pure chance does not exist – but while I was out shopping this morning, I happened to pass by one of those small Italian café bars, and I did something that I do not usually do.'

Morph and Chris both glanced at each other for an instant and then turned their attention back to Ali. 'Which was?' they asked in unison.

'I went in and had a coffee.' Ali looked in turn at each of their faces and the 'So what?' expression written across them. 'You see, I never drink coffee, only tea in the morning, but today was different. It was like there was some unseen force that was urging me to go inside.'

'Well, sometimes you have to live a little dangerously, break the routine, take a chance once in a while and go for it.' Chris leant over and drained the third bottle of wine of its remaining contents into his glass, smirking at Ali's seriousness over something that his mother would have described as just 'giving way to a whimsy'.

Ignoring Chris's obvious mirth he continued with his story. 'Well, there was a television tuned to an Italian channel and I started to watch it. It was then that I saw his advert.'

'Whose?' asked Morph.

'Mago Marco the Magnificent's, of course.'

Morph's face took on a dumbfounded expression. 'And is it normal for these people to advertise on TV?' he asked, incredulous.

'Oh, yes,' replied Ali, quite matter-of-factly. 'How else can they let people know about their services?'

Morph sat silent for a short while. 'But offering something like that is not exactly the same as informing someone of a new washing powder that gets your clothes even whiter. I mean, I know they aren't all good Catholics in Italy, I said so myself before, but doesn't the Roman Church object to that kind of thing as heresy or something?'

'Yeah,' cried Chris, 'whatsa the Pope gotta saya about alla thata?'

Ali leant back casually, one elbow propping him up precariously on the edge of the huge cushion where he had been squatting for most of the evening. 'Usually,' he began, trying with all his might to fight the alcoholic dampening of his thought processes and, at the same time, to assume a certain air of credibility, 'where orthodox religions are strongest, belief in the occult and the supernatural also lie deepest.'

'Hmm,' said Morph thoughtfully, as he watched Ali slide backwards off his cushion, hairy legs flailing in the air. He took another sip from his glass.

'But if everything mechanical that you touch breaks down, how can you expect us to arrive in Piacenza with you travelling in the car?'

'Aha!' exclaimed Ali, pulling himself back up to a more dignified posture. 'It is not exactly true that everything I touch ceases to function, sometimes it just goes a little awry.'

'That's true,' verified Chris. 'The video recorder still whizzes and clicks but doesn't make much sense, and all the wrong things seem to happen when you push the buttons.'

'Aw, that's the same with all videos.' Morph himself still hadn't figured out most of the functions on his own machine, even though the instructions had clearly stated 'easy to use' and he'd had it for over three years. 'Still, I have to admit to not fancying the idea of something going "awry" with my brand new Volvo.'

'But you do not have to worry about that,' said Ali. 'That is precisely what I was coming to. It would seem that... hic...' Wayward pupils rolled around in the gradually reddening whites of his eyes. 'You see, there is a way of temporarily insulating the machines from any adverse effect... woahh!'

'What he means,' said Chris deciding to help out while his uncle once again climbed back up on his cushion, 'is that if he gets pissed – like he is now – machines are quite safe from him. Something to do with the... er... inverse proportion of... err...

something of the sort, right?'

Chris looked over at Ali for help as he suddenly realised that even if he had understood what he had been told that afternoon, his mind was beginning to feel so foggy that he was darned if he could remember it now anyway and, to be honest, he didn't really care. So, instead of trying to pursue the lost cause any longer, he wisely reached across the table for his own glass and slid forward, banging his nose hard on the low but reassuringly solid pine table he was seated in front of.

Morph rubbed his eyes in disbelief at the drunken display of inadequacy that was being acted out before him. Must be some kind of family trait, he reasoned, a genetic susceptibility to alcohol. He looked back over to Ali in the hope of some form of clarification or, better yet, further acrobatic stunts.

'That is right!' exclaimed Ali as he stood upright and straightened his gown out, oblivious of Chris's tragic table nose-butt. 'It was a theory developed and tried out by myself and a very learned and most genial Irish doctor.'

'Another pissh-head,' whispered Chris, in a confidential manner to an understanding pile of empty sunflower seed shells next to his head.

'Apparently the machines' allergic reactions diminish in direct inverse proportional rates to my increasing personal incompetence.' Ali stopped, thought and then mumbled, 'Or something like that, anyway.'

'So it's all okay, then,' said Morph, quite uncertainly.

Chris looked up from the table, nursing his quickly swelling nose. 'Why dow't you pwove it to us then?' he challenged.

'I will.' Ali took three wobbly steps to reach where Morph was sat cowering. Bending over, he took his intended victim's left wrist in his palm and touched his watch. Morph couldn't help noticing the unintentional force in that grip and realised that the Arab had not always been a gentleman of leisure.

'There, you see, nothing has happened to it,' said Ali, sounding rather pleased. Then, on closer inspection of the watch he added in a tone of disappointment, 'Oh, but that is no good. It seems to have stopped almost three hours ago. It must have been when I passed you that plate of couscous.'

Morph stared down in dismay at his faithful family heirloom.

'You know, I suppose it is quite ironic that I seem to have this effect on machines,' Ali continued unhappily, lining his body up over his own cushion in another improbable attempt at reseating himself, 'because years ago, I used to have the honoured position of chief handyman in one of the Shah's palaces.'

Chapter Eighteen

His mind spinning ecstatically in a whirlpool of data, Belvois threw himself down into the awaiting embrace of his favourite armchair and reached automatically for the TV remote control unit, then changed his mind. Instead he chewed at the end of his moustache and began massaging the sides of his head in small, comforting, circular motions, just like it had said in one of the books he had recently read on self-relaxation.

His mind was on fire, flashing and burning with new knowledge, new sensations. It was a peculiar sensation he thought, going from being merely bright to a living library in the space of a week.

At the beginning it was as if there had been two different personalities in his head, a new all-powerful, all-knowing, dictatorial side, and a small, cringing, insignificant Belvois, frightened by the awesomeness of his newly discovered potential. But that didn't seem to him to be the case any more. It was actually fun. He smiled to himself as he recalled the ease in which he had dealt with those meatball types at the academy that morning and the look of gobsmacked surprise on the face of the sergeant. Hell, it was stuff he'd always dreamt of doing as a kid when he used to read all those superhero mags. He now had a huge, almost unlimited, capacity for knowledge at his command and he wanted more. At the same time, however, there was still a little voice inside of him calling out to stop it, that he was getting lost in there. It was like being a drug addict of sorts. There was something inexplicably exciting, almost sensual, in being inundated with new thoughts and ideas. He felt a little bit like one of those fanatic collectors who, until now, he'd never been really able to understand. Like a stamp collector who, having just been bitten by the bug, had no intention of quitting until he'd got hold of that most sought after of all philatelic treasures, the penny black.

Of course, right then, he had absolutely no idea what his own personal penny black was, but he had every intention of finding out. It seemed he only had to think about any one of the subjects that he had 'learned' and it would all come searing its way back from stored to active memory in precocious detail. It certainly was a little chaotic, but he felt he was getting the hang of it.

He yawned deeply and stretched. He knew he should rest and his cute blonde doctor had seemed particularly insistent on it, but sleep was out of the question. He felt far too awake and much too alive. What he really could do with right now was a nice cup of coffee.

'Coffee. Turkish word *kharre*, Arabic *kahwa*, probable origin of word through the Dutch *koffie*. A cup of coffee: a refreshing stimulant drink of brown colour in a spherical or tubular shaped container made from the seeds of a shrub of paleotropical genus: *Coffea* mixed with hot water and frequently drunk with milk and sugar. The effects of such stimulus can...'

Stop! Enough!

Belvois got up and stomped irritably out into the kitchen. He really would have to learn to control this kind of thing or else he'd end up boring himself and everyone else in earshot to death.

Cathy had warned him of some trivial physiological side effects in the early stages while his mind was learning to handle all the new input, but he certainly hadn't been expecting to blurt out inane trivia every time he thought about something in particular. It had to stop. While driving home that evening he'd had no idea how many times he'd found himself instructing the steering wheel on the fabrication and use of traffic lights, traffic regulations, and the consequential economical and sociological effects on countries that had developed or improved methods of transport. That would teach him for having absorbed almost the entire works of the *Encyclopaedia Britannica* before supper.

It was only when he had made himself a coffee and was wandering back into the living room to watch a bit of TV that his own personal computer caught his eye.

'Get your input here,' it called to him. 'I'm connected up to the Internet too. I can take you on a voyage to almost anywhere you like. Come with me,' it cooed enticingly, 'I'll show you a good time.'

Chapter Nineteen

At 9.30 on a Thursday morning, a huge French superstore was the last place he would have expected to find himself. Usually all the world consisted of at that time of day was dribbling into a big spongy pillow until way into the afternoon.

Morph had agreed to take Ali to Italy and was quite happy to bring Chris along for the adventure, but only on the condition that he bought some new clothes. 'I'm not taking you across the border into Wopland dressed like that. They'd have us all arrested and deported immediately on the grounds that we were showing total disrespect for their country's prominence in the world of fashion,' he'd said.

It certainly had been a shock to his system though. When Morph had said an 'early start' he had naturally not assumed that he would be woken up at 8.30 and dragged down to the supermarket to buy clothes and some strong alcohol to keep Ali pissed up throughout the journey.

These places just got bigger and bigger, he thought to himself as he gaped down what appeared to be an almost endless shelf display of cheeses. He glanced around for Morph but failed to spot him; they had lost each other somewhere near the vegetable racks. He touched the shirt pocket from where his passport rudely protruded and reassured himself that the money he had just changed in the little bureau de change at the other end of the shopping mall was still there. Then, armed with his very own trolley, he headed determinedly in the direction that he thought the clothing section would be, flip-flops flapping happily beneath his feet.

'Anything you need at all you can get in that place,' Ali had shouted from his apartment window as he'd watched them climb into the car. 'You are bound to find something that takes your fancy. Enjoy! Enjoy!'

But the symbol of western capitalism, a symbol of freedom for most, also holds great dangers. Dangers that can afflict any of us at any time. Dangers that prey upon the unsuspecting consumer and are expert at separating the incautious from their wads of dough.

Chris suddenly found himself with lots of money in his pocket and not even a shopping list to follow. Ripe, then, for the cunning, predatory psychology of the superstore consumer specialist.

He hit the music department first, a basket full of discounted CDs caught his eye and he began to rummage.

And rummage.

Never before had he realised that he so desperately needed so many things. So many of these cassettes were absolutely essential for his music collection. A *Best of the Platters* jumped into his hand, and briefly he wondered who they were before spotting the price – it was so cheap! He flung it in his trolley with the others, and flip-flopped a bit further on. Then the clothing section loomed into view, so he made eagerly onwards.

By the time Morph found him, Chris's consumer delirium had reached feverish proportions. A quick glance at the way he was frenziedly filling up the trolley with junk told Morph that something was seriously wrong. He had seen the same thing strike his mother many years back, and now the hippy had also fallen victim to what the papers had termed 'Megastore Madness'.

'You don't need all that,' he cried out to him in earnest. 'Think! Think what you're doing, hippy!'

'I am and I do, man! I really do!' came the reply from the deepest recesses of a discount shelf.

'But most of these are women's clothes, Chris.'

'Bargains! Bargains! Cheap! Cheap!'

Morph realised that no amount of reasoning was going to do any good, and so he took the only responsible and logical action possible. As quickly as Chris was loading the items in Morph began throwing them out. Slowly they headed down the aisles, passing through the different sections, objects being transferred from shelf to trolley and then back to shelf again or simply finishing up on the floor, all in a flurry of movement.

Underwear.

Blouses.

Plastic sandals.

Handmade, ceramic flowerpots.

Miracle mops with a free subscription to *Domestic Life* magazine.

Wankel rotary engine screwdrivers.

'Stop!' cried Morph. He couldn't keep it up any more. He was knackered. Leaping over the trolley, he grabbed Chris by the shoulders and began shaking him. For an instant, a semblance of intelligence seemed to appear in Chris's eyes (which in itself was quite odd, Morph reasoned later, as he hadn't seen it there before), but then the consumer-crazed hippy caught sight of the…

'Cream! Oh, wow, man! Look! Spray cream!'

Naturally Morph was not too stunned by the presence of cream in the dairy section of a huge supermarket, not even if it was spray cream. Nevertheless, the level of excitement that this rather mundane fact seemed to whip up distracted him momentarily, long enough for Chris to slip out of his clutches.

There wasn't time to react, and Morph could only look on in horror and bewilderment at the scene that now confronted him. Snatching a can of spray cream from the shelf, the hippy flicked the top to the floor and, keeping the can perfectly upright, put his mouth over the nozzle, pressed, and deeply inhaled the gas propellant that was emitted. He continued to inhale for what seemed a good fifteen seconds before the can itself protested and spat out a gush of thick, white, gooey froth which filled his mouth and dribbled down his chin. Aghast, Morph watched on as the hippy repeated the process with a second can and then collapsed to the floor in a helpless, giggling pile.

Much distressed by the inexplicable nature of the scene, Morph ran over and tried to help him to his feet.

'Are you okay?'

'Nitrous oxide, man!' he squeaked back at him, sounding like some absurd cartoon character. 'It's fuckin' great.' He burst into another fit of hysterical giggles.

'Nitrous oxide?' asked Morph, failing to understand. He picked up one of the cans and began to read its ingredients.

'La laaaa laughing gas, man.' He was beginning to screech and the few customers who were around in the store at that time of the morning were beginning to gather at a safe distance and stare. A management type, obviously attracted by the disturbance, started to make his way politely through the small group of curious onlookers to see what was going on.

Deciding escape was definitely the best solution, Morph slipped away to finish buying his own supplies for the journey ahead, abandoning the giggling wreck on the floor to his fate.

He had just had time to place his supplies in the boot when Chris emerged with his trolley filled with plastic bags. He was still grinning.

'They made me buy the cream cans, man.'

'Naturally.'

'So I scored a few more fresh ones as well,' he said, pointing to one of the carrier bags. 'And thanks for trying to help me out in there, man. Everything just went blank for a while. I really don't know what came over me.'

'Mostly cream, I'd say,' replied Morph, dryly. 'Think nothing of it.'

It wasn't until they were sat in the car that Morph requested a further explanation.

'Oh, it was one of the few useful things I learnt from school chemistry classes. For some reason, they use nitrous oxide – laughing gas – as propellant in spray cream. We used to get off on it as kids before my mum finally caught on and stopped buying it – took her some weeks, though, before she realised why our grades kept dropping in home economics classes at school. It makes your voice go all funny too.'

Morph sat and mused for a minute and then spoke. 'All right, I'm game. Let's have some then.'

Five minutes later, the car engine started and drove jerkily out of the store car park and out on to the main street, its two occupants, their faces splattered in cream, laughing hysterically at insanely high pitches.

A very curious sight indeed for your average Swiss shopper.

Chapter Twenty

'Looks to me like you've got a bit of a job on your hands this time, Caissa.'

'Oh, do you think so?'

Blitzkrieg stared at the ancient marble chessboard with its antique, hand-carved ivory pieces. He wasn't such a good player himself, but when you'd been knocking around with a chess goddess for a couple of centuries you tended to pick up one or two things.

'Isn't it considered pretty bad positioning to have a piece straying so far from the others at such an early stage in the opening?'

Caissa came over from the drinks cabinet carrying two glasses of freshly squeezed orange juice and handed Blitzkrieg one. She looked down at the board.

'Oh dear!' said the goddess. 'That could get a little awkward, couldn't it?'

Blitzkrieg regarded the glass and its orange contents with disapproval. It wasn't that he didn't like fruit juice, but there was nothing like his beloved amber nectar at any time of day. Still, some restrictions to his drinking he'd had to accept from her. He slugged it back and belched loudly. Caissa threw him a look of rebuke, but she had given up trying to teach him good manners years ago. It was a lost cause.

'You can't really expect much else from a beer deity, dear,' her friend, Helena, had commented one day while they were sat taking tea out in the summer house and Blitzy was pissed up, lying flat out on the ground under the big oak tree, singing unintelligibly.

'I heard that,' he'd mumbled, and then had simply farted.

Still, when he wasn't pissed up or being uncouth or just generally doing what beer deities have to do from time to time, he really could be romantic, thoughtful and quite a hunk. She also knew that, given half a chance, Helena would be in there like a shot – the little floozy. Anyway, Blitzy was a vast improvement on that awfully aggressive and badly scarred God of War, Mars, who had kept on hassling her for so long.

True, it had been thanks to Mars and his obsessive desire for her that, out of pure desperation and advice from one of her sister water nymphs, he had gone and asked Euphron, God of Sport, for a present with which to woo her. Euphron had obligingly invented the game of chess in her honour, and, as a delightful consequence, caused her promotion from wood nymph to goddess in one go. But she felt she'd quite paid her debt to him from that point of view a long time ago. A lot of water had passed under the bridge since then…

'Well, looks like I'm going to have to do something about that, and pretty sharpish too,' she announced, tossing her long, dark, mane back behind her shoulders again.

'Do you want a hand?' Blitzkrieg watched her as she sauntered out into the bathroom to prepare herself to go out. Her cute little ass looked even more enticing than usual inside tight, ripped and faded denim jeans. He licked away the saliva from the side of his mouth.

'I don't think it's going to be difficult, but you can come along if you like, it might be fun.'

Chapter Twenty-One

The implications of his new-found ability were just beginning to dawn on him. In fact, it had been their major topic of discussion since he and Maria had left Piacenza that morning and headed towards the casinos of San Remo, the Italian version of Monte Carlo.

'You're so lucky,' Maria was saying. 'Just think, you'll never have to pay cinema entrance again.'

'Or for pop concerts.'

'You can look up girls' skirts without them knowing.'

Done that, thought Max.

'And rip off rich casinos in San Remo.'

'We hope,' he grinned. He had to admit that it had been a pretty nifty idea of hers, and certainly a different way of spending a day off than hanging out by the open-air swimming pool. A day on the beach, swimming, snorkelling and sunbathing, and in the evening making some wad in the casino of their choice. It was also good to escape from the stifling humidity and voracious mosquitoes of Piacenza; and a night playing at being James Bond on the blackjack tables in the classy atmosphere of the Costa Azzurra appealed to both of them. It was something neither of them had done before, although they'd often played cards with friends in the bars and knew how to play most of the games.

'You mean, you're not sure if you can do it.' Maria placed her hand unconsciously on her credit card.

'Well, if it doesn't work out and we start to lose, we can always get up and leave,' he said. 'And anyway this is gonna be one smooth operation, you'll see.'

'Do you think it's immoral?'

'What?'

'What we intend to do. Cheat in a card game in this way.'

'Like Maverick or maybe Doc Holliday or a dozen other illustrious, wild west heroes?' Max laughed at her concern. 'Well, it's a bit late to think of things like that now. But seriously, no. Besides, think of the money. If it works out, a couple of trips and we'll never have to work again. Easy Street for both of us and then who knows, if it makes you feel better, we could always give some away to charity every year, no?'

He glanced away from the motorway for a second and caught her look of consternation, guessed what she was thinking and sighed inwardly in frustration. How could she come up with such a foolproof plan for making them rich, and then start having second thoughts? Typical female capriciousness, he decided.

Having been raised by ex-sixties hippies turned bar proprietors, Maria's unwavering faith in her philosophical melting pot of concepts such as karma and capitalism was not too surprising. He also knew that the ideals and practice of karma were as real to her as the wrath of Allah to a Muslim, the existence of paradise to a Christian, voodoo to a Haitian, or a Swiss bank account and a second house in the Caribbean to any politician. What to most god-fearing folk would seem just a trifle, to her was a sponge, custard and jelly-filled horseman of the Apocalypse.

'You're worrying about your karma again, aren't you?'

She nodded and smiled a little weakly. 'I really don't know what put the idea into my head in the first place,' she said. 'I mean, whichever way you look at it, it's still stealing. And sooner or later we're going to pay for it.'

'Well, personally,' he began, determinedly – he had absolutely no intention of backing out without a fight now that they'd come this far – 'I thought it was brilliant. I still do.' He pulled sharply over into the left lane to allow a coach travelling at twice the speed of sound to pass them. The air-drag from the massive vehicle threw the little Citroën CX into brief instability, and Max had to fight with the steering wheel to regain complete control.

'And what if we're only a small part of the inevitable retribution that the casino owner himself has to pay? You don't exactly get to being the owner of a casino by being Mother Teresa of Calcutta, do you? And besides, everyone knows that nowadays all these places are Mafia run.'

'I suppose you're right.'

She sounded almost convinced. He moved in quickly to give

the *coup de grâce*. 'Whatever happens to them in that way is what they probably have coming. Besides, places like those aren't going to notice the loss of what we intend to take. It's a piddling amount to them.'

'Next left,' interrupted Maria, abruptly. She'd only just spotted the turn-off sign in time.

Max changed down a gear and the engine revs rose almost responsively. Very soon they'd be there. They were both eagerly looking forward to a dip in the warm waters of the Med.

'Well, anyway,' she said resignedly – it was obvious Max had his mind set on the idea and, after all, if it worked out, she certainly could make good use of the money – 'it all fits in rather nicely with Siddle's theory of anti-karma.'

Max grinned. If she was joking about this guy, it meant he had succeeded in swaying her doubts. 'You mean a little bad karma might be good for us?'

She was, of course, referring to the controversial theory originated and developed by the Englishman, Ken Siddle, a Yorkshire domestic appliance repairman and author of the best-selling philosophical work, *Ken and the Art of Domestic Appliance Maintenance*.

Mr Siddle's idea was that if the basic premise of karma is: 'What you do to others eventually comes back on you, and for every bad thing that happens to you there will, in turn, be an equally compensating good one', then the contrary is also a logical and viable conjecture – meaning that for every good thing that happens to you, there will eventually be an equally compensating bad one. His cryptic analogy was that it was much like the hot water thermostat appliance found in most domestic buildings. In order to maintain constant a comfortable room and water temperature, the thermostat had to continually compensate by cooling and reheating.

Taken a step further, then, and applied to everyday relations, Mr Siddle's theory came out something like this: 'If some bugger tries to do you a favour in some way, best thing is to tell him to "bugger off". One, because he's only doing himself the favour by increasing his own "good" karma and thereby consequently diminishing yours, and two, because if something good does happen to you, sooner or later the law of balance requires something equally bloody horrible to come along in return.' (*Ken and the Art of Domestic Appliance Maintenance*)

According to Mr Siddle's calculations, backed by precise flue-piping installation measurements, the best defence against any potential do-gooder was to immediately pick an argument with the fellow and then get yourself beaten up by him, thus alleviating, immediately, any bad karma you had coming. This was far better, he had reasoned, than having to live in fear of the inevitable, not knowing when and where the equalising retribution would strike. Of course, he himself had admitted that this was indeed a drastic and somewhat painful solution, and that really the best thing to do was to maintain a policy of complete non-involvement and non-interference with the rest of the human race.

The theory was condemned by most spiritual leaders worldwide as 'misanthropic', 'basically flawed', and just 'pretty damn silly'. To which Mr Siddle's astute reply had been, 'Sod off, ya buggers! Ah don't needs none a ya anyway's.' And had himself, in fact, 'sodded off', vanishing mysteriously and completely from the public eye. Rumour had it that he had gone to Switzerland.

But the book was not without effect, and from it arose two more completely useless and unnecessary religious sects who held minor squabbling differences as to its correct interpretation. These were called the 'Sod Offs' and the 'Bugger Offs', who likewise 'sodded off' and 'buggered off', respectively, to live in complete isolation from the rest of the world and each other.

Chapter Twenty-Two

'Hi hu hu hu err. Pi pu pi blur glu blur…'

Beep beep beep beep.

'Shit!'

Cathy slammed the phone angrily back down on its base, hovered over it uncertainly, and then snatched it up again and dialled a different number.

'Hello, can I speak to Mr Andersson, please? Cathy McDonald speaking.'

Damn it! What was this thing about her and answerphones? It seemed that it was virtually impossible for her to speak coherently into one, even when she had understood exactly after which beep she was supposed to talk. She had wanted to leave a message for Belvois, asking him to contact someone at the lab the second he got back, but, once again, had found herself without the ability to articulate the correct sounds into the answerphone. Never mind, maybe Belvois, with his new linguistic potential, would be able to make some sort of sense of it.

'Yes?' demanded Andersson's voice. 'McDonald?'

'Yes, I'm ringing from the lab. It's about Belvois. He hasn't turned up this morning, and nobody's answering the phone at his place in town. I was wondering if you…'

'What? But wasn't he supposed to have reported in this morning at nine to run some more tests?'

'Exactly, and frankly I'm more than just a bit concerned. I never was that keen on the idea of letting him out from under our observation after the episode yesterday.'

The line on the other side went quiet for a moment.

'Listen. I'm in the car right now. How soon can you meet me over at his apartment?' His voice sounded a pitch higher than its usual B flat bass.

'About ten minutes.'

Cathy put the phone down, picked up her handbag with the

car keys and exited the building. She had a bad feeling about this. Something inside her began to twist up.

She'd already lost Robert, her husband, when their first experiment of the type had gone awry. He'd insisted on being their guinea pig, saying that it was morally and ethically wrong to pay someone else to test out their theories. He had argued that, anyhow, it was their brainchild and that they were the only people qualified to give an accurate account and interpretation of the data they could collect.

Previous animal experiments had not been too encouraging. Even their greatest achievement up to that point – the successful programming of the use of an entire computer keyboard into the memory of a female chimpanzee – had had its drawbacks. The young chimp could ask for anything she desired simply by keying in the correct sequence. She'd even been able to memorise codes of up to seven figures long – no small feat if you think that most humans have difficulty remembering each other's names and telephone numbers. But the chimp, an eight year old called Sally, had turned out to be rather capricious, and they'd had to draw the line when she started asking for a four-bedroomed, detached house with a swimming pool, commanding spectacular views of the Victoria Falls, and had refused point-blank to be reconciled by a doll's house and a poster.

And then poor Robert. Everything had gone so smoothly for those first few early experiments. They'd been amazed at his almost total recall of any programmed data, even though, at that time, the data-holding capacity had been somewhat limited. How they had been delighted when one evening, on a whim, they had gone out, and Robert had walked away with first prize in the County Trivial Pursuit Championship. But then, that one fateful morning, to find him dead in the lab like that, with the prototype translator device still attached and flashing. The coroner's verdict had been death by gross self-negligence. He had been so involved in the memory-recording process that he had forgotten to take his heart pills.

When Cathy arrived at Belvois' apartment, she found the main door of the apartment block, together with Belvois' own door, conveniently ajar. She knocked and timidly gave the door a push so that it opened sufficiently for her to peer inside.

Andersson was already there, standing with his hands on his hips and looking carefully about him. Behind him stood a short, stocky man in his late twenties, dressed in suit trousers and a white cotton shirt. She recognised him as Deklan Cruz, Andersson's driver and bodyguard, nicknamed 'Pecdek' by most of the employees at MEGA Industries because of his excessive pectoral development.

'Come in, McDonald!' Andersson gestured for her to join him. 'Take a look at this place.'

Cathy cast her gaze around the room.

'My God!' she cried out, unable to contain her horror at the dirty plates, clothes and old magazines that lay liberally scattered about. A thick smell of stewed coffee hung in the hot, mid-morning air, threatening at any moment to suffocate the last particle of oxygen left in the stuffy room. Men really can live like animals, she thought.

'Oh, this is nothing for a bachelor's pad,' said Andersson, grimly. 'You should have seen mine as a student. I wouldn't like to even imagine what the inside of his fridge looks like.'

'Ugh!' came Pecdek's gagging reply from the kitchen, and they heard the sound of the fridge door quickly slammed shut.

'Seriously, though, there're no signs of a struggle – not that I think there'd be many who'd stand much of a chance against him after seeing that little demo he gave yesterday.' He paused, grimacing slightly in thought. 'I'd say there's more chance that he's gone AWOL. It doesn't look as if our boy got too much sleep last night.' He indicated with a nod towards the computer in the corner of the room, still on, and humming informatively at its small audience of seven or eight coffee mugs that were paying absolutely no attention whatsoever.

'Maybe he's just gone out shopping,' Cathy suggested lamely, not believing it herself.

'I'm calling Chief Ciambella,' announced Andersson, ignoring her last remark. He drew the cellular phone from out of its holster on his trouser belt. 'I want an all-out search. McDonald, get on to the others at the lab, get them off their backsides and out there looking for him. We need everyone involved. We can't afford for him to go walkabout like this.'

As she was leaving, Cathy found herself puzzling over the last thing Belvois had obviously been reading on the computer screen before disappearing. It was *Rock 'n' Roll's the Only Way To Go*, the semi-autobiographical novel on the life of Hill Waily, the seventies rock star, electrocuted at the age of sixty-five by his own guitar after spilling beer all over it.

She began to worry just a little for Belvois' sanity.

Chapter Twenty-Three

The old man sat and watched through squinted eyes as his fourth customer of the day loomed into view. He dabbed at the sweat that trickled down his temple with a yellowed cotton handkerchief that had seen better times. Not many passed by these parts nowadays, now that the new super bypass had been built, but you could pretty much guarantee that if they did, they'd stop at his service station for a wash and to fill up. So he just sat and waited in quiet certainty as the car approached.

Red dust clouds rose up and dispersed into the hot afternoon air as the wheels of the dark blue Volvo pulled up to a halt. There was a moment of expectation while the smooth whirr of the car engine went from tick-over to off, and then three of the doors burst open at once.

Leaving the car doors wide open, the three travellers bundled over to where the old man sat. Two of them were limping badly, but the third, wearing a white dress, made even poorer headway. Every other yard he fell to the ground, picked himself up again and then fell again, staggering, crawling and gambolling forwards. The other two were of minor importance, thought the old man, but this third - now, he was interesting.

The two strangers who had been at the front of the car arrived first and spoke to him in a foreign tongue of which he understood nothing. But he understood their gist. He handed them the keys and pointed over towards the toilets, never even for a moment taking his eyes off the third as he fell once more to the ground.

'Oh, don't worry about him,' said the one with hair like a girl's. 'He's just pissed as an Arab.'

The old man, failing to understand, pointed courteously once more in the direction in which Morph was already headed, and continued to watch as the third, with great effort, managed to prise himself out of the dust and zigzag after the other two. His gaze followed them into the toilets and nodded knowingly at what he presumed to be sighs of relief echoing from the station bathroom.

'Man, I thought I was never going to walk again! Those pins and needles were killing.'

'I thought I was never going to make it to the bathroom in time.'

'I... hic thought I was neber... hic goita mak it, either.'

'Oh, man! What a state! Hey, Morph, get a load of Ali, man.'

'I know. You're tellin' me. I would have had to have stopped the car anyway; I couldn't stand all the singing any longer. Chris, pull his head from out of the urinal, will you?'

'Oh, maan! Oh, no! Not there. Ahh, man, now you'll be stinking of piss for the rest of the journey.'

'Here, I'll give you a hand to stick his head under the tap in the basin.'

The British, in general, do not fare too well abroad when confronted with a serious language communication problem; and a guaranteed ninety-nine per cent of the time this problem is inevitably due to the fact that the person with whom they wish to communicate does not speak English.

'Do you speak English?'

'Eh?'

The fatal and most feared reply. Now the ardent traveller must begin to draw upon all the innate communicative talents he can muster. These can usually be broken down into three or four well-defined stages:

Stage 1: speak louder – it's possible that he or she is merely slightly deaf, but do be prepared for a similar response in volume increase.

'DO YOU SPEAK ENGLISH?'

'EHH?'

Stage 2: speak slowly and loudly – it's possible that he or she is a little backward as well as slightly deaf.

'DO... YOU... SPEAK... ENGLISH?'

'EENGLEESH?'

The parrot effect. This can be deceiving as well as frustrating, needlessly and cruelly raising the hopes of the erstwhile communicator.

'Yes, yes, English.'

'NO. NO SPIK EENGLEESH.'

Stage 3 (and perhaps the most cunning of all): wave your arms in large exaggerated circles, repeating, simultaneously, both stages 1 and 2.

'Whash he doin'?' asked Ali, mystified, as he leant unsteadily against the car boot where Chris had placed him.

'No idea, man. Appears to be some kind of feeble impression of a helicopter or something.'

The old man took two paces back for personal security reasons and held up the pump handle in front of him as further protection.

'NOO. I DON'T WANT MORE PETROL. I WANT TO KNOW THE DIRECTIONS FOR THIS HOTEL WHERE... IS... THE... HOLIDAY INN... HOTEL?'

Morph was getting just a little desperate and about to enter stage 4, which is to assume that the person you are attempting to talk to is a blithering moron, give it up and walk away. He decided on one last try and, fixing the old man (who had by now taken shelter behind the more substantial mass of the four-star petrol pump) with his most determined stare, he changed tactics and drew a large rectangular shape in the air.

'HOLIDAY INN... HOTEL,' he shouted. 'ON... THIS... ROAD... SOMEWHERE.'

It was all just too much. The old-timer dropped the pump handle and, abandoning his outpost behind the pump, fled as fast as his age-enfeebled bones would take him into his office, locking the door behind him and then proceeding to stare back through the glass door at Morph.

Morph sighed and turned despondently towards his two travelling companions.

'He's really quite sprightly for his age, isn't he?' said Chris, agreeably.

'I was hoping he might be able to tell us where the hotel is. I know it's on this road or near here.'

'Maybe *she* can,' said Chris, pointing to a young girl in her early teens who was coming across the road towards them.

'Are you looking for a hotel?' she enquired in sweet adolescent tones.

'Oh, far out!' exclaimed Chris. 'Could you hear him from all the way down that road?'

'Oh, no,' she answered simply, 'it's just that those hand gestures your friend was using were one of the first things we studied in our English lessons at junior school.'

It had taken a lot of perseverance and convincing finally to raise Ali from his hotel bed, but a couple of hours later, they were all sitting together in the pizzeria which was conveniently located in the basement part of the hotel itself.

'You'll feel better once you've eaten something,' Morph was saying. 'Never drink on an empty stomach.'

Ali focused on Morph's nose with bloodshot eyes. 'Uugh!' he managed and went back to burying his head in his arms folded on the table.

As a source of stimulating conversation, Ali was not the business tonight, Morph thought, and went back to reading the English version of the menu. Finally, he looked over the table at Chris. 'What are you going to have, hippy?'

'Babes. Sexy babes.'

'I think you'll probably find they don't serve them here,' said Morph.

'Wanna bet, man?' Chris nodded to the side, a few tables down from where they were sitting.

One look at the long tanned legs and miniskirts and Morph was obliged to admit to the same. A blonde and a brunette! The longhaired brunette glanced over, caught Morph's drooling stare and flashed a polite smile at them before turning nonchalantly back to resume her conversation with her friend.

'Foowaw!' said Chris, with all the eloquence he could muster.

'Babes, sexy babes!' salivated Morph, reiterating his friend's initial judgement. It sounded good, but deep down Morph knew that was about as far as it would go. That was about as far as it nearly always went, staring, dreaming and drooling. His confidence just wouldn't allow him to go any further, so he made the usual cop-out excuse.

'They're too classy for us, man.'

'Naw, they're not,' said Chris. He eyed Morph for a minute and added, 'And look at you, dressed to the nines. You're looking well groovy.'

Morph grinned. Even though he'd never really felt totally comfortable in anything other than a business suit, he knew his Lacoste shirt and Armani jeans were a safe bet. 'Always buy famous-name clothing if you want to be in.' He had always kept to his DJ friend's advice when he did his shopping, even if, to tell the truth, the only difference as far as he was concerned was in the price. But then Morph had always found ideas on fashion difficult to comprehend. His music collection was simply a compilation of good sounds that friends had put together for him. Whenever someone asked him, 'Hey, that's cool! Who's that?' he was usually forced to bluff, or um and ah a bit until they lost interest.

He studied Chris critically. There were some people, he guessed, who managed to look cool even when dressed in cheap supermarket rags.

Chris fished in his jeans pockets for the packet of cigarettes he'd bought that morning. He took one out, lit it, and inhaled as sexily as he could, then screwed up his face in disgust as he had done periodically all day, every time he'd tried to smoke one. They still tasted like a cross between rabbit droppings and wood.

'It's your own fault,' Morph chided. 'Told you not to buy those French things.'

The waiter, with a nose so noble it would have made even the early Caesars look like peasantry, came over to them.

'Si, Signori?'

'I'd like pizza number two and a big beer, please.'

'Same for me,' said Chris. Having taken more notice of the girls than the menu, he reckoned it was the safest bet.

Morph reached over and shook the snoring mass. It awoke.

'Wha?'

'The same for my friend,' said Morph, realising it was useless pursuing the subject.

'Very good, sir.' The waiter spoke good restaurant English, Morph thought. 'Three number twos and three bears.' He left them and returned almost immediately with the bears.

Chris and Morph thirstily grabbed theirs and downed good healthy gulps of the cool amber liquid.

'Aahh!' commented Morph, wiping the froth away from his mouth with the back of his hand.

'Aahh!' concurred Chris, wiping the froth away from his mouth with the back of his hand.

'Ooaah,' moaned Ali, after raising his head from off the table and spotting the contents of his glass. His face took on a strange shade of Martian green. He got up surprisingly quickly and ran off to the toilets, which were helpfully indicated by a tasteful plastic sign of a little boy pointing the way with his own member.

'Buurrp!' commented Chris.

'Buurrp!' concurred Morph.

Taking another healthy swig, Chris leant over the table towards his friend, and pointed after Ali with his cigarette. 'He left in a hurry, didn't he?'

'Yup,' Morph affirmed and assumed his best Dorset farmer accent. 'Gawn with the wind, oi reckurn.' He too had noticed the unusual little public convenience sign and had wondered about its marketing possibilities in hospitals: male wards this way, and perhaps something similar for the women…?

'That aniseed liquor stuff he drinks is evil medicine, man. Where do you think he gets it from, some kind of rocket fuel dealer?'

'It's called ouzo and it's Greek, and I think a more appropriate question should be: why do you think he gets it?'

The pizzas arrived and the wordless ritual of their dissection and rapid consumption began.

'Mmmm?' asked Morph, just making conversation.

'Mmmm,' replied Chris, not wishing to seem impolite.

When finished, they both pushed their empty plates aside.

'Burp!' observed Morph, eyes bulging slightly as the pressure was released.

'Burp!' remarked Chris, coolly maintaining his savoir faire.

Their heads turned at an incline and eyed Ali's pizza which was still sitting there, whole and untouched.

'Hi, guys,' said the pizza, sounding a little nervous about the situation. 'Now you wouldn't be considering eating me now, would you? Just because I've been left hanging around with all my juices going cold and this warm melted cheese seeping its way through my crispy base…'

'Burp!' reflected Morph and Chris in perfect unison, smiling and rubbing their bellies in a satisfied manner. Three plates now lay empty before them with just a few oily crumbs to tell the tale.

Ali returned and took his place at the table. He looked much less green. The other two looked at him in somewhat guilty embarrassment.

Chris decided that he should try and apologise, but Ali, having already noted the three empty plates and the absence of a third pizza, merely held up his hand to silence him.

'I do not think I could have managed it anyway on this stomach,' he lamented.

'Oh, that's all right then.' Relieved of his part in the pizza orgy, Chris got up and wandered determinedly in the direction of the 'babes'. 'Coming?' he asked of Morph.

'Uh, yes. I'll just finish my beer.'

'Chicken! I'll put in a good word for you all the same.'

Morph turned to Ali and studied him through his black-rimmed glasses.

'You're looking a tad healthier, I might say.'

Ali nodded. 'Yes, it was a bit rough on my stomach, I am not as young as I once was.' He paused and looked thoughtful. 'But then I guess nobody ever is as young as they once were.'

Morph raised his eyebrows. 'Very true.' He had noticed that every now and again – even when completely rat-arsed in the car – Ali had an aptitude for sagely remarks.

'But it worked, did it not?' he announced, sounding somewhat reconciled. 'Nothing went wrong with the car. Nothing seems to go wrong with machines when I am in a state of total alcoholic intoxication.'

Morph looked down at the cheap digital watch on his wrist that he'd had to buy at the supermarket that morning and sighed. 'But now you're sober, so I'd be grateful if you'd keep your distance.'

'I think it may have had some lasting effects. You know I have always been afraid of these modernised bathrooms, until now, that is.'

Morph peered dubiously at him through his glasses, remembering his beloved watch and the damage to all the electronic equipment in Ali's apartment to which he freely admitted responsibility.

Nevertheless, Ali went on to explain how the gadgets in the toilet he'd just paid a visit to were all electronic, but they were all still working when he'd left. 'Perhaps this time the problem has gone away for good.'

Morph raised his glass, keeping his doubts to himself. 'I'll drink to that. My grandad always swore that this stuff was a cure-all.'

Ali reached up and called the waiter over.

'Do you think I could get an aspirin and a glass of water?' He grimaced as he watched Morph gulp back his beer.

'And can I have another one of these?' Morph held up his empty glass. The noble-nosed waiter vanished behind the bar.

Morph wondered briefly whether he should have ordered Chris an extra, but then one glance over in his direction told him that he needn't have worried. The hippy seemed far too busy with the girls, waving his arms about wildly (in quite the correct manner) and sounding like a tape recorder at half speed with the volume full up. Impressive communicative technique, thought Morph, and, with only a further leering glance at the long, tanned legs under the table, turned his attention back to Ali who was swilling his aspirin down.

A waiter suddenly dashed by them in the direction of the toilets, returned just as quickly, and ran past again with a bucket and mop in his hand. Water was seeping out from under the toilet door and into the restaurant corridor.

'Oh, dear,' Ali sighed resignedly.

The waiter opened the door and entered. Sounds of banging and cursing floated out with the water which was now beginning to gush out from under the toilet door at an alarming rate. The waiter came out looking somewhat distraught, and discreetly closed the door behind him. A futile gesture. He vanished out into the back of the restaurant. Some excited shouting soon rose up and a short time later he reappeared, together with what was probably the manager and two other waiters. In turn, they all tried the door. It appeared blocked.

'Was the lock on the door electronic too?' asked Morph inquisitively.

'No, no.' Ali seemed equally puzzled by the little scene.

Morph looked over at Chris to see if he'd noticed the growing fracas. The scene over the other side, however, was no less curious. After a good five minutes of trying to understand Chris, the look of initial amusement on the babes' faces had been replaced by a mixture of growing fear and consternation. Continuing to nod and smile agreeably, they had begun to edge backwards away from their table. Aware of this fact, Chris began moving slowly forward, arms still drawing great unlikely shapes in the air in a vain and desperate attempt to clarify any misunderstanding.

Noticing the girls' uneasiness, Noble-nose (one of the few waiters not involved with the flooding incident) approached. Unwisely, he was carrying a tray of drinks.

A flailing arm shot out, accidentally connecting with the waiter's tray and sending it spinning up into the air. It finished noisily on the girls' table in a confusion of liquid and splintered glass.

One of the girls screamed, and a young hero courageously leapt over his table to help the distressed damsels. At the same time, Noble-nose took control of the situation and grabbed Chris by the arms, holding them tight behind his back in a judo lock while the young hero shielded the girls with his own body.

Chris started to wriggle and protest vehemently, but the more he did so, the tighter he found himself restrained.

Meanwhile, over the other side of the room, the management and waiters had decided to force the door. A double shoulder barge cracked the flimsy barrier from its hinges, and the reason for its blockage suddenly became apparent as gallons of water tidal-waved out into the room. The waiters and management vanished momentarily from sight, engulfed by the avalanche.

'Bravo!' shouted an enthusiastic customer, voicing the opinion of many. They hadn't been so entertained for quite a while – two floor shows for the price of one pizza!

Morph and Ali placed some money on the table and decided it was time to leave.

Chapter Twenty-Four

Belvois' eyes widened, and he growled through the hair on his face in irritation while his answerphone forced him yet again to listen to its merry little jingle – a four-bar extract from Beethoven's Sixth – before deeming him worthy of hearing the message.

He found himself asking the same question he had done for the last twenty-four weeks and three days since he'd first made the grievous error of renting from the phone company. What kind of depraved maniac could design such an infernal device and have the extraordinary bad taste to choose that particular piece as a jolly little jingle?

Looking mournfully out of the lounge window, he wondered how many other tortured souls there were like him out there.

'Cheap, crappy, rented shit,' he grumbled under his breath in tune with the catchy melody, knowing that there were another twenty-seven weeks and four days to go before the contract expired.

Click!

At last.

Beeep. 'Hi hu hu hu err. Pi pu pi blur glu blur...' Beeep.

Bastards! He'd been forced to listen to all that just so some wacko could vent off on his time.

Then the jingle started up again as the tape started to rewind.

'Nooooo! Stop! No more!' he cried. 'Here's where the little man fights back.' And, ripping the machine out from its umbilicals, he sent it hurtling through the open window. It gave immense satisfaction as it made not one, but two pleasing crunching sounds of splintering plastic on the road below. Now *that's* value for money, he thought.

Pecdek yawned and opened a pair of sleep-puffed eyes. He stared at his watch and attempted to focus. For nearly four hours he'd been stationed outside Belvois' apartment on the off chance that he should show up. It had been pleasant at first, isolated from the heat and humidity of the late afternoon in the small air-conditioned pocket of his car, but now he really had to get out and stretch his legs. He opened the car door and stepped out.

The hot, damp air rushed at him in an all-over body embrace. Even though it was dusk now, the city had not cooled much. In another twenty minutes the relief watch should arrive, and he could knock off and go down the gym. In anticipation, he began doing some light, callisthenics exercises to wake his muscles up. Then, keeping his short, stocky legs straight, he bent over and touched his toes.

A thought suddenly occurred to him, as thoughts usually do in this and other often more inappropriate positions: what if Belvois had come back while he'd been napping? He shot a glance up to the apartment windows and saw that the lights were switched on inside.

Without wasting further time, he reached back into the car, and extracted his cellular phone from his light, crimplene Valentino jacket. Better call in and ask for instructions. He hit the button which held in memory Andersson's personal number.

'Er, hello, Mr Andersson? Pec... er... Deklan here. I... Wha...?'

Alas, that was all the time he had in which to deliver his vital information. Immobilised by surprise, Pecdek had but a few brief milliseconds to stare in wonder and bewilderment at the rapidly growing, square-shaped object that was spinning above his head. A split second later he was prone, unconscious on the ground with a broken nose, his cellular phone in pieces and an 'EZ Speak' type of answerphone lying safely intact on his chest.

Once free of the annoying little machine, Belvois did not even bother to view its fate. It was gone and good riddance, he thought, and he turned his attention to something far more worthy. He walked over to his table and picked up the case that had been lying patiently on top of it.

Placing it gently on the ground, he slowly, and with great reverence, opened it up. A brilliant light shone out, almost dazzling him for an instant, and he suddenly realised that he had been unconsciously holding his breath. He reached inside with both hands and gently extracted it from its casing, like a baby from the cradle.

'Come to daddy, little one.'

The polished chrome of the 1970s Gibson electric guitar looked so beautiful he felt little shudders of pleasure run down his back and into his groin.

'Better than sex,' he whispered, quoting the great Hill Waily.

He turned to the newly bought 150 watt amplifier and switched it on.

PUMFF!

He took out a long, red cable, plugged himself in, and ran his hand down over the strings.

BRIONG, it sang sweetly to him.

It was time to put into practice what he'd only learned as theory last night.

Andersson arrived just in time to see his driver's unconscious form being loaded into the back of an ambulance. There were also three police Alpha Romeos at the scene. He spotted Chief Ciambella's rotund form in the midst of the armed officers, ordering them to take up strategic positions in the street and to block any possible back exits. All much to the entertainment of the small, but growing, crowd of excited civilians at the corner of the street. On spotting Andersson, Ciambella sauntered over with an important air. These were the times when he really got to enjoy himself.

'Just like your American films, eh?' he said, grinning. He had to shout over the sound of the police sirens.

'Yeah, right!' Andersson shouted back. He glanced up at Belvois' apartment windows and then back to Ciambella, grimacing at the grating sound the sirens were having on his nerves. 'Just what the hell has happened here?'

Ciambella nodded towards the ambulance that was closing its doors.

'Nothing too serious, I don't think. However, initial deductions lead us to assume that your chauffeur was struck down by an answerphone. A rented answerphone, registered to your boy, Belvois.'

Andersson put his hands over his ears in protest.

'Can't you do something about the racket those sirens are making?' he screamed above what seemed to him the ever-increasing volume of wailing.

'What sirens?' retorted Ciambella. 'That hellish screeching is coming from one of these apartments, and I'd hazard a guess at it belonging to the same hand as our answerphone sniper.'

Andersson looked dumbfounded. 'What is it?'

'Put your hands in the air and rock!'

Both Andersson and Ciambella abruptly whirled on their heels to face the origin of the unexpected command.

'"Put Your Hands in the Air and Rock",' repeated one of the bystanders who had crept close enough to eavesdrop their conversation. 'It's a rock song by Hill Waily.'

Andersson's jaw dropped as if its hinge bolts had just been removed for further lubrication. 'That noise – it's a guitar?'

The sergeant was having the time of his life. Sure, it was risky, but that's what a policeman's life was all about, wasn't it? Not being stuck behind a desk shifting forms from in-trays to out-trays all day long, which was usually what he found himself doing. And it wasn't every day that he had the opportunity to kick open an apartment door. One either side of the door, backs rigid against the wall, guns poised, the other officer and he waited like coiled springs ready to be released.

'Remember, don't shoot him unless there's absolutely no alternative, and then only in the leg or something,' whispered Andersson nervously. 'He mustn't be damaged.'

'Don't fret it,' said the sergeant, waving the anaesthetic dart gun at him that he'd just been specially issued with.

His officer giggled. 'Good one, Sarge.'

'What's with you?' demanded the sergeant.

'Don't FRET it, get it?' explained the other by placing his gun between his teeth and pretending to play a guitar.

'Oh, oh, yeah,' replied the superior officer, his own pun finally dawning on him. 'Guitar, fret it, get it, yeah. Hah hah!'

Andersson glanced desperately from one policeman to the other.

The sergeant turned, all business again, and rapped politely on Belvois' apartment door, but there was no answer.

'Try knocking louder,' suggested Andersson. It was obvious that Belvois wasn't going to hear a discreet little tap like that above the racket coming from his room.

The officer looked over at his sergeant, who pursed his lips and shook his head in silent agreement. They had absolutely no intention of missing out on the door-kicking bit. It was the best part and what they'd both been trained for.

One well-placed leather boot and the door flew open. The two policemen burst into the room, weapons outstretched and ready. A smiling Belvois, guitar in hand, turned to greet them.

'Hi, guys,' he said warmly. 'Come on in.'

Dressed only in a pair of jeans, his greying hair greased back away from his face and a red handkerchief tied around his forehead, he really looked the rocker.

'Just hackin' out a bit of Hill Waily. If you want a beer, help yourselves, they're in the ice box.' He seemed totally oblivious to their aggressive intentions or their forced entry, completely oblivious to everything, in fact, but his playing. He went back to strumming energetically on the Gibson.

Realising that the loony was no real physical threat – except perhaps to their eardrums and musical sensibilities – the two daring crime busters lowered their guns and turned questioningly towards their chief, who was just making his entrance alongside Andersson.

'Hey, this chap's pretty good, Chief,' said the sergeant, bobbing his head a little to the rhythm.

'Yeah, right on!' echoed the other officer.

'Hill Waily! Of course!' A spark of recognition lit up Ciambella's face. 'I thought I recognised the tune. My son plays it all the time in his room. He's become a real fan ever since he died. Quite a cult figure, you know.'

'Sure,' snorted Andersson, obviously unimpressed. 'One man and his fuckin' legacy.' And, reaching into his jacket pocket, he pulled out his own tranquilliser gun and fired.

Belvois glanced down at the dart protruding from his leg and had time to throw its originator an accusingly hurt look before he and guitar dropped unconscious to the ground in a chaotic chorus of echo and reverb.

Chapter Twenty-Five

The huge, brassy revolving doors of the casino opened a different world. It was like suddenly becoming aware of the existence of two separate realities. Energy and noise suddenly exploded in rich reds and golds all around them.

Sure, it was noisy outside too. Few places in Italy could be truly classed as tranquil – the caloric exuberance of the people and their horn-happy driving saw to that. But outside it was only playtime, holidaymakers on the loose, in search of a good meal in a nice restaurant, maybe some entertaining cabaret, and, by day, a good suntan. Here inside they played for real. Fortunes had been won and lost in these casinos. People had gambled their life's savings in a night or, as was so often the case, the life's savings of others.

You could lick the air and almost taste the adrenalin and tension in it. A bittersweet cocktail of fortune and misfortune, winners and losers, twenty-four hours around the clock. This wasn't just the playground of a privileged few. It was a humming, thriving monument to the undisputed spice of capitalism – money. Here it was in its purest and most unabashed form, and the people inside had swarmed straight to the source.

Like moths to a flame, thought Max, talking of which, he was beginning to feel some flutterings of his own.

Max held out his hand and Maria placed her smaller one inside it. Her face was lit up with the same anticipation he was feeling. The energy that ran through these places was irresistible, you couldn't deny it. It wasn't just electric, it was nuclear. If it were possible to tap it, he was sure there would be sufficient to illuminate an entire city.

They walked over to the other side of the big hall, passed the cheeky, winking one-armed bandits, passed the sparkling wheel of fortune with its obligatory crowd of fortune seekers and spectators. Maria glanced at him.

Max shook his head. 'Forget it. That's just luck.'

He was right and she knew it. There was nothing there that could be manipulated by Max's particular ability.

They arrived at one of the active blackjack tables. It was a minimum stake table.

'This will do for starters,' Max announced. The butterflies had gone kamikaze in his stomach, diving and rebounding off his stomach wall.

With the typical self-consciousness of once-in-a-while players, they stood and watched, trying to get a feel of the situation and the etiquette of play.

Some of the punters were doing worse than others, and the one next to Max considerably worse than most. Pretty soon the stool became free, and Max, seizing his chance, slid on to it. Slipping through the small crowd of onlookers, Maria came and stood by his side. He threw his cash down on the table – as he'd seen others do before him – and the dealer swiftly replaced it with the equivalent in gambling chips of various colours.

'Thanks, Frank,' said Max, having read the dealer's name tag fastened to his waistcoat.

The dealer simply nodded at him.

Maria picked one up and examined it curiously, then replaced it on the small pile.

'Bets, please.'

The game had begun. Max was dealt a four of hearts. Not the best number to receive. The others started placing their bets down. One, two, three people to his left, but it was useless looking at the cards now – he had no idea how many they would take, or whether they would stay or go bust. He decided not to raise his first stake; the butterflies seemed to be feasting away on what was left of his confidence. What if he couldn't…?

He stepped out of his body and walked through the table to where Frank was sat, finger poised over the box that held the cards. Sticking his head up through the table, he literally eyeballed the next card. It was a peculiar sensation having your eye – even though it was physically insubstantial – poked right up between table and card. The pure vicinity made it kind of hard to focus.

The jack of clubs. If the player next to him twisted again, he'd go bust. He did.

An audible groan of sympathy rose up from the small crowd, and the punter, shaking his head despondently, got up and left the table.

'Card.'

Max had to restrain himself from calling 'card' a second time before the dealer had had time to respond to his first call.

Nine of clubs.

'Card,' he choked, and cleared his throat with a grunt.

Eight of hearts.

'Twenty-one,' declared Frank, professionally aloof to the hum of appreciation from the onlookers, and turned to the man sitting to Max's left.

Max had no idea if he would win the hand, but he knew he couldn't lose it. At the most, if Frank pulled out twenty-one they'd only be quits. Obviously, he had no real way of manipulating exactly what the dealer would turn up, but at least he could guarantee that he himself would never go bust. That had been the plan and, eight or nine turns later, it was going very smoothly indeed. There certainly was a big and very pretty pile of multicoloured chips growing before him.

'You're doing well tonight, sir,' commented Frank, while replacing the cards inside the machine with new packs. It was just a casual aside – a compliment in its way – aimed at increasing the rapport between punter and dealer, but the other players looked over at him enviously.

Max responded with a grin, shrugged his shoulders and deliberately went bust. They had decided previously that losing every now and again might help throw suspicion off them.

However, there was to be one hitch that neither of them could have foreseen, and it happened while Max had his head protruding through the table and was eyeballing the next few successive cards.

'Tut, tut, Max. Shame on you. That's really not very sporting now, is it?'

Max twisted his ghostly frame around in surprise, his body literally divided in two by the card table.

No one there.

'Up here, darling.'

Max looked up. 'Who?'

'Well,' came the voice in a mock injured tone, 'I wouldn't have thought anyone could have forgotten our first meeting so quickly.'

'Caissa!'

It was a very odd sight indeed. Sat cross-legged, she was hovering in mid-air above. She floated down gracefully and stood on the table.

She was dressed elegantly in loose, white trousers and top, as if ready to dine out for the evening. She reached down, placed an index finger under his chin and effortlessly pulled him up through the table so as to be at eye level with her. She was, in fact, actually much shorter than him, and so Max's feet and ankles remained buried in the table.

'Don't gape,' she said. 'Didn't anyone ever teach you that it's rude?' And a deft upwards motion of the same dainty pinky closed his jaw for him with a 'clop'.

'Hello, Max. Told you we'd be seeing each other again soon.'

She pouted at him disapprovingly as he continued to stare.

'Uh, sorry. I guess it's because I've never seen you with a body before,' he retorted without thinking. But what a body!

'So, do you like it?' She laughed and provocatively ran her hands swiftly down her slim, curvaceous frame.

Max felt the ethereal equivalent of his blood pressure rise briefly, and then, suddenly remembering where he was, glanced at Maria and around the table in embarrassment.

Jeez, Maria and all these people were watching them!

But they weren't. Besides the fact that he knew they couldn't see him anyway, they all appeared to be frozen, completely immobile, even Maria.

'How...? How do you do that?' he stammered.

'Neat, huh?'

Incredulous, Max observed the people who were sitting or standing, captured in mid-action, word or thought, like a snapshot in a photo album. A glass that one of the clients on a nearby table had apparently just clumsily elbowed off remained suspended in the air, along with some droplets of its spilled liquid. An eerie silence pervaded the casino.

Caissa smiled at him. 'Lesson number two. Once free of your physical body, time does not have to behave in the same way as you're used to. What can be a fraction of a second for them can be a week, a month or more, for you.' She paused and added, 'It doesn't even have to be necessarily linear, but that you'll discover by yourself in time.'

It wasn't clear if he'd heard anything she'd just said. Max just continued to stare dumbfounded at his new freeze-framed world.

She glanced over at Maria leaning up against Max's physical form and nodded her approval.

'My compliments Max. You make a fine couple.'

'Er, thanks.'

'Now, down to more important business. *My* business.' She glanced down at the quite substantial pile of chips that he had accumulated and pouted again.

'I must admit to being a tad disappointed though. Is this the best you could think of doing with your new-found gift?'

'Er.' Max shuffled uncomfortably. He felt a little like a schoolboy about to be severely reprimanded.

'There are so many more and better things you can do with it.' She looked him straight in the eyes. 'And then, your promise to me to win the tournament that starts in two days meant nothing?'

'Oh, I'll be there for that,' he said, earnestly. 'Wild horses couldn't keep me away.'

'But you have to win. You're one of the few who stands a chance against…' She stopped.

'Against?' he prompted.

'Against an opponent who threatens to dethrone me if he wins,' she finished evasively. 'But I'll explain it more a little later.'

Max couldn't help wondering whether her faith in him wasn't just a little misplaced. Certainly, when he was in an ethereal form, his mental prowess was indubitably improved – probably because he had no physical distractions of any type and, as a consequence, less mental restrictions. The studies he'd done while laid out on the beach that day had gone very smoothly indeed; he'd been able to take in a vast amount of material and in a relatively short period of time. However, all the study in the world was no real substitute for genuine talent.

Caissa waved her hand in front of his eyes. 'Yoo hoo, I'm still here.'

'Sorry. I was just feeling a little stressed out at being your main hope and not knowing why.'

'Okay, I admit you're not my only hope,' she replied. 'I'm not so bad a player as to place all my hopes on one lone defender.'

Max thought he understood. 'You mean, you haven't put all your eggs in one basket, then?' he said, feeling somewhat relieved.

'Absolutely not. But as to your second point of not knowing why – before explaining that, I have something to show you.'

Max glanced down at his physical body, sitting unmoving at the table. 'Do I need that?'

'That, you can save for your lovely friend,' she answered. 'Besides, you'd never be able to take it where we're going.' She regarded him a little curiously. 'You've had quite a lot to contend with in the last few days. Are you sure you can handle this?'

A chess goddess, floating heads in his washing machine, turning into Peter Pan virtually overnight. Sure he could. Max felt that there couldn't be much else left to surprise him with. What was left: Asgard? Never-never land?

'No problem.'

Famous last words.

'Well, in that case, you'll be needing something to wear.'

Max suddenly looked very unhappy. The problem of clothing hadn't occurred to him. He looked down at his own astral form and realised that he had absolutely nothing on. He was naked, in all his morning glory, in front of this stunning goddess. If he'd had blood, he'd have blushed a deep scarlet.

'Oh, don't bother yourself,' Caissa said nonchalantly, but she couldn't hide her amusement. 'I assure you I've seen it all before. But where we're going now requires some sort of covering, all the same. Just a matter of good taste really.'

Max was standing on the table, his hands hiding as much as he could of his nether regions. 'How...?'

'Just think what you'd like to be wearing,' she answered, foreseeing his question and still grinning widely. 'It's all here.' She tapped the side of her head.

Max decided that what he'd like to be wearing most of all was what he'd come to the casino in.

'Close your eyes and concentrate.'

Desperately, he took her advice, and, much to his relief, when he looked again, he was fully dressed: trousers, jacket and tie.

'That's it! Slightly more socially acceptable than before,' she commented. 'Although perhaps less interesting.' She giggled again at Max's expense. 'You see, it's your mind that creates the image you are seeing now, an image that also serves as a kind of extra protection for your astral form. Kind of like the way your clothing protects you normally.'

He made a mental note never to go about spiritually naked ever again.

Caissa reached out in front of them and it seemed to Max that she was turning some kind of invisible door handle. Then suddenly, the very fabric of space and time seemed to crack open in front of him, a crack that widened as she drew back her hand, finally revealing a rectangular portal of light. He took a nervous step backwards, awed, dazzled and strangely humbled by its intensity.

'There's nothing to worry about,' said Caissa as she stepped through into the light. She turned and reached out her hand to take his. 'Coming?' She laughed at his obvious trepidation. 'Don't worry, you'll be back before they have a chance to miss you. For them, no time will have passed whatsoever.'

Trustingly, Max let himself be drawn through the portal, and it closed up soundlessly behind them.

'Pretty cool, eh?'

He heard her voice, but wasn't really able to respond because what happened next seriously messed with his reality yet again.

He didn't know how to react. A split second before, he had been engulfed by a warm, intense light, the next, he was standing in probably the biggest casino he'd ever seen. It was so huge, he couldn't see the walls or the roof. All around him lay table after table of roulette wheels, card games, one-armed bandits, fruit machines, wheels of fortune – every gambling device he'd ever heard of, and others besides. The place was buzzing with activity.

'Wow!' It wasn't really an adequate description, but it was the best he could manage under the circumstances.

'Yes, isn't it?' said Caissa. 'Everything on the physical plain has its equivalent here.'

'Where's here?'

'Hmm, I think I'll let you figure that one out by yourself.' She walked over to a roulette table and placed what resembled a kind of golden ankh on it. The croupier changed it for a number of chips and she placed them all on the number thirty-two. 'My lucky number,' she grinned.

'Thirty-two pieces on a chessboard?' Max hazarded.

She smiled and turned her attention back to the table, but Max had by no means finished.

'What do you bet with?'

'A kind of universal currency.'

'Thirty, red,' declared the croupier, and swiftly raked away all the losing chips.

'Oh!' Caissa pouted and held out her hand. In her palm appeared half a dozen more ankh-like objects. Once again the croupier changed them for chips which she placed strategically over the numbers on the table and waited.

The wheel span again and the little ball whizzed busily round its edge.

'Fourteen, red.'

'Yippee!' She scooped up her chips. 'That's enough with games of chance. I don't go that much on them myself.' And she walked over to a small kiosk nearby. The lady inside changed them into a number of other ankh-shaped objects, which Caissa immediately swallowed.

'Yummy,' she commented.

'You just ate your money,' observed Max, looking slightly aghast.

'It's not money, you silly, it's positive karma.'

Okay, this subject he knew something about.

'People gamble with their own karma here? So that's what those ankh objects are!'

'Exactly. What other currency do you think would be universally acceptable?'

Max set his jaw firmly. 'Can I play too?'

'Of course.' She laughed at the infantile expression that had come over his face. The little boy who didn't want to be left out.

'Hold out your hand like this.' She stretched out her palm and Max imitated. 'Good. Now think of the last time you did something for someone else for free and out of pure goodwill.'

Max raised his eyebrows at her.

'Go on. There must have been at least one occasion,' she teased.

For a moment nothing came to mind, then he remembered some programming work he had helped a colleague out with the other day – or what seemed like the other day. A bronze ankh materialised in his hand.

'Bronze, eh? Hmm. It wasn't *that* good a deed, then. Well, you can't spend that here, the minimum bet is silver. You'll have to go over there.' She pointed to a row of tables further down.

'So this stuff is pure positive karma, then?'

'Pure as it comes.'

'And what happens if I lose?'

'You simply lose that piece of karma there. And if you win, you get some that you don't have to earn in the physical world.'

Was everything beginning to make a sort of jumbled sense?

'Positive karma which you earn by doing good deeds?' It wasn't so much a question as a kind of clarifying of his own thought processes.

'Messieurs et Mesdames, place your bets please.'

There was something extremely familiar about the French croupier, but Max couldn't quite place him. He put his little ankh down and it was quickly exchanged for some blue chips. He placed them on number three and then, changing his mind, scattered them over the table as he'd seen Caissa do.

'No more bets, please.'

The wheel was spun.

'Well, what about real bad guys who've caused countless suffering through the ages like Hitler, Charles Manson, Julio Iglesias, and probably never even participated in bob-a-job day?' asked Max, keeping his eye fixed on the slowing ball.

'They have great karma debts to pay, especially to the people they've hurt. I suppose they have to either work here or go and get reincarnated, and then spend their lives continually doing favours for others. They say that reincarnation is the fastest way of doing it. However, it's not guaranteed that you won't make the same mistakes again because you don't remember anything of your previous life.'

'And if they refuse to pay up altogether?' Max couldn't imagine those guys willingly paying their debts off.

'They simply cease to exist. Essence and everything – poof!'

'Vingt-deux, rouge. Twenty-two, red.'

'You lost,' said Caissa, rather unnecessarily.

'Oh.'

'Do you want to try again?'

'No, at least, not until I know what they all use it for.'

'Use what?'

'The karma. What if someone wins a fortune in the stuff?'

'Well, it's positive energy. If you have enough of the stuff, your spiritual presence becomes more solid. If you choose to return to the physical world, things go right for you more often. You achieve higher spiritual levels according to the amount of good karma you have. You can even get to be a deity, or more. And, of course, you get closer to the truth.'

'What truth?'

'The Great Truth, of course.'

'Oh, that truth,' said Max, not wishing to sound completely ignorant. All the same, curiosity soon got the better of him. 'What Great Truth?' he asked finally.

'Don't know,' Caissa answered honestly. 'I'm not on that high a level myself yet. Maybe never will be.'

Well, that certainly cleared a few things up.

On an impulse, he stretched out his palm and thought right back to his schooldays when he used to do sponsored charity runs. Three shining golden ankhs appeared.

'Ooh!' exclaimed Caissa.

'I think I'm getting the hang of this,' he declared. He exchanged them for some chips and asked Caissa to place them for him.

While they were standing waiting for the others to finish their betting, Max studied the little French croupier again.

'Poirot! It's Hercule Poirot!' exclaimed Max in astonishment. 'I'm sure it is. He's just how I envisioned him in the books.'

The croupier, who had obviously heard him, continued as if nothing had been said.

'Could well be,' said Caissa, looking at the short, balding, little man with the immaculately kept moustache. 'A lot of fictional characters manage to make their way here and become as real a presence as you are, even more so in some cases. It just depends on the amount of people who believe in them, that's all. It's more or less the same for certain minor deities, like yours truly.' She paused and added, 'Which brings me to the point of why I brought you here.'

'Huit, noir. Eight, black.'

'I won!' Max almost shrieked with delight, and had to struggle to contain his excitement.

Caissa grinned and then shrugged nonchalantly. 'I am a goddess, after all. Things often go right for me.'

Picking up the huge handful of chips she'd just won for him, Max turned to face her.

'What point? What did you bring me here to explain?'

Caissa slipped her arm through his and led him away from the tables.

'You see,' she began, 'if people lose faith in a deity, then that being receives less energy – less karma – and consequently becomes less potent.' She paused for a breath and then added sadly, 'Many of my friends have vanished over the centuries. We need belief, like people need food, to sustain us. My presence, my very existence, comes from all those who worship me – albeit indirectly – through chess.'

Max thought he'd spotted Porky Pig serving drinks at a table, but declined to mention it, wisely judging the moment to be perhaps somewhat inopportune.

'The seduction and interest in my game is what feeds me. I live to protect it and, at the same time, protect it to live. Without its following – which has been growing rapidly in recent times – I would eventually start to lose my power and control, even the right as protectress of the game.'

It *was* Porky Pig, he'd been right.

'If I lose this game, I'll probably end up going back to being just a wood nymph. Which isn't so bad, but it's a bit of a demotion. Besides, there is something even more important at stake. The time-honoured game of chess and its symbolic struggle, a struggle of human and immortal consequence, the game of warriors and great thinkers alike, must never be reduced to a mere sequence of binary numbers. That must never happen, ever.'

'Binary numbers? You mean computers?'

'If Belvois wins this tournament, people will lose interest in the game.'

'Belvois? What's he got to do with it?'

'He's no longer a man, but half computer.'

Oh, well, that explains a few other things, thought Max. Pierre Belvois, half man, half machine! Who would have thought it?

'And if a machine wins, my followers will become disenchanted with the game. Knowing that machine thought is supreme in chess, they'll eventually go in search of other challenges, leaving the machines to get on with their calculations. My presence will become progressively weaker as people lose interest.'

'And sooner or later no more Goddess of Chess.'

'Exactly.'

Max's brow furrowed. He suddenly felt very concerned for her. 'I really had no idea it was all so important.'

'For me it is,' she said, and then laughed light-heartedly. 'Oh, but don't worry. You just do your best for me, that's all I ask. And anyway, it's not so easy to beat me at my own game. What do you say to a drink? I have a friend here waiting for me.'

Max gazed in wonder at the myriad activities and forms of entertainment around him. They stopped in front of a table that was particularly odd. Many people were gathered around a kind of box. At the bottom, jets of flame shot out at random intervals and sharp, wickedly jagged objects jutted up from the base. A rope was fastened lengthwise across it and a tiny human figure was attempting to walk it.

'They bet on whether he makes it or not,' Caissa explained.

Max looked shocked. 'But it's barbarous! Who do they find to do something so precarious?'

'Debtors,' she answered, and then upon seeing his confusion added, 'bad guys.'

On closer inspection, Max thought he could recognise a small moustache and swastika. And – ridiculous – the guy taking the bets was definitely Roy of the Rovers.

They arrived at a bar area and seated themselves at one of the many white marble cocktail tables. A huge blonde man came over and pulled up a stool next to them.

'Max, I believe you and Blitzkrieg have already met.'

'Hiya, Max.'

Max stared at the chiselled features and the piercing blue eyes. 'You! You were in my washing machine!'

'What scandal! But you'll never be able to prove it, never, I'll deny everything. And I refuse to say any more without my lawyer being present,' cried Blitzkrieg in mock defence. He turned to Caissa. 'Have you been here long?'

'No, just arrived,' she answered.

A delighted grin suddenly spread over his face as he saw the bar.

'Drinkies' time!'

'Oh, dear,' said Caissa. 'Can't you wait till later?'

Blitzkrieg looked at her as if she'd gone mad. 'Why?'

'Perhaps Max, here, would like your expert opinion on what they serve, before you… er… begin,' she said, desperately trying to think of a reasonable argument to stall him with. When he got started, he could be so embarrassing at times, especially after the transformation. She turned to Max in explanation. 'Blitzy's a beer god, you see. He can't help it, it's in his nature.'

'Oh?' said Max, unsure of how to react to such information. 'A beer god? You mean there's more of you?'

'Yes,' replied Caissa. 'But he's my favourite.'

Blitzkrieg was beginning to look a little agitated. 'Whose round is it?'

Max jiggled the chips in his trouser pocket. 'Mine.'

'Hah hah!' boomed the beer god. 'I believe I'm getting to like this lad.'

He whacked Max good-humouredly on the back and called

for service.

A tall, skinny man with cropped, straight black hair approached. He was wearing a blue uniform and Max noticed that he had pointed ears.

'Can I get you something? Fermented vegetable juices? Fruit juices? Cocktails?'

'Two of your best house beers and a grape juice for the lady.' The beer god winked and grinned in Caissa's direction.

The waiter left and returned almost immediately with two frothing tankards and a glass of red grape juice.

'Excuse me, but aren't you—?' began Max.

'Nothing like Vulcan efficiency, is there?' interrupted Blitzkrieg. The waiter turned and promptly left, after relieving Max of some of his winnings.

'But he's an actor, a real person!'

'No, that's just his fictional personage,' explained Caissa, sipping from her glass. 'They often get jobs here, it's as good a way as any to earn your karma.'

Blitzkrieg raised his glass to him. 'Bottoms up. Good stuff this. Got a bit of a belt to it, it has.' And he drained the tankard in one almighty swig. 'Ahh! That just puts me in the mood for another,' he declared, slamming the empty vessel down on the table and calling for service.

Max put the tankard to his lips and took a healthy swig himself.

'It's superb!' he exclaimed in astonishment. 'I've never tasted anything quite like it.'

'But of course you haven't. Very few people on earth have,' Caissa explained. 'That stuff really doesn't travel well.'

'Nectar of the gods, that is.'

Blitzkrieg's voice had distinctly deepened – if it wasn't already so before – quite gravelly in fact, and he seemed to Max to have grown slightly bigger physically. Perhaps it was just the effect of the strange beer playing games with his eyes. He took another gulp and suddenly belched. Red-faced, he put his hand up to his mouth in polite apology.

'Ha ha!' observed the beer god.

Max glanced over at Caissa in embarrassment, but no amount

of social grace or etiquette could prevent the cruelty of what happened to him next. A second, altogether involuntary and extremely strong, exhalation of trapped air sent him and his swivel-head stool into a fast spin. He rotated three or four times very, very quickly before gravitational force thrust him outwards and backwards across the casino floor.

Somewhat dazed, he was helped to his feet by a little white-haired gentleman with a distinct Scottish accent. 'Aye, first time, was it, laddie? Ne'er yea mind, sonny boy, you'll soon get used to its kick. You noo wanna give up now.'

Rubbing the back of his head and, despite the rather undignified circumstance which had led to his unexpected flight, he couldn't help but notice that he seemed to be as solid here as in his world, and a fall of that distance still hurt like a fall of that distance. Frowning thoughtfully, the Vulcan leant over the bar, where he had been in the act of mixing one or two cocktails, and spoke in a confidential manner to one of his clients, a gentleman of some demeanour and obvious education who had suddenly produced a pen and begun to scribble furious notes on a beer mat.

'A further confirmation of your eleventh law, Sir Newton?' he asked, raising a questioning eyebrow.

Maria counted the wad of notes for the third time. It was a lot of money, a hell of a lot. They'd just earned in one night what would have normally taken them six months. But they'd been right to stop when they did. Best not push their luck too far, and anyway, they could always go back whenever they needed more.

'So what you're telling me is that up there,' – she waved some lira towards the car roof – 'loads of gods and fantasy characters are running wild.'

'Well, I wouldn't say "wild" exactly,' Max corrected her a little pedantically. He changed up a gear and continued. 'More like busily solidifying their presence by the accumulation of karma – or positive energy, if you prefer – in one way or another.'

'And any one of these characters, gods, dead people or whatever, can return to earth, reincarnated, as a quicker means of achieving greater karma?'

'That's what she told me, more or less. Except I suppose the term "reincarnated" wouldn't exactly apply in every case.'

'Don't get finicky,' Maria snapped, afraid of losing her track and at the same time finding his tone just slightly irritating. 'Let's say incarnated then, if it's their first time.'

'Okay. Sorry.'

Maria looked at him and swallowed hard. 'Taking this to its logical conclusion, then... Oh, my God! You realise what this means, don't you?'

'Er, no.' Uh-oh! Here we go with another one of Maria's wacky theories. But so long as it didn't lead to the ruin of three of his best pairs of socks, he couldn't see what harm it would do enquiring. 'Go on, then.'

'It means that someone passing me on the street one day could be the incarnation of the spirit of Porky Pig.'

Food for thought.

'And another thing,' Maria continued. 'Did she give a hint as to who runs that karma casino joint?'

Chapter Twenty-Six

'How is he now?'

'He's in his room, probably playing the guitar or studying. After a good night's sleep he claims to feel like a new man. Apart from being slightly over-preoccupied with existential and religious... er... things, he appears quite rational and, despite early fears, shows no signs whatsoever of serious disorientation or mental instability.'

'So, in your considered opinions, he's not gone wacko then.'

'No.'

'So what got into him?' demanded Andersson, as he extinguished the remains of a Havana cigar in the crystal ashtray on his desk. 'Why the unwarranted attack on my driver, and, worse still, why the Hill Waily impression?'

Cathy glanced over at Menti, who was next to her on the other side of Andersson's desk. They had just left Belvois after an exhaustive session and now had to face another with only a handful of suppositions to go on.

'Well,' began Menti. He adjusted himself to a more upright position and fingered nervously the leaves of a notepad and a bunch of papers on his lap.

'Best make the explanation seem as professional as possible; we'll just have to try to baffle our way through,' Cathy had suggested as they were making their way over from the room where they had left Belvois.

'It would seem that the attack on Deklan, according to the subject's own account of the proceedings, was completely unintentional. Apparently, the patient had no knowledge whatsoever of Deklan's presence under the window, although he does admit to having thrown his answerphone out of it.'

Andersson put his hand up to his mouth and coughed to clear his throat. Then, reaching over the huge executive desk, he poured himself a glass of water from the bottle on the silver tray and waited with visually restrained impatience.

'In fact,' continued Menti rather hurriedly, 'he displayed genuine signs of distress at the thought of having caused harm to yet another human being, requesting, and I quote, "To be taken immediately to the victim and allow him to break my nose in return."'

'What's this? Your nose? Why would he want to do that?' cried Andersson, looking shocked.

'Er, no, sir. Belvois' own nose. He wanted to offer it as a gesture of goodwill or something.'

Andersson started forward in his chair. Not the words he would have expected from his super soldier. 'He *has* flipped out then! Is this what you meant by being "overly preoccupied with existential and religious philosophies"? Is this some kind of eye for an eye, tooth for a tooth in reverse? Don't tell me he's suddenly turned into some kind of religious maniac? Because in my experience there's not a lot of difference between a wacko and a Gandhi gribbly. They're both unstable fruitcakes.'

'Er… perhaps over-enthusiastic altruism might be a more gentle term. He also claims to have fully forgiven you for your actions yesterday evening,' put in Cathy quickly.

Andersson grunted disconcertedly.

'It seems he's been quite affected by the works of a number of radical philosophers, in particular a certain Siddle, an Englishman, who wrote *Ken And The Art Of Domestic Appliance Maintenance…*'

'A Gandhi gribbly then,' Andersson groaned, reselecting from his own more colourful technical terminology. He'd never read the book himself, but he remembered a number of heated debates about it on various TV chat shows a few years back.

'It's not something anyone could have possibly predicted.' Cathy decided it would be wiser to keep the discussion on a more scientific basis. 'Belvois' psyche is showing an ever-increasing need to express itself in altruistic terms.'

'Exactly. This regard for others as a principle action for being could be construed as a natural by-product of the search for his true or new self. He's no longer able to identify with himself as he was and he can't quite accept what he has become. He needs to find a balance,' concluded Menti.

A distinctly glazed look was slowly forming itself in Andersson's eyes. If he wasn't mistaken, their baffle strategy seemed to be working.

'It's almost as if the more he learns, the more he feels the need to justify his own existence and purpose philosophically. It would seem that his vast and sudden accumulation of knowledge has opened up an equally vast spiritual chasm that he feels he needs to fill in one way or another.'

Andersson fell back again into his great leather armchair. 'This is ridiculous! I mean… well… isn't he Catholic?'

'Er… yes, I believe so.'

'And that's not enough for him?'

'Apparently not.'

'Bloody hell,' Andersson mumbled from under his moustache. 'Next time we choose a Muslim or a Buddhist or something.' He rubbed his chin thoughtfully. 'But all this doesn't explain the Hill Waily business, or does it?'

'Quite the contrary,' said Cathy, relaxing back into her own seat again. They'd won. He'd swallowed it. Menti had been particularly brilliant, she thought – he almost had her believing it. Anyway, the most important thing was that Menti had proved his worth as the project's psychologist. She crossed her legs under her white overall and continued. 'Belvois told me that he'd read somewhere of some sixteenth-century missionaries who used to convert the native Indians with the guitar. The principle being that learning three chords on any instrument would get you closer to God.'

'The mystical link between music and spirituality is well known and documented,' said Menti. 'And the patient, by learning to imitate a rock 'n' roll hero, was, and I quote: "…trying to increase my positive energy rating to this aim."'

Silence.

'From super soldier to saint in one night. So what the hell can be done about it?' enquired Andersson finally. The idea of a 'positive energy rating' had to be the equivalent of some kind of holy scoreboard read out to everyone in paradise on a Saturday night, like the football results.

'I recommend no further action to be taken at this present

time,' said Menti, sounding pretty sure of himself. He rose and professionally tapped his papers back in order on the side of the chair. 'The best thing would be to let him find his own answers. It's the only way I see of achieving a complete restabilisation of his psyche – his emotional and spiritual needs. Besides, there's no harm in it, he's only in search of answers like the rest of us.'

'The only difference', interrupted Cathy, 'is that maybe he's got a better chance of finding them.'

Andersson chewed on his moustache a little. It must be part of the identity crisis they had warned him about before. Well, he couldn't see how it should change his plans in the long run, as long as certain precautions were taken. Unless…

'So you're sure that none of this lunacy will affect his performance in the tournament?'

'Absolutely not,' Menti assured him. 'There's no reason why a few healthy philosophical questions should interfere with his capacity for logical reasoning and chess-playing ability.'

Andersson breathed an inward sigh of relief.

'Well, make sure he has everything he needs and wants, but I don't want him on the loose again. We don't want to risk anything happening to him if he should decide to go walkabout. And the police chief, Ciambella, won't be so willing to do me any favours a second time around. After the tournament is finished and I've proved my point to the General, then he can go and live in a convent for all I care. We can make plenty more like him, and better.'

'No problem,' replied Menti. 'The office apartment on the third floor has been designated for him. The room has everything he needs, or he just has to make a call for it. It's security-locked tight until the day after tomorrow when we leave for Salsomaggiore. No one gets in or out without passing the guards, and only security-cleared staff, besides you, Dr McDonald, Ms Lee and myself, will have access.'

'Excellent.' Andersson looked decidedly happier. 'There's just one thing that bothers me about all this philosophical music business, and that's the idea of Belvois' particular choice of music getting him closer to God,' he added as both the doctors were leaving the room. 'I mean, wasn't rock 'n' roll once condemned by the church as the devil's music?'

Devil's music or not, thought Cathy as she sat listening to Belvois, he sure plays a mean guitar, and he's got a really neat little butt.

Nature can play some strange tricks. Logically, the most physically attractive part of a man to a woman – apart from his wallet, obviously – should be his wide shoulders or rippling muscles, things that, in nature, might have served as protection for her and the family. But no. Nothing like that. When asked, seven out of ten women prefer... his ass!

So much for primordial instinct.

At times he seemed to her like the proverbial little lost boy who had suddenly found himself alone in the world and needed to find answers; and, at others, like the other day at the military academy, he was quietly confident and in control. She admired his courage and had wondered what had driven him to accept the part of guinea pig in their experiment. A decision that had required great courage? A noble, self-sacrificing gesture in the name of progress and the betterment of mankind? Or maybe he'd had nothing to lose – like her. At least she'd still felt that way up until about a couple of hours ago.

Since the death of Robert she'd suddenly found herself alone. It had been frightening. Hell, they'd been together ever since university days in Glasgow. And then an American company had offered them a very respectable five-year research grant, and so they'd got married and gone to Washington to live. They had passed nearly all their study, work and play hours together, and then suddenly she'd found herself alone.

Sure, she hadn't been short on offers from men since then. She'd even gone out with one or two, but had lacked the interest to follow it up. It simply hadn't been the same. Even the lovemaking, the tender caresses, had felt mechanical – just going through the motions. Acting. It had been satisfying physically – she needed that; after all, she was still a young woman with natural needs and desires – but it had always left her feeling emotionally empty the next morning. And then there was her work. So in the end she'd simply lost herself in it and tried to forget. Time heals.

She'd only known Pierre Belvois for a few short weeks, but they had spent a lot of time together and she'd grown to feel comfortable in his company. She liked him, his honesty, his simple directness, his sensitivity, and his cute ass. And now the guitar. Since a young teenager she'd always been inexplicably fascinated with musicians. She marvelled at the dexterity of his fingers as they ran up and down the fretboard. The movement captivated and sent little tingles right through her. He was making her feel that age again.

He stopped playing and came over to where she lay naked on the white sheets of the apartment bed. He bent down to kiss her and she responded with moist lips and hot breath. He loved the perfume of her skin. It was so natural – no additives, no preservatives. She just looked and smelt great.

He certainly hadn't expected this much, not even dared to hope, but it had happened and he was ecstatic. He was in love, or so he reckoned.

Apart from the Swiss account with the very generous sum deposited in it by Andersson, the other major reason for accepting his part in the experiment had been when they'd told him who he'd be working closely with. It hadn't been the first time that his dick had done the talking, the smaller head thinking for the bigger one, but he was grateful to it now.

And how.

Oh, yes, she was lovely. Bee... yoo... ti... ful. The girl of his boyhood dreams. The type that had constantly invaded his thoughts while he'd been trying to do his homework. Difficult and distracted times. To be honest, his education had been a losing battle to the erotic fantasies of early puberty. He hadn't achieved great grades at school. In fact, every time he'd sat himself down at his desk, desperate to do some study, the monster would rear its shiny red head again. Still, he may not have had contented schoolmasters, but he must have helped put a smile on a few manufacturers' faces when they'd seen the annual sales figures for man-sized tissues. IQ of 154, a genius – he knew because it was in the confidential personnel files he'd hacked – and so very sexy. Not only had she turned him into a fuckin' superman, but she was fuckin' him to boot.

'This never happened in Mary Shelley's *Frankenstein*,' he joked.

She brushed his hair from off his forehead with her hand. 'No, and you can't even see the stitches.'

He'd been delighted when she'd come back to the office apartment to see him for the second time that morning just before lunch, saying that she didn't like the idea of him being confined there like some kind of prisoner. Light-heartedly, he had replied that he actually liked the place and had asked her to stay for lunch. He couldn't believe his luck when she'd agreed.

He was a fine cook – always had been – and he'd discovered that she also shared a similar passion for the culinary arts. The apartment was well stocked with a wide variety of foodstuffs, including perishables brought in that morning – another reason why he didn't mind staying in the place. It was cleaner and tidier, and also he wasn't afraid to open the fridge.

They'd laughed and joked as they'd perused the kitchen cupboards. They'd prepared dinner together, chatted about everything and anything. It had all been so natural. Then, after an excellent white wine and *pasta con pepperoni*, she'd asked him to play her something on the guitar, and he'd been only too happy to demonstrate his newly acquired musical talents. The time had passed so quickly and easily that it was almost without realising it that they'd found themselves in each other's arms.

'Yup, guys, there's basically only one way to pull if you're not an incredible hunk or you don't have five Porsches in the garage: learn to play an instrument.'

The immortal advice given by Hill Waily to some pimply, teenage fans a few decades back, and it still rang true. Belvois, however, had another ace up his sleeve that not even the great Hill Waily could have known about.

Among the vast amount of knowledge he had recently accumulated was a particular study done by some American psychologists into the astounding effect of the male hormone, testosterone, on women. It seemed that it stimulated female sexual desire. Women just couldn't resist it. Sprayed on to chairs in the cinema, they were magnetically attracted to those particular seats without the faintest idea why. Attempts to extract and synthesise it into a cosmetic perfume had always led to poor results – something to do with the individual nature of the wearer's skin. If it wasn't your own testosterone, it didn't work.

But it was his, and all Belvois had to do was stimulate the gland that produced it – a little like he could do with his adrenalin.

'Mmm, come here, lover boy,' she purred, writhing sensually on the linen sheets. 'Now play me with those fingers.'

Chapter Twenty-Seven

Cappuccino with cocoa powder sprinkled on the top is for tourists, and only foreign tourists would drink one while eating croissants at three o'clock in the afternoon. Still, so long as they paid, the barman thought, as he polished a wine glass and kept a wary eye on the longhaired hippy who was sitting by the window in the corner of his bar.

Chris sat and munched his third croissant and supped from his third cup of cappuccino. It was good waking up late again, and breakfast always tasted so much better at this hour. He wasn't into mornings: only the olds, his folks, and sad people with jobs got up at that time.

He plonked the empty cup down on the table, the froth from the coffee lining his upper lip with a complementary moustache, and reached for the magazine that was lying on the window sill. He looked at the front cover and tugged thoughtfully on the goaty, blonde beard that hung scraggily from his chin.

It seemed to be a kind of 'What's On Italia' local entertainments guide. Skipping through its pages, it began to dawn on him that the only things he could understand were the occasional band names in English. Maybe if he studied it a little, he might be able to find them something to do that evening other than eating pizza served by some hyper-aggressive Italian waiter.

Ali entered the bar and, spotting Chris by the window, went over to him after ordering another two cappuccinos for them both.

'How did it go with Mago Marco the Magnificent then?'

Chris studied Ali carefully, half expecting to see some kind of physical change, perhaps a pair of horns or red eyes – no, the latter he had anyway – or maybe a magic wand. He hadn't had much personal experience with witches, even though, after all the horror films he'd watched on late-night TV, he considered himself no small expert; if you had werewolf, zombie or vampire hassles, he was your man for advice.

'I don't know.' Ali sighed, and raised the coffee that had just arrived, to his lips. 'He was not very happy, and looked rather dubious at first when I admitted to it being my fault that his door intercom had ceased to function. But he gave me an emergency sitting after his Rolex exploded all over the floor when we shook hands.' He took another sip. 'Anyway, after passing some kind of medallion over me several times, he did seem to be quite convinced that I could be cured.'

He began to fumble in the deep recesses of his gown. 'He said that I was right in considering it a kind of allergy and prescribed me some things to take.' He produced a silver metallic Celtic-style bracelet and some leaves enclosed in a plastic packet.

'The tea is to drink. He said that it would help to cleanse me from the inside and that when I ran out of the stuff, I should write to him for more. It is very expensive, though.'

Chris opened the packet and sniffed it curiously, then closed it again and raised his eyebrows. He made a mental note to buy some cigarette papers on their way back to the hotel – that stuff was well worth a trial toking session.

'And the bracelet?'

'Some kind of charm that will help reduce the negative impurity that my body absorbs and which, in turn, affects machines.'

'And I bet that was expensive too.'

'Yes, actually. Not only that but he charged me for a new doorbell and a revision of the entire electrical implant system.'

'Ouch!'

'And a new watch. But if it works, it will have been worth it.'

'Oh, wow!'

'Well, I do hope so,' said Ali, pleasantly taken aback by the unexpected enthusiasm for his personal well-being.

Chris glanced up at Ali for a second, questioningly, and then went back to the page he'd just found in the magazine he was reading. 'No, I mean, Oh, WOW!'

Ali leaned over to look at the page. There was a picture of a dark-haired girl dressed in a short, black skirt and jacket, very pretty, but, as far as he could see, nothing to get so excited about.

There were plenty of pretty girls in magazines.

'So what?'

'It's her, the chick who's been appearing in my dreams for weeks and weeks. I know it's her. Her face is imprinted here.' Chris tapped his heart with his forefinger.

Ali tutted piteously at him and shook his head. 'I think you have drunk too much coffee and you are getting excited about nothing. It is probably your imagination or something.'

'No, man. We've astral-travelled together. Now I know that it wasn't just a dream. I read about this kind of stuff in a Carlos Castaneda book once. People do it in their dreams.'

Ali gave the picture another look. 'The girl of your dreams, eh?' He began to read the information printed below. 'Well, it looks like you may be right, dear nephew. It seems her name is Jacqueline King and she is hosting some kind of two-day chess tournament in Salsomaggiore, starting tomorrow.' He paused and his brow furrowed briefly. 'And by a most curious coincidence, that is exactly where Morph is headed, if I remember rightly.'

'Destiny,' said Chris. The word just kind of dribbled out of his mouth along with his lolling tongue. 'It's my destiny to meet her.' He was beginning to feel most peculiar.

Max was discovering just how damaging city driving could be to his spiritual integrity. Every time he stopped his car to allow courteously another road user to pull out, someone else behind would start to honk in frustration at him. Any positive karma gained by being nice to one person seemed to be almost immediately negated by the irritation he had unintentionally caused in another. He could almost feel the energy build up and then vanish again, ebb and flow as if moving with an invisible tide.

Partly because of his experience in the casino the night before, he now seemed to be able to feel his karma as an almost tangible presence, once free of his physical form. It would have been a very hard thing to explain to most people, but not to Maria. She didn't seem to have any problem with the concept – the advantage of having flower power parents, he supposed. She'd always talked to him about the importance of having good karma, its vital importance in the role of things, but he guessed that up until the other night he had never really taken it seriously.

It made sense. Every major religion in the world had, as its basis, the necessity of being good (or at least pretty nice and chatty) to your fellow man. They all preached that one particular idea, although the wordings were often slightly different and the interpretation, at times, alarmingly suspect. But any followers who adhered to and practised that part of their faith were, whether they realised it or not, simply increasing their potential and growth as spiritual beings. Despite the dogmatic differences particular to every different kind of religious philosophy, if their fundamental principles were followed correctly, they all seemed basically valid.

Max laughed wryly to himself. Still, no matter how ancient the wisdom they were founded upon, none of the major religions, until now, had ever come up with a reasonable solution to the antipathy felt towards one's fellow man when sat in peak rush-hour traffic.

Oh, well, to hell with it! He decided to return to driving like every other Italian on the road. There were, anyway, other much more effective methods of spiritually fortifying himself, and driving certainly wasn't ever going to be one of them. He gave the car horn a quick blast and felt that pent-up feeling of aggravation flow from his body. He vented himself again, this time at the dodderer two cars ahead who was holding everyone else up, and a chorus of similar sounds honked and gaggled goose-like around him.

He'd had a feeling that afternoon, when he'd first climbed into his little Citroën, that he was going to find the experience very trying. But someone had had to take all that cash to the bank, and anyway, at least he'd made his bank manager very happy.

Pleasing people (even a bank manager) was a sure-fire way of bathing in the soul-warming vibes of good karma, and being good to others certainly had its reciprocal merits. He was beginning to feel a little like James Stewart in one of his classic movies where the philosophy of being pleasant and honest and just plain nice to everyone always paid off in the long run. Yeah, he guessed it was a bit like that, and how much nicer the world would be if...

Max was suddenly determined on his path. What if he really could teach other people how to leave their bodies, to experience and get to know the joy of being immersed in good karma? It would be his own personal contribution towards the betterment of mankind.

When he and Maria had tried to list the potential advantages of such an ability, it had stupefied them both. The ecology would be helped by people not needing to use conventional forms of transport so often. Common illnesses and their discomforts need no longer be suffered – just get out of your body, go about your business as usual, and return to it only when it had got better. There'd be no need to diet if overweight because, free of the parasitical demands of the physical form, unnecessary hunger could be completely ignored. Major surgical operations could be performed without the inhibiting drawbacks and dangers of anaesthetics...

He stopped at a zebra crossing and watched an old couple struggle slowly across it. Even time itself need no longer necessarily bring with it the often cruel and debilitating effects of old age. All the insults, the pains and evils associated with growing old: arthritis, rheumatism, and the loneliness brought on by the inability to get out and about; all that could be escaped from, and returned to, only when necessary, when it was time to feed, wash or exercise your body. There would be no reason not to go and visit old friends, even, maybe, those officially deceased!

A thought suddenly occurred to him: what would happen if someone's body died while they weren't in it, while they were out and about? Would they continue to live on, or would the spirit form be dragged off to its eventual destiny regardless of conscious objections? He didn't know; it was just something else that he had to discover. Hell, it was all so new, so exciting, so mysterious! The possibilities and questions seemed to unroll before him like an infinite red carpet.

He pounded on the car horn out of pure exhilaration. He could help, he could make a difference, help to ease some of the suffering. If he could somehow find a way of teaching his little ability to others... Maria would be his guinea pig.

Magnanimously ignoring the indignant beeps from the cars

behind him, he allowed another two – this time rather odd-looking – men to cross in front of him. Quite a gesture of goodwill, seeing as in Italy, as in most continental countries, the zebra crossing is there only for the convenience of the road user and not the pedestrian. The driver might stop, but only if he was having a nice day.

'I'm feeling a little weird, man,' said Chris, as he and Ali were sauntering back to their hotel. 'Don't know if I like it or not, actually.'

Ali, who had been lost in thought since they had left the café bar, now turned round and regarded his younger companion with a certain concern.

'Please define weird.'

'Kinda dizzy-like and irritated at the same time. And my heart's beating real rapid, man.' He put his hand over his chest. 'Whoa! And I keep breaking into hot sweats. I think I may have caught some kind of exotic disease.'

Ali cocked his head to one side slightly. 'Just how many cappuccinos did you have back there?'

Chris thought while trying to find his wrist pulse. 'Don't know. Four, maybe five.'

Ali snorted knowingly. 'It is the caffeine. The only thing exotic that you are likely to catch in Italy since Mussolini wiped out malaria is something from one of the many ladies of the night who live here.'

'But coffee's never affected me like this before. I mean, I drink loads of the stuff back home.'

Ali chuckled at the worried expression on Chris's face. 'Your metabolism is still used to that horrible instant stuff that the English are so fond of drinking. What they drink here is like rocket fuel in comparison. But, that being said, it is still not as strong as what we used to get in the old country. Back in Persia the coffee is real. After all, it is the place where coffee originally came from.' His tone was suddenly sentimental, and he gave a short sigh. 'Ahh, Persia, I may never see you again. The tall palms, the sweet dry air...'

Oh no! Chris thought. On top of everything else, the old

bugger was getting all nostalgic on him.

'Do not worry,' Ali continued, drifting back to reality, 'you have just had too much caffeine intake. Now take some deep breaths and remember to drink a lot of water when we get back to the hotel and you will be fine.'

'Far out! Is that all you reckon it is then?' cried Chris, relieved at the certainty with which Ali had delivered his diagnosis. He filled his lungs with air. 'Thanks, man. Deep breaths, yeah, deep breaths.'

And so they continued down the street: Chris with one hand on his heart, and wondering whether or not he shouldn't actually be enjoying the caffeine buzz he was experiencing, and Ali dreaming of his Persia, his long white robes swishing around him majestically as he strode.

Together they stepped off the kerb and on to the zebra crossing, oblivious of the herd of impatiently growling, snorting traffic and the loud offensive horns.

Max sat and waited for the odd couple, the Arab gentleman and a hippy, to cross in front of him, his previous enthusiasm now a fixed and determined idea. He watched them pass, a distant smile on his lips. A little smile that hid behind it the possibility of new hope for a better world, but to any casual onlooker would probably have been misconstrued as somewhat cretinous. A smile can be a most mysterious thing.

The hippy was obviously having respiratory problems, Max noted, from the way his chest was rapidly heaving up and down, although his Arabic companion seemed unconcerned – or maybe he hadn't noticed.

The lights turned to green, and the revving engines that had anticipated the change now fumed, impatiently wondering at the hold-up. Max waited; he couldn't go because the hippy had just collapsed on to the crossing and the Arab was struggling to pick him up.

'*Tutto bene?*' called Max, as he leapt out of his car to see if he could help. It seemed to him that the situation was rather serious and his own question slightly fatuous.

'Hyperventilation, I think,' Ali responded, glad of the help the

Italian gentleman was offering. He was discovering just how difficult it was to lift the dead wait of a completely limp hippy. Every attempt he made to get a firm hold on a body part failed as it kept slithering loosely from his grip and flopping soggily back down on to the road again.

Max took his feet and Ali held him under the shoulders, and together they managed to carry him to the pavement.

'There!' Ali nodded towards the hotel at the corner only a few yards away. 'The Holiday Inn Hotel.'

Max nodded his understanding. 'Okay.' He was desperately trying to recall some of his old school English and began to wish that he'd paid more attention in class.

For Enrico Furia, the interminable delay was too much. He honked his horn again in frustration. He'd already been caught at the last three sets of lights, and now this imbecile, two cars up, refused to move. In a moment they would turn red and it would be all too late. It was time to take matters into his own hands. Time for action. He turned the steering wheel and hit the accelerator, mounted the kerb, passed the first stationary car in front of him and screeched to a halt barely two centimetres away from the leg of a horrified Arab.

Ali heard Max's warning shout and the sound of screeching tyres and swirled round to his side. A car was half mounted on the pavement, its radiator grill grinning menacingly at the side of his leg. Instinctive self-preservation took control and, screaming, he dropped both Chris's legs and slammed his hands down hard on to the bonnet of the car, denting it slightly.

The driver began to shout furiously and gestured rudely from him to the traffic lights, which were still tantalisingly green. And then his engine stopped dead.

Satisfied that the red and raging man in the car was no longer an immediate danger to them, Ali turned back to the task at hand and, with Max, carried Chris into the reception hall of the hotel. They placed the human bundle into an armchair where it proceeded to moan feverishly.

'More… more drugs.'

Max looked in concern at the hippy. 'He is okay?'

'Oh, yes. He will be all right after a glass of water. He just got carried away with his breathing and hyperventilated, causing the blood to rush to his head.'

Max wasn't sure if he'd understood what the Arab was saying to him, but the bellboy seemed to. He came over to them with a glass of water in his hand. Ali took the glass graciously, turned to the slumped Chris and casually threw the water in his face. Chris jolted upright, eyes wide, shocked by the sudden coldness on his skin.

'Old Persian treatment for dizzy spells,' Ali explained, smiling at their surprised faces. 'My mother often used to have fainting spells in Persia – she suffered at times from the heat – and my father would always favour the effectiveness of that particular method on her.'

Max decided it was best to return to his car that he'd left running with the keys still in it. The situation here didn't seem to him to be so dramatic any more.

'Well, I go now. The car…' He was trying his best, but it had been so long since he'd spoken any of that language.

'Thank you very much for your help,' said Ali, slowly and clearly so that the kind Italian gentleman would have no problem in understanding, and then repeated it in pretty fluent Italian.

'You're welcome.' Yeah, at least he'd remembered that particular phrase. Pleased with himself, Max held out his hand, shook Ali's and left.

Ali bit his lip guiltily. Why did he always forget that one? He hoped the nice gentleman wasn't carrying anything electronic, or worse, electronic and expensive.

Enrico Furia sat in his car, still partially mounted on the pavement, and watched helplessly as the owner of the little Citroën returned, smiled and waved cheerfully over at him and got into his car. Then the lights turned green, and all the traffic moved off without him. He was stranded. Some pedestrians complained and rapped on his windscreen as they attempted to squeeze by between the wall and his car. Italian streets are notoriously narrow.

Lost for something to do, he tried turning the key in the ignition for the hundredth time. It just clicked. He couldn't understand it. The car was only a few months old. How could anything be wrong? Perhaps it was just a loose battery connection. He turned on the radio to check. Sound suddenly blared out at him, confused sound, like all the radio stations in the country were transmitting on the same channel, and then sparks began to fly out and the little plastic knobs on the front blew off and whizzed passed his head. He started backwards in his seat, mouth gaping wide. He'd never seen anything like it. Radios weren't supposed to do that.

A police siren suddenly wailed his attention from behind and he glanced in his rear-view mirror. Enrico Furia groaned and slunk down further into his seat. On top of everything else, he was going to get a fine for being illegally parked.

Chapter Twenty-Eight

Cathy had promised to return later that evening, and since then Belvois had assimilated a very large amount of literary material, largely to do with music, philosophy and, of course, something that he figured might be of help to the latest interest in his life.

He'd read a fair few Mills and Boon romances and not an inconsiderable number of guides to good relationships and agony aunt columns from various magazines. Actually, what had surprised him was not the variety of information there was available on the subject, but just how contradictory it could be. There had to be a lot of very confused people out there, Belvois had finally concluded.

However, they were all agreed on one thing and that was the importance of a healthy, quality sex life. 'Do it often and do it well,' had been the general advice, and he'd had no problem finding material on that particular subject. The only obstacle had been in its selection. In the end he'd decided that the ones with the illustrative photographs were the most useful. Cathy was going to be pleasantly surprised when he saw her later. But she wasn't going to come back until around midnight as she said she'd got so much to catch up on, work that she should have completed that afternoon. Belvois grinned to himself. He'd kept her far too busy to think of her job, that was for sure.

Now, though, the problem was keeping himself occupied until then – until midnight. He glanced at his watch. Half past eight. It was still only early evening. He certainly didn't feel like doing any more reading, and sleep was out of the question, his mind was far too active.

He glanced around the room. His guitar sat in the corner where he'd left it earlier that afternoon. Playing relaxed him, made him happy. Sure, even locked up in the room 'for his own security', as Andersson had put it, he was still happily ecstatic: he had his music, a new satisfying philosophy on life, and Cathy.

He wanted to play, to perform, to express himself in front of an audience, maybe fill them with some of the same good vibes that he was feeling, and he knew just the place.

To hell with all this security bollocks. Didn't they want him in perfect condition for that dumb tournament tomorrow evening? Hadn't they said that he was to relax and take it easy? Well, what better way to relax?

His mind made up, he went over and packed his guitar in its case. He could slip out, have a quick jam, and be back before midnight for Cathy's arrival. What could be simpler and more rewarding? And then he'd make them all happy by winning the tournament, and finally he'd be free of his obligations to Andersson and the firm.

He turned to the computer, still hot and humming, and entered a password. A map of the building's security systems and guard rota came up. His fingers shot over the keyboard and in the space of twenty seconds all MEGA's state-of-the-art security systems that might have alerted the guards as to his intentions were diverted. Another five seconds and the main door to his apartment clicked open, the digital access lock on the other side neutralised. Andersson was a fool if he'd honestly believed, even for one minute, that their feeble precautions could keep him locked in if he hadn't really wanted it.

Guitar case in hand, he walked down the empty corridor, boot heels reverberating in the hollow emptiness. Pulling up the bar that opened the fire escape exit, he stepped out with a clang on to the fire escape stairway and into the hot, sticky, night air.

Morph sat and stared at the remains of his expensive beer. He wobbled the glass in tiny circles on the table and watched the golden liquid swish around the edges, sometimes rising almost as high as the rim.

It was funny how a day could begin exceptionally well and then peter out into near obscurity. The day's sales had gone excellently, and he'd enjoyed a new culinary experience in the form of a dish called risotto Milanese. He'd also discovered a new and surprising passion for Parmesan cheese. In England, it had always smelt and tasted like the scrapings from between a marathon runner's toes – one who always wore particularly tight and sweaty sneakers – but here it was beyond doubt one of the greatest things he'd ever eaten, served up in huge chunks. And then the story of the hippy's collapse in the road and Ali's experience with the rip-off 'Mago Marco the Magnificent' – well, that had just about highlighted the day. Now, however…

It had been Chris's idea to come and see this group called DMC which he had sworn were one half of a famous American rap band – the other half being called 'Stagger', or 'Leg It', or something – on a tour of Europe. Instead, they'd paid their money and were being subjected to various degraded versions of old sixties and seventies numbers. It reminded Morph of the occasional Sunday evenings as a boy when he'd had to go to his dad's local conservative club dances. Sad stuff. Musicians who seemed, even to him, to display no more musical talent than the family dog. Actually, that was being a bit hard on the dog who had always demonstrated great passion when it came to soap opera theme tunes and would howl his guts out to them. 'Stuff from the heart if not always perfectly pitched,' as his mum used to say.

Morph was dreading the inevitable rendition of 'House of the Rising Sun', and decided at that point he would really have to leave. He looked over at Chris and Ali. They didn't seem to be too overawed with it all either. Perhaps the evening could be saved yet, and they could all go back to the hotel and watch some Sky Sport.

Unfortunately, what none of the trio could have known before coming to the Graffiti nightclub was that DMC, far from being a super-hip multi-talented rap band, were in fact a collection of amateur musicians who jammed together every Friday evening.

The initials DMC actually stood for Dyslexic Musicians Club, which was originally formed by an English immigrant who played sax. However, lacking any particular talent for his instrument and musical rhythm in general, he had realised that playing the professional circuit was probably not the best of ideas, no matter how impassioned he was. So he'd placed an ad in the local paper asking for other enthusiastic but basically hopeless and frustrated musicians to come forth. And so DMC was born. Fortune, being the lady she is at times, even ensured that the owner of a local nightclub, a guitarist of sorts, would become one of their most sympathetic members, and thus DMC found themselves a place to regularly gig in. Lucky indeed, as no one else would have booked them more than once.

Friday nights at the Graffiti, then, soon became a meeting place for poor and frustrated musicians of all kinds. An opportunity, once a week, to sit down and jam and basically get it out of their systems. Even Hammond organ players were welcome.

The locals, of course, had soon grown wise to this, and would, as a general rule, avoid the place like the plague on that particular evening. The Graffiti club, normally a very chic and popular hangout, was usually pretty much deserted on that particular night, the only people there being the musicians themselves and the unhappy bar staff.

Teachers at the highly respected classical music academy on the other side of the city would often threaten lazy or lax students with forced attendance of the club on that night as a punishment.

Obviously, all – or nearly all – the musicians knew that they were fundamentally crap, but this only served to bond them together. There was a great spirit of camaraderie among them. They put humorous slogans and stickers on their instrument cases and in the rear windows of their cars which read: 'Dyslexic musicians do it wetter', or 'DMC – 'Dis tune, Dis chord, Disband' or 'Musical dyslexia isn't an affliction – it's a way of life!' or 'Rock 'n' roll ain't noise pollution? – If you believe that then you've never heard us play.' And so on.

Morph tried draining the dregs from his glass for the third or fourth time while suffering and occasionally wincing at an exceptionally well-muffed solo to Led Zeppelin's 'Stairway to Heaven', exceptional even for DMC's standards. It was a strange thing, but every time he looked inside his glass there always seemed to be one last drop that he couldn't quite finish off. He decided it was probably best to get a refill. He looked over at his two companions to see if they were ready for another yet.

'Hey, man!' the hippy shouted back at him over the whine of abused electric guitar strings. 'Looks like your doppelgänger's about to take the stage.'

Morph looked from Chris back to the small stage in the corner of the bar where the group was sitting and performing.

A bearded type sporting Armani jeans, a Lacoste shirt and Rayban classic sunglasses, who did indeed seem to bear a more than remote resemblance to Morph himself, was headed towards the stage, winding his way past the empty chairs and tables.

'He probably knows as much about playing the guitar as you or me, judging from the rest of the evening's performance so far.'

'Hey, that's not true, man! I can do a fair old version of "Blowing in the Wind" on the guitar myself.'

'Oh, yeah?' groaned Morph. 'How d'ya like this blowing in the wind then?' He lifted up his right leg and farted, wafting it in the hippy's direction.

In retaliation, Chris stood up and aimed one back at Morph. A distressed look came over Ali's face, and he wrinkled his nose. The evening's entertainment seemed to be lacking a certain class. Still, any distraction was really a most welcome change, even though this particular change certainly couldn't be regarded as in any way refreshing.

Meanwhile, the mysterious guitarist had reached the stage, and, much to the other musicians' surprise, brazenly plugged himself into the spare amp. It burst into life with a deafening crackle of static, drowning out the singer completely - which was probably just as well.

Even the singer didn't really seem to mind, as it happened just at the point when he realised that he'd forgotten all the words to the last part of the song; and anyway, the drummer and bassist, having lost interest after the first refrain, had dropped out and were up at the bar having a smoke. Actually, all said and done, it was a most fortuitous interruption of events.

Finally, realising that the song had come to an end, the acoustic guitarist stopped strumming. Everybody watched in passive silence as the newcomer tied a red and white spotted hanky around his forehead, pulled his white Lacoste shirt off over his head and flung it inside his guitar case, revealing a classic 'white string vest and a hairy chest' look.

The band stared.

Chris, Ali and Morph stared.

The barman and his girlfriend stared.

The other seated musicians who hadn't yet consumed enough alcohol to get up and play stared.

The posters on the wall and the people and things in them all stared.

The bottles of spirits and all the glasses, ashtrays, tables and chairs stared.

Oblivious to it all, the newcomer placed his guitar on its strap, hung it round his neck and beamed over at the remainder of the band.

'Do you know any Hill Waily?' he asked finally.

She'd decided to surprise him. It was still relatively early and she knew he wasn't expecting her for at least another couple of hours. Cathy had finished what was vital and had decided to leave what wasn't until the following day. As she was going to the MEGA offices, she passed by a bar and bought a bottle of white wine. She'd never really liked turning up at people's places empty-handed, even though this time she was pretty sure that wouldn't be what Pierre was expecting from her.

She smiled as images of the afternoon she'd just spent with him flashed through her mind. It was so easy with him. He was good, relaxed, and simple company. And he made her feel like a woman again.

She thought about her late husband, Robert, and then Pierre. There was something else they had in common: although full-grown men, they both had that air of the little boy about them; both so capable, but at the same time, vulnerable. She liked that in a man, always had done.

She wondered what Menti would have to say about it, that stoic Freudian. Oh, she could make a pretty good guess. He'd probably say that she suffered from a classic mother complex. It could be true. Having lost her mother at the age of six, she had been raised by a loving but distracted and, as a consequence, inattentive physicist father, whom she'd had to learn to look after in turn: cook, do the washing, tidy the house. Menti would say that she'd taken over both the role of daughter and mother to her father, and so now any man in her life represented a mishmash of the paternal figure, the lover and most probably also the son – Freudians loved all that closet incest stuff. Therefore, subconsciously, any man now had to fulfil all three prerequisites before being accepted – or something like that.

Whatever, the fact remained that she had unexpectedly fallen in love, and now it was too late. Besides, in a few more days, Pierre would be free of his contractual obligations to Andersson and MEGA Industries and therefore would no longer be her patient. They could see each other when and where they wanted.

She parked the car and walked up to the glass entrance doors of the huge building. Cameras twisted and sized her up and she heard a click as the lock on the door was released to allow her in.

'You're working late tonight, Dr McDonald,' remarked the guard sympathetically from behind a wall of TV monitors as she passed by the main reception desk.

She glanced over at him. Had she sensed something strange in his tone or was it just her imagination? And then she realised that he'd seen the bottle of wine she was holding. Even when wrapped in paper, a bottle of plonk always looks like a bottle of plonk.

'A little private celebration,' she said, unable to disguise the embarrassment in her voice. You idiot, McDonald, she thought, and slipped quickly inside the lift while its doors were still opening.

The lift stopped and pinged its doors apart for her. She stepped out into the warm humidity of the third floor corridor.

Wait a minute. Warm? Humid? This place was supposed to be as air-conditioned as the rest of the building. Maybe it had broken down? She'd tell the guard to send someone to repair it immediately. But no! She could hear the whirring hum of the system; it was still working. She glanced down towards the end of the corridor and, suddenly, her suspicions were confirmed.

The exit door was wide open to the night.

Pierre!

Bottle still in hand, but now brandished as a makeshift weapon, she broke into a sprint towards the apartment. His door was open too. Tentatively she gave it a push. It swung open, exposing an empty room. A computerised voice greeted her.

'Hi, Cathy,' it said. 'This is just a little message to let you know where I am in case you decide to come earlier than planned…'

'Great technique, almost machine-like in its clean precision and confident execution; an exciting style coupled with an infectious enthusiasm for everything he plays…'

'Three beers and a champagne cocktail, Antonio,' commanded the waitress as she arrived flushed and flurried from a table over at the far end of the bar.

Antonio put down his pen. He would have to finish writing his article for the local entertainments guide later; right now there were just too many people coming in. He rammed a half-litre glass under a tap and flicked the switch. While the glass was filling slowly up, he grabbed the cocktail mixer, threw some ingredients inside and began to shake it.

'Paula,' he said, addressing his waitress girlfriend, 'this guy's really hot, right?' It was a tone of comprehensible uncertainty and surprise. He'd never heard anything quite as good before on a Friday night – not since he'd been working there, anyway – and he wasn't sure whether he was imagining it or not.

'Uh-huh,' she nodded in confirmation. 'Makes a bloody change. People are actually coming in of their own free will.' She leant over the bar and pushed her serving tray to one side while watching him top up the one remaining glass of beer. 'This is much easier than having to trick or drag 'em in off the streets and then tie them down so they stay good,' she joked in a loudish whisper to make herself heard above the music, 'as we usually have to do on a Friday evening.'

The audience burst into an enthusiastic applause; the place was alive and electric. On the stage up in front, a small group of stunned musicians stared back at the crowd. They were experiencing a genuine novelty. There was nothing particularly original about a standard twelve-bar rock 'n' roll progression, but they'd never been subject to real, honest-to-goodness, earnest applause. And no one had ever begged them for an encore before. It was their first true taste of being real musicians.

Forgetting himself for a minute, perhaps carried away on a tide of emotional elation, the drummer suddenly stood up, drumsticks in hand, and called out to the rest of the band. 'Yeah, man! All right! Let's hit 'em with another!'

The other members just looked at him in astonished silence. This wasn't a Hollywood musical where a bunch of guys who'd never met before get together and are able to perform with great fluidity and expertise all the breaks, refrains and other tricky intricacies of a new song. Hell, no! It's not that easy. It takes hours of practice and rehearsals, bloopers, swearing, insults, a couple of crates of beer and a large amount of tobacco and other substances before anything reasonably passable happens. And despite the fact that they had known each other for years now, they were all still basically hopeless. Everything said and done, they were, and always would be, DMC.

'Okay, okay,' said the drummer, his self-consciousness suddenly returning. He pointed to where the newcomer was sat casually on his amp. 'He starts, and we'll just see what we can do, okay?'

The rest of the band seemed quite happy with that, and they all turned expectantly to the bearded, string-vested rocker with the headband.

Belvois had made it. He was in heaven. It was really true then that learning three chords on the guitar could get you there. He smiled at the faces in front of him. He beamed at the band beside him. He looked down at his 1970 Gibson electric with loving tenderness in his eyes and broke into a lightning run of notes which culminated in a well-known Hill Waily riff.

Much to their own eternal bewilderment the rest of the band joined in at the right place and, even more surprisingly, at the same time. It was a moment to be cherished; a moment that would be talked about at the bar for many years to come; a moment that, at the end of the evening, would lead to yet another sorry misquote from one of the great Bard's works. When all the audience had gone and the band were having a last celebratory drink among themselves, Dave the drummer would find himself compelled to stand, and drunken enough to say with tears in his eyes, 'And let other members of DMC hold their manhood cheap that they did not play by our side this day.' Or something like that.

The joint was jumping. People were jigging, twisting and singing along to the words of the song – not even the lead singer was having any difficulty remembering them. And some couples, who had obviously been to lessons, were doing the jive.

It was inspiring stuff, and Ali offered Chris and Morph another round of drinks, but was unable to get the waitress's attention. He decided it would be quicker to go to the bar himself. He rose from his seat, and suddenly found himself grabbed by the arm and dragged into the middle of the dance floor.

Chris was delighted. Morph was a little jealous. The girl who had pulled Ali in the midst of the fray, was the one whom he'd had his eye on for the last five minutes or so.

'Hey, sweetie, nice outfit! Where'd you buy it? Is there some fancy-dress party to go to later?'

She seemed rather forward, that much was true. He had always been used to the much more timid Arabic girls who wouldn't even walk with you unless they'd known your mother, her sisters and cousins (both first and once removed) for some years, but perhaps it was the Latin way. His initial apprehension passing quickly, Ali swiftly fell into the mood of things. It was easy, the music was so contagious, so full of energy.

'No party,' he answered, copying her twisting hip movements. 'I always dress like this.'

'Oh,' she responded, and, laughing, she turned to her two female companions dancing beside her. 'No fancy-dress party, I'm afraid. Sorry, guys.'

Her friends didn't seem to mind, they were having a good time anyway. Ali's partner turned her attention back to him. She took hold of his hands and started to spin herself around.

This is rather easy, thought Ali, nothing to it. It seemed to him that the upper body movements of this type of dancing were very similar to those employed in the waltzes at the Shah's palace, at which Ali had become quite adept at one time. He started to twist himself, raising her arm and ducking under the other, spinning her round in circles, all to the rhythm of rock 'n' roll. He would have made an unusual sight even in the most liberated of Arabic countries. A little circle of spectators formed around them, and a rhythmic clap rose up along with some cheers of encouragement.

And it was then that tragedy struck.

A fifth foot from somewhere among the tables suddenly appeared between the jiving couple's feet and Ali stumbled forward. First he collided with a main speaker amp, and then fell headlong on to the lead guitarist. Belvois let out a yelp of pain as his guitar was knocked violently against him, and the pair fell to the ground in an orgy of electric feedback, amplified bangs and flailing legs. Everybody gradually stopped dancing, the band stopped playing, the waitress stopped collecting glasses, and the barman stopped mixing cocktails. A shocked amplifier crackled and spat some more, and then seemed to recover its former control and equilibrium and fell into a low, pulsing hum. Silence reigned supreme.

Dave the drummer was the first to react. Dropping his sticks, he climbed out from among his little nest of drums and jumped down from the stage to where the two stunned protagonists of the sudden drama still lay groaning. He helped Ali off the unmoving form of Belvois.

'Nifty little dance sequence, matey.' The accent was Australian. 'Shame about the finale though.' He returned for the fallen guitar hero and pulled him up, seating him on the edge of the low stage.

'Oh, my God! Pierre! Are you all right?' This time the accent had a slight Scottish tinge to it.

A pretty blonde pushed her way through the staring and bemused crowd; some of them were beginning to snigger and smirk at the duo's misfortune.

'Pierre, are you all right?' Cathy repeated in a concerned tone. Her Celtic lilt always became far more pronounced when she was worried or stressed, even after her years lived in Washington DC.

'He's fine,' said Dave, in an attempt to console her. 'He's just a little stunned from the fall. He'll be okay after a good stiff drink.' He called to the waiter and gestured for something strong. The waiter nodded his understanding.

'Hey, Pierre! That was really class playing, lover boy.' She was trying to get some kind of reaction from him other than the blank stare, but it didn't seem to be working.

Belvois heard the familiar voice and tried to respond, but he couldn't. His mind was on fire. A million pieces of irrelevant data kept finding their way into his mind, zipping from one cerebral cortex to another, then exploding into lots of little penguins that turned their backs and waddled away again into the back of his mind. It was a most disturbing experience, and it left him with a strangely uncontrollable urge to giggle.

He never would find out the significance of the penguins, but the fact that he giggled at that particular moment in time put everybody else's mind at rest. He was all right then, thought the crowd, and a general relieved laughter rose up among the spectators as they began to return to their seats in the belief that no real damage had been done, and that the entertainment had every probability of continuing.

Thinking it a rather professional thing to do, the band decided the show should go on, and one by one, they fell into that old tried and tested favourite: 'The House of the Rising Sun'.

'Ca… Ca… Cathy?'

'I'm right here, lover.'

'Ca… Cathy?'

'Yes, Pierre?' She was stroking his forehead. The giggle hadn't convinced her. He didn't look at all well.

'Git…'

'Huh?'

'Guitar.'

She glanced around and saw it lying at the foot of the stage, still intact. She picked it up and handed it to him. He took it into cradling arms.

The waitress handed Cathy the drink obviously destined for Belvois. She sniffed at it. It wasn't whisky, more some kind of local herbal brandy, but it smelt strong and would probably bring him round quicker. She gave it to him and he swigged it back. The strong liquor burnt its way down the back of his throat, melting away any ice that stray penguins might have left lying around there.

'Ahh!' he announced after a few seconds.

Cathy looked at him straight in the eyes. He was focusing at least. 'Tell me you're okay. I was so worried.' She threw her arms about him, hugging both him and the guitar.

'I believe I'm fine now,' he said after their embrace had unwound itself. 'I've really no idea what came over me. It was such a silly little fall. I can't understand why it left me so dazed.' Brave words but they weren't true. He knew there wasn't much time; a king penguin had just politely informed him so in passing.

'Cathy,' he said with some urgency in his voice, 'we have to get back to the lab, fast! Help me pack.'

He bent down and opened his guitar case, and was most distressed at the sight that greeted him.

The remarkable thing about an electric lead or wire is that no matter how carefully it's rolled up and attentively placed in a drawer, left overnight, you can pretty much guarantee that it will have mysteriously tied itself into unravellable knots by the morning – knots that even a master fisherman would find himself hard-pushed to dream up, let alone undo. A similar effect can be observed behind any household hi-fi or TV and video system.

And this was exactly what Belvois was experiencing at that precise moment as he desperately tried to pack away his guitar. His father, albeit a superstitious farmer with a poor education and an embarrassing tendency to fart loudly in public, used to say that there were Hobgoblins that lived in 'those damned electrical thingamajigs'.

Not for the first time Belvois felt that his father had been granted an elite insight into the supernatural. It seemed only an hour ago that he'd packed this stuff into his case before going out, coiling up the wires with loving care and attention and placing them in their own separate compartments in his case. Now, however, it was like trying to disentangle a room full of horny, slithery things on heat who had been attending an introductory group participation course in the art of the Kama Sutra and had got a little carried away. And he was quickly running out of time.

Ali stood and watched horrified as the beautiful girl gently brought round the stricken guitarist with the soft caresses of her hand across his forehead.

'It's all right, mate,' the drummer said, placing a consoling hand on Ali's shoulder. 'These things happen and there's no harm done.'

Ali nodded his gratitude, but still felt like a dirty rotten, clumsy party-pooper. 'I am so sorry.'

Another pair of hands reached out and pulled Ali away from the scene. Chris and Morph led him as discreetly as possible in the direction of their table in the corner.

'I am really so sorry,' Ali kept mumbling, shaking his head as they led him away. 'So very sorry.'

'Er, I think we should leg it, man,' said Chris under his breath to Morph as they reached their table. 'If Ali's touched any of that techno stuff they've got there, it's gonna be junked in no time; he hasn't had enough to drink tonight for it to be safe.'

The band struck up some chords, and Morph, recognising the tune, hurriedly nodded his agreement and desire to escape the ugliness. He had absolutely no interest in anything anyone had to say about certain houses in New Orleans.

The trio rose to go and, as they were exiting through the saloon-style swing doors on to the street, the song the band were attempting to play was suddenly drowned out by a series of electrical explosions. One by one the instruments, amplifiers and speakers, interconnected by an intricate (and probably extremely tangled) webbing of electrical leads, all experienced the domino effect of Ali's touch.

Chapter Twenty-Nine

Blitzkrieg bent his massive frame over the small coffee table on which the marble chess set lived. The one set that nobody was allowed to touch.

To him it lived because the pieces really did seem to have a life of their own. Every so often they would move themselves around the board, even, at times, removing themselves from the playing area completely, as was the case with the five pawns that sat on the edge of the board.

'Hi, little guys,' said Blitzkrieg in a light-hearted salute to the glorious fallen. 'How's the battle raging?' They were gathered in a little clump and looked exactly as if they were having some kind of secret discussion. Maybe even some kind of union meeting.

'Ooohey, hark at him, lads! "Hi, little guys,"' mocked one of the white pawns in a decidedly sarcastic tone at Blitzkrieg's unhearing ears. '"How's the battle raging?" he asks as if he were really interested and gave a damn.'

'Yeah, right! And how would we bloody well know anyway?' grumbled back another. 'Nobody tells us anything. We were all damned well wiped off right at the beginning of the game. I hate bloody gambit openings, I do.'

'Fair rights for pawns and more respect!' shouted a black pawn angrily.

'Yeah,' agreed the others.

One of the other three white pawns piped up. 'And why is it always us guys in the middle that have to go first? We're always out of the game before the others, we are.'

'Yeah! Right on, brother!' the others shouted.

'We're just as important as any of those trumped up bishops or rooks that strut around menacingly as if they own the place. Full of their own self-importance they are.

'Yeah! You said it, brother. We're the heart and soul of the game, us. Without us to lean on, those stuck up hoity-toity types wouldn't even have a game to play. Hell, they'd be slaughtered straight off.'

'Yeah. How would they like to be always placed on the front line? They should try being cannon fodder once in a while.'

'Yeah. Right on, brothers. It's not all death and glory, is it? There's also this damned interminable hanging about on the sidelines afterwards. Soul-destroying it is at times.'

'Yeah! And the least those bastards could do is get our names right.'

'Yeah, right!' they all shouted together. 'For the millionth time, we're not bloody prawns, we're broody PAWNS.'

Apart from this unusual aspect, the chess set had nothing particularly remarkable about it at all from a visual point of view. Blitzkrieg admired its symmetry, the sharply cut lines. It was beautifully simplistic in design, exactly like those used in any ordinary tournament. But then that in itself was odd, as one would have expected the Goddess of Chess to possess a set of intricate sculptures, something exceptionally original. Apparently though, the sets that people like to display are not the most practical to play with, or so she had explained to him once.

Anyway, it all looked very complicated. There were pieces all over the chequered board. 'We seem to have reached a dizzying intricacy of middle game tactics,' were Caissa's exact words before popping out to do some shopping.

'Coiled springs ready to be released at any moment. Most exciting.' The voice came from behind him and had a heavy French accent. 'Who eez her opponent?'

Blitzkrieg lifted his steel-blue eyes from the table and grinned pearly white teeth back at his interlocutor. Their eyes met on the same level, even though the Frenchman was standing erect to his full height and Blitzkrieg was still sitting in the chair.

'Actually, I thought it was you.'

'Non, non, monsieur! It eez not me. Of that I can assure you.' The small Frenchman placed a hand across his chest by way of surprise and demonstration of innocence, then slipped it back inside the lapel of his jacket.

'Actually, I'm not sure who it is just yet.' Caissa materialised in front of them, placed two plastic shopping bags down and removed her denim jacket, dropping it over the back of the plush, white, four-seater sofa beside her. 'But whoever he is, he's a cunning devil and that's for sure.'

She looked over at her guest, dressed in his gold-braided, military blue uniform and then at her watch. 'Oh, but I'm late. Please, you really must excuse me, but I've had so much to do lately. I hope you haven't been waiting long.'

The Frenchman replied with a stiff little bow of his head. His finery made her feel slightly scruffy by comparison.

'You really must forgive my appearance also. I haven't had much time to change.'

'A beautiful lady eez always a beautiful lady, madame.'

'You flatter me, sir,' she said, falling into his own antiquated style of speech. 'But it is unpardonable of me to have kept waiting one of the greatest military tacticians ever.'

'*The* greatest!' he corrected her, raising an index finger in the air. A grunt arose from the armchair behind him.

'Wellington whipped your ass around a bit, though, didn't he?'

The Frenchman stabbed Blitzkrieg with a sharp sneer, then turned back to face his charming hostess. 'May I enquire as to who will be my adversary this time?'

'Aha! I have invited someone very special for you to play against,' Caissa replied evasively.

She went over to the side of the room and opened a cabinet displaying a large and varied choice of alcoholic drinks. 'Would you like something to drink while we await your opponent's arrival?'

'Cognac.' The Frenchman's tone was one of agitated excitement. 'But, please tell me who…?'

As if in answer there was a sharp knock on the door. Caissa went over and opened it.

Standing in the entrance was an impressive-looking gentleman sporting a pair of thick black eyebrows. He was dressed in the style of the late nineteenth century: a brown suit, matching dicky bow tie and a gold chain of a pocket watch looped out from his waistcoat. His thinning dark hair was greased flat, as was the fashion in those days. He bent over and, taking Caissa's hand in his, kissed it.

'Paul, how lovely to see you again!' Caissa exclaimed with genuine joy. 'Please come in. Your illustrious opponent is waiting.'

'Thank you, my dear. It's always a pleasure.' He had an unmistakeable Mississippi drawl.

The Frenchman suddenly looked quite taken aback. 'Paul Morphy?' he exclaimed in disbelief. 'The same enigmatic Morphy from the 1850s who came from out of nowhere, defeated all the world's best players in the space of two years, and then mysteriously disappeared again?'

'Ho ho, Boney baby,' Blitzkrieg chuckled. 'Looks like your French goose is cooked again.'

The Frenchman turned once more towards the annoying ruffian in the armchair. What on earth did a beautiful lady of obvious class and education like Caissa see in such an uncouth boarish churl? 'That, monsieur, remains to be seen.' And raising his chin indignantly in the air, he walked up and greeted his opponent with a sharp bow and outstretched hand.

Caissa led the two gentlemen through into a back room. It was magnificently furnished in the style of the old country mansion gaming rooms of the last century, quite a contrast to the modern layout of the living room they'd just left. The walls were panelled with stained wood, huge beams lined the ceiling, and all around the room were bookshelves and display cabinets separated by the occasional hanging picture. Light from a bay window illuminated a dark wood dining table on top of which, at one end, were a silver tray with assorted glasses and a crystal decanter containing what was undoubtedly a quality brandy. It was as if they had just entered another world and time.

A sudden electronic whizzing and wheeing invaded the tranquil sobriety of the room. Caissa closed the solid oak door behind her, effectively shutting it out completely.

'Mon Dieu! Your collection of chess sets never ceases to charm me every time I see them. Most admirable.'

'They sure are beautiful, ain't they?' agreed Morphy, as he sauntered over to join him in admiring them.

'You're welcome as always to choose one to play with,' said Caissa.

The Frenchman looked up at Paul Morphy.

'No, no. You choose, sir,' replied the Mississippi gentleman.

They walked up and down the row of cabinets for a few minutes.

'Alors. Let us see. The last time I chose thees one 'ere, but thees time perhaps... Yes, thees one.' The Frenchman pointed at the set he fancied.

Caissa opened the cabinet and carried it carefully over to the table. 'An excellent choice,' she complimented.

'Spanish, nineteenth century, I'd say at a guess,' mused Morphy, fingering the length of an eyebrow.

Caissa nodded. 'Eighteen seventy-six, Seville. José Juan Carreras, a true craftsman.'

She walked back to the door they'd come through. 'I think you'll find everything you need here, gentlemen. Help yourselves to drinks. There is a selection of titbits and other drinks if you prefer in the cabinet.' She signalled the corner of the room. 'And there are restrooms through the door on the left. If you need anything else, just let me know. Enjoy your games.'

She turned and opened the door. Electronic beeps once more flooded into the room. She closed the door quickly behind her and walked over to where Blitzkrieg was sat in front of the TV playing a video game.

The two opponents sat on opposite sides of the table and chatted amiably for a short time while sipping at the rich, strong cognac they'd poured themselves.

'To Caissa, Goddess of Chess and most charming host,' declared Morphy, raising his glass to that of the Frenchman.

'Yes, I adore coming 'ere to play. You never know who you will meet and the cognac is simply excellent.'

They clinked glasses, and then the Frenchman, who had the white pieces, hovered a little uncertainly over the board before deciding on a king prawn opening.

Chapter Thirty

'Foo!'

Cathy and Menti had been up most of the night nursing their patient, clicking keys on computers, and chewing on strands of long hair – in Menti's case that meant nibbling on his upper lip – and generally shaking their heads in concerned bewilderment. It had been a long and fruitless effort. They hadn't managed to establish anything concrete.

Cathy was in emotional turmoil. Why the hell had she had to go and get intimate with her patient? It was so foolish, so damned unprofessional. She'd broken rule number one and now they were both paying the price. In the state of worry and confusion she was in right now, she wasn't any good to anyone, least of all poor Pierre. She had to get a grip on herself, take control of her emotions and start to reason logically. It was the only way. She rubbed at the dark lines that were appearing around her eyes and sighed. Right now she needed to be nursed and comforted as much as Belvois.

'I just can't understand it. Everything was going so well. Why should a simple bump on the noggin have sent him so totally doolally?' Menti asked rhetorically for the hundredth time. He picked up Belvois' cranial X-rays and shook his head at them, also for the hundredth time since he'd been called that night.

'Foo,' dribbled Belvois nonsensically. He was still clutching his guitar case. He'd absolutely refused to relinquish it, no matter how hard they'd tried to prise it free of his iron grip.

Menti looked at him puzzled and nibbled his lip some more.

Belvois still lay on the same stretcher he'd been wheeled in on after his breakdown. His mobility certainly hadn't been facilitated by the cumbersome guitar and at one point had actually got jammed between the lift doors. Apparently, as Cathy had told him later, Belvois had started screaming something about penguins, and then had just keeled over in the passenger seat. Since his return to consciousness – if it could be called that – half an hour later, the only thing he'd uttered had been complete gibberish. Menti would have rather had the penguins – at least they'd have had something coherent to work with.

'I mean, there are absolutely no signs whatsoever of cerebral damage. The chip seems to be functioning perfectly, but he doesn't seem to respond to outside stimulus of any sort.'

'Fooooo!' cried Belvois, grasping the handle of his guitar case even tighter than before.

Cathy went over to where he lay and stroked his smooth forehead with her palm. She felt like crying, but couldn't, not there, not in front of Menti. She had to hold it together for Pierre.

'It's almost as if he's short-circuited,' Menti continued.

'We're going to have to remove the chip,' Cathy said decisively. 'It's the only way to find out exactly what's gone wrong.'

Menti looked up from his computer screen where the fourth test on the chip's functions was being performed and simultaneously displayed. It was responding perfectly.

'You're talking a five-hour surgical operation,' he said dubiously, slumping down into his chair and then discovering that it was virtually impossible to slump into a moulded-back, plastic seat, and barely managed to stop himself from tipping over backwards. 'You're talking missing the last phase of the old man's big test tomorrow, er, I mean this morning,' he added, and glanced at his watch. Hell, it was late, or early, or something. Whatever, he didn't like being deprived of his sleep. 'You're talking possibly ruining, or at least delaying by some months, his company's long-awaited rise to stardom. He's not going to be too happy, especially since all the tests show that there's nothing wrong with either man or machine.'

'You're damned right he's not going to like it. He's not going to like it one bit.'

All eyes turned in the direction of the booming voice coming at them from the other side of the laboratory. Andersson stood framed in the doorway, the faithful Pecdek just behind him, still sporting a rather large and ridiculous-looking bandage on his nose.

Menti cringed visibly. He hated it when the old man started talking about himself in the third person; it was a sure sign of trouble.

'Oh, foooo!' commented Belvois, acutely summarising the secret thoughts of the two doctors beside him.

'So my boy's suddenly become a blithering ding-dong because of a night out on the town,' boomed Andersson again, this time with some irony in his tone. He stormed over to where Belvois lay and scowled at what he saw. 'And how the hell did he manage to get out of here in the first place to have caused such a catastrophe?'

Actually, neither Cathy nor Menti had been informed on that front.

'Errm,' mumbled Cathy.

'Ahem,' coughed Menti, making a vain attempt at throat clearing.

'Foo,' offered Belvois helpfully.

'Grrr!' growled back Andersson, and spun round to face Pecdek.

'Well? How the fuck did he get out?'

'Whaa?' exclaimed Pecdek, in wounded surprise at the unjustified attack.

'Foo!' joined in Belvois, becoming really quite chatty.

'Stop!' cried Andersson, desperately placing his hands over his ears. 'Somebody speak to me in fucking English. I don't understand this jungle lingo. It's like being in a fucking zoo.'

'He reprogrammed the security system from inside his own room, and, using a plan of the building's interior, chose the nearest exit, down the fire escape. Smart stuff.' Miss Lee entered the laboratory from behind them, closely followed by Tangenti, the staff department head, brandishing a bunch of papers.

'Thank you, Miss Lee. Efficient and timely as ever. What would I do without you?'

His half-Asian secretary shrugged her shoulders in response. 'Who knows?'

Andersson swung around to face his captive audience once more. 'Now then, would someone be so kind as to explain how a twenty million dollar investment ended up like that.'

Everyone turned to look at the prone form of Belvois and guitar case.

'Foo,' said Belvois, sounding a little self-conscious.

Although Andersson had already heard the story over the phone at two that morning, Cathy briefly summarised the sequence of events as they had happened, with omission of course of certain more personal details like the bottle of wine. She didn't think the guard would spill the beans and, anyway, it was the least of her worries right at that moment.

Andersson grimaced. 'Is that it?' he asked in amazement. This didn't bode well. 'And that was enough to send him completely mental?'

'Fooooo!' Belvois assured him.

Andersson shook his head in disbelief, and his bushy eyebrows knitted themselves into their habitual hairy caterpillar form. It just didn't make sense. The same guy that had taken out three huge, military combat experts without even breathing hard, had been rendered a virtual veggie by a simple bump on the head. He began to regret seriously having shot him the other evening with the tranquilliser gun. What if...?

'You don't think it could be some kind of delayed reaction or allergy to the er... stuff I... er... that put him... er... to sleep the other evening?'

Menti shook his head. 'Most doubtful hypothesis.' He was a good linguist.

Cathy sighed. 'The safest method is to remove the chip, run some checks on it and replace or substitute it. It's possible that in some way the ECO readouts aren't showing up a malfunction. It seems to me it must be that that's causing Pierr... Belvois' mental blockage.'

'And therein lies our problem,' came in Menti. 'That's exactly the point. All the technical data we have gathered up to now shows absolutely nothing wrong with the chip or any physical signs of cerebral damage, and leads me to conclude that the cause is psychological. His symptoms are those of a typical trauma case. The poor fellow has just had too much to assimilate in too little time, and his mind has shut down.'

'Like a nervous breakdown?'

'Yes, if you like. A serious nervous breakdown due to stress-related causes.'

'Does that mean you think he might come out of it soon?' asked Andersson. Hell, the bloody final showdown began that morning and would be finished in the turn of thirty-six hours. Years of planning to be thwarted by this.

'In these cases one never really knows. We have to wait till he comes out of it – if ever,' added Menti.

'McDonald?' Andersson turned to her. He needed a second opinion.

Cathy shook her head. She was so mixed up - torn between her feelings and concern for Pierre, her duty as doctor and scientist, and her duty to the company. 'He may be right. There may be nothing wrong with the chip at all. It may be all psychological. We can't be sure unless we remove it altogether.'

Andersson looked from one scientist to the other. Removal would mean a certain end to his plans. By the time he got another buyer and everything organised, the bloody Chinese, Japanese, or the Russians would probably have developed something even more devastating. No, he had to go for it now. 'No chip removal, not yet. There must be something we can do. I mean, isn't there some kind of drug you can give to patients in these circumstances?'

Menti nodded. 'There is a type of strong amphetamine that is sometimes administered to help stimulate cerebral activity. Yes, I was, in fact, about to suggest it as a possible alternative.'

'Then for God's sake do it, man. Anything's worth a try at this stage.'

'No!' cried Cathy in outrage. 'There's a danger of permanent damage if you do that. I can't allow it. If the chip is faulty and he's artificially brought back to the chaos that right now he's somehow managed to escape from, his sanity might not be able to handle it once and for all.'

They were not going to touch him. She placed herself between Belvois and the others, her hands and arms outstretched in warning, suddenly a tigress protecting her injured mate.

'If you even make a move to approach him, I'll go straight to the authorities and report us all and the experiments we've been doing here,' she snarled. 'I created the chip. It's my responsibility. I'll remove it and then we'll be sure…'

'Okay, okay,' said Andersson, palms in the air in the age-old gesture of surrender. 'You're absolutely right. A man's sanity is too high a price to pay for a few paltry dollars. I'd never be able to live with myself if something like that happened. Come now.'

He walked slowly towards her. She backed off a little warily, unsure, her pulse rate fluttering unevenly. Maybe she was overreacting, but she couldn't help it; after all, how could Andersson have known? He suggested it, but surely he could see that it was wrong.

'It's okay,' continued Andersson, a soothing quality to his voice that no one in the room had ever heard before – almost mesmeric. 'Nobody is going to harm him. Trust me.'

He placed an arm tentatively around her tired shoulders. It was so nice, warm human contact, and she was so tired, too tired to think, let alone fight. She let herself be comforted, her head sunk into the soft, perfumed shoulder of his jacket, and she began to sob.

'And I think right now you and Menti should really get some rest. You've both been up all night.'

Cathy shook her head in protest, but Andersson insisted, still in that soft, calming tone, and her eyelids were beginning to get so heavy…

'Before continuing, you both should rest. It's what's best for the patient as well, and you know it too. He'll be fine here until you both return this afternoon, and in better hands than now.'

'Yes, yes, I suppose you're right. I don't know what came over me,' reasoned Cathy, slowly. 'He needs us with our minds clear; like this we're no good to him at all.'

She glanced over at Menti and he nodded back at her. Then she looked over at Belvois and suddenly the fatigue seemed to vanish, temporarily replaced by a reluctance to leave his side. A torn expression shot across her face. 'But I don't like to leave him like…' she began again.

'You don't have to,' continued Andersson's steady but soothing drone. 'You can stay in one of the apartments on the top floor, and as soon as you're ready, you can come straight down and start work.'

That seemed to pacify her somewhat, and she smiled weakly. 'Yes. Who knows, we may even be able to resolve everything before the tournament.'

'Well, in that case,' said Andersson, in a tone of mock severity, 'don't oversleep.'

He nodded to his secretary. 'Go with Miss Lee. She'll show you to your room and see to your needs for a few hours. Go now. Sleep. You'll feel better for it after, more awake, more alert. Go now.'

Miss Lee walked over to Cathy and slipped an arm through hers. 'Come along. The sooner you get some rest, the sooner you can return with a fresh mind on the situation.'

And with a final glance round at the prone form of Belvois and guitar, Cathy and Andersson's secretary left. The room's other occupants quietly watched them out, and the lab door swung closed behind them.

Menti started to leave too. He certainly wouldn't say no to catching up on his own lost sleep of that night. He looked at his watch again. Nearly five. A couple of hours' kip at home was just what the doctor ordered, and he should know because he was one. But, as he passed Andersson, he felt himself forcefully grabbed by the collar, and he suddenly became aware that both Pecdek and Tangenti had begun to applaud.

'Very well done, sir,' clapped Tangenti, enthusiastically. 'Excellently handled. May I ask where you learned to do that?'

Andersson grinned for a moment at his two appreciative employees. So they weren't as dumb as he had assumed. 'Oh, out of the many business courses I've attended over the years, one of the most useful and memorable was a short introduction to hypnotic suggestion. Works a treat under the right conditions.'

He turned his attention back to the slight form of Menti who he was still holding by the scruff like a naughty puppy.

'I hope you weren't seriously convinced by that little scene, just now?'

Menti turned his eyes upwards to look at his captor – it was easier than moving his neck. 'Er... no?' he asked, uncertainly.

Andersson's voice had suddenly lost all its soft, soothing

charm of moments before. Instead, it held the old, fearsome, gruff tones that were his usual trademark. His eyes looked down in menacing, steel-blue coldness. 'No, you weren't, were you? Because you haven't finished just yet. There's still that little matter of an injection to see to.'

Chapter Thirty-One

For the uninitiated, cruising down an Italian motorway can be a most harrowing experience, with people who overtake on both the outside and inside lanes, flash their lights at you if you're not going at least fifty kilometres an hour over the legal limit, and show an alarming disregard for safety distances.

The Highway of the Sun, as they call it, is the natural route to take when travelling down to the south of Italy, but Morph was beginning to wish he'd taken one of the slower roads. The AA guidebook had not prepared him for what he was undergoing.

'No, I'm bloody well not pulling over for you, you impatient little bastard,' growled Morph at the little Citroën that was wildly flashing its lights from a distance of about five metres behind them. 'I'm already doing twenty over the limit.'

'Ho ho,' laughed Chris from the passenger seat, while looking at the inebriated form of Ali distended over the back seat, 'and I'd say that Ali's about forty per cent proof over his limit.'

Needless to say, Morph had not been overly convinced by Mago Marco the Magnificent's herbal remedies. 'By all means try it out,' he had said. 'But not in my car. Either you're completely wasted when you get in, or you don't get in.'

'Whaassat?' hiccuped Ali upon hearing his name mentioned, and then returned to the arduous task of extricating his index finger from the neck of the almost empty whisky bottle. If he could just get it out, he'd be able to finish up that last drop that was splashing about so teasingly at the bottom there.

'Grrr!' Morph growled as the little Citroën darted forward, flashed its lights again, and then backed off a little way, repeating the manoeuvre every few seconds, a bit like an excited dog waiting to be let out for its walkies. It was the kind of technique that they all seemed to use, but he'd had enough. He was having none of it. He saw no reason why he should inconvenience himself by pulling in and slowing up behind the convoy of trucks travelling illegally down the centre lane just because the lunatic behind him didn't want to moderate his own speed at all.

It was the fifth or sixth time it had happened in the last twenty minutes or so, and this time he was determined not to give in. Hell, driving was difficult enough when your steering wheel was on the wrong side. The dickhead behind would just have to wait until he, Morph, had overtaken the convoy in his own sweet time. Oh, sure, if he wanted to, he could accelerate and get things over with much quicker, but why should he burn more petrol just for that idiot's convenience?

It had become a matter of pride and principle. Besides, it was he who had the bigger engine capacity and if he really wanted to, he could leave that little rust-box standing.

The Citroën closed in, barked at him, flashed its lights and backed off again. Morph glared into the rear mirror and, holding up his fist, uncurled the middle finger in a truly international gesture of understanding and cooperation.

'Ha! Sit on that, sucker!' cried Morph, rebelliously. He glanced again into his rear mirror to see what effect his act of defiance had achieved, but the car was no longer there.

'Whaa?' he blurted, incredulous. 'He's vanished into thin air!'

Chris also twisted and looked around him, but the car was nowhere to be seen.

Then suddenly the Citroën reappeared up in front. It had obviously overtaken both them and the convoy of trucks by means of the inside lane.

'Beep, beep!' announced the little car, triumphantly, as it zoomed off into the distance.

A heavy rumble from behind them caused Morph once more to nervously glance in the mirror. The convoy of trucks was now travelling in the outside lane, and the leader was flashing his lights at him. The monster bellowed at him, a deafening, primordial sound that seemed to awaken feelings long passed into the collective racial subconscious, some prehistoric predator preparing its attack. The blood literally drained from his face, and his bowels began to dangerously relax themselves.

It was just too much. He couldn't take the stress any more. His heart leapt into his throat, rebounded down again off his

Adam's apple, and began beating out rapid and painful Latin-American bongo rhythms on the inside of his ribcage. It was horrible.

Instinct and reflexes took control. He dodged right into the middle lane, and then swerved quickly back again to avoid a motorcyclist who shouted and hammered angrily on his car roof as he passed by on the inside. Oh, shit! He was back in the fast lane again! He glanced in his mirror and saw only the huge, savage, snarling fangs of a radiator grid. They were almost on him! Move! He had to move and now! He hacked a right into the middle lane again. Just in time! The trucks thundered by, one after the other, and the vibration caused the windows in his beloved new Volvo to rattle violently.

Gripping tightly on to the steering wheel, he watched them charge down the fast lane together like a herd of stampeding dinosaurs and disappear over the steaming tarmac horizon. They would have flattened him if he hadn't got out of the way.

'Oh, wow! Have you just farted? What a stink, man!' Chris hit the button that opened the electric window, and stuck his head outside, inhaling great lungfuls of warm air that, to be honest, didn't smell an awful lot better.

Defeated and humiliated, his hands still shaking, Morph pulled right over into the slow lane. He decided to take the first turn-off possible and find a washroom.

Chapter Thirty-Two

It was a good three hours later before Cathy finally re-entered the lab.

'Why didn't someone wake...?' She stopped dead in her tracks. Perhaps it was because she'd just woken up and hadn't had her coffee yet, but her first impression was that she'd walked in on a scene from an old Hammer Horror production.

An immobile form draped in a white sheet was sat upright on an operating table in the middle of the lab, surrounded by a myriad leads, flashing lights and beeping noises. Meanwhile, a sinister figure in a laboratory coat flitted from one computer station to another flicking switches, pushing buttons and other such ominous things.

The normal practice for heroines at this point was to either scream and faint, or make for the exit, grab the first crucifix at hand, and leg it to the nearest church. Instead, the look of concern on her face soon passed to one of delight. He was awake.

'What's up, Doc?' asked Menti good-humouredly, as he turned from the readout screen to face her at the entrance of the swinging lab doors.

'He's come out of it, then?' cried Cathy, her mobility returning to her. She passed swiftly over to where Belvois was sat. She had to restrain herself from hugging him, and contented herself with taking his hands into hers and gazing into his eyes. But her joy and enthusiasm at seeing him up vanished as quickly as it had arrived.

If he felt anything or even registered her presence, he gave no acknowledgement. The eyes, wide open, stared unblinkingly outwards at a world that she couldn't see. The smile dropped from her lips as she peered into the black void of his unnaturally dilated pupils. She'd seen that look before when she and Robert had gone scuba-diving off the Florida coast together. A chill passed down her spine exactly as it had done then, when suddenly, out from behind a rock, she'd come face to face with a two-hundred-kilo tiger shark. Its eyes had held that same awful emptiness.

'I'm just giving him the once-over,' said Menti. Despite his efforts he was unable to totally conceal the nervousness in his voice. 'Everything seems to be back in order. In a minute I'll unhook him from the "translator" again and you can see for yourself.'

'You mean...?'

'Yes,' came Andersson's voice as he entered the room. It seemed to be his speciality: timely dramatic entrances and cutting people short mid-sentence. 'That idea of Menti's worked tickety-boo. One hit of that amphetamine substance and he came round like a shot and sat bolt upright like he is now. Oh, sure, he screamed for a little while, but he calmed right down once Menti here plugged him back into the network.'

Cathy glared in horror. 'He screamed?' The words nearly choked in her throat.

'Well, yes.' Menti swallowed for her. 'But I assure you that it's a very common reaction for people who suddenly wake up from coma-like states after such an injection. Well documented.'

'And why did you plug him back into the network? I mean, wasn't that what you had theorised as being to blame for his state? Too much information consumption and not enough environmental assimilation?'

'That's just it. He's not learning anything new. He's linked up to a special program called Compulax that induces a relaxed hypnotic state. It's been used with great success in the States. For the last few hours, he's been enjoying a wonderful and highly therapeutic mind massage. He's even finally relaxed his grip on that guitar.' Menti pointed to the case leant up against the far wall of the lab.

Cathy had heard of the program. She even remembered some publicity spot on TV once with a famous Hollywood actress saying how much it had done for her.

But still something didn't ring right. He was, after all, sat most unnaturally bolt upright and completely inert. This, together with the fact that his unseeing eyes were fixed wide open and his pupils dilated to the maximum, gave a very disconcerting impression indeed. He seemed about as mind-dead as someone who'd just spent an evening at an annual convention for retired game show hosts. Frankly, he looked stuffed. Whoever his taxidermist was, he'd done a thorough job. She prodded him tentatively on the chest in an attempt to make him move in some way. Nothing. Stiff as a board.

'So why is he sitting up like that, and not lying down in a relaxed position?'

'Again, because of the effects of the amphetamine. His cerebral readout is perfectly stable – see for yourself. We just can't seem to get him to unbend physically, that's all.'

She turned round to the computer monitor next to her and punched up on the keyboard the results of the last four hours of tests that Menti had been running in her absence. Physiologically he was fine, but physiologically he'd been fine before. It proved nothing. She gritted her teeth together, trying to contain the frustration and feelings of betrayal she was feeling. How stupid of her! How naively trusting! She just prayed they had done the right thing and, most of all, that Pierre was all right.

'Don't worry, McDonald. He is fine.'

Andersson approached the other two doctors, smiling; that same fake smile he'd used to convince her to leave the lab the first time, Cathy thought. Well, it wouldn't work again. She ignored him, but he insisted.

'You'll see. The day after tomorrow we'll all be in the news. And they'll probably give both of you a Nobel Prize.'

'It's finished,' announced Menti. He nodded at Cathy who, in response, went over to Belvois and removed the translator device from off his head. She placed it carefully inside a small, hinged, black box on the table, and then all three turned to watch in anticipation.

'Let's hope he doesn't throw another wobbly on us,' said Andersson, concerned.

'A wobbly?' asked Cathy, shocked into incomprehension. Could anybody be so truly callous and insensitive?

'A wobbly?' questioned Menti in turn. This was a term he hadn't come across during his period in England.

'A wobbly.'

Silence fell as all attention became focused on the origin of the last voice.

The rest of his body motionless, and using only the minimum number of muscles required to perform the action, Belvois' head jerked itself round to observe the mute trio.

'A wobbly,' he repeated, suddenly jumping down from the bed he had been sitting on for the last four hours or so. Bare, flat feet slapped down on to the cool, hard marble of the laboratory floor, and the sheet that had been covering his otherwise naked form fell to the ground. Extending himself to his full height and stretching his sleepy muscles into reawakening, he turned unabashedly to face his audience, dressed as mother nature had intended him.

'A wobbly,' he said again, in a helpful and informative tone.

It wasn't clear as to whether he was simply repeating the first thing he'd heard upon waking, like any personality-disordered being with a neural implant might.

'To throw a wobbly – noun; definition: colloquial usage. A fit of panic, temper, insanity, etc. To lose one's calm in a fit of panic, temper, insanity, etc.; act unpredictably. Also possible: a wobbler…'

Chapter Thirty-Three

'It probably was for the best that we got out of that city,' Chris was saying to his two companions as they lugged their possessions into the new hotel. 'After the way Ali blew up that gig last night. Really far out, man! Never seen anything like it. Bummer in a way, though, that guitarist was hot. Still, the fireworks were great, the way all those people legged it out of the club with sparks and things flying out after them was such a crack.'

Chris turned and patted Ali consolingly on the back as they reached the dark and rather grubby reception desk of the Hotel Paradiso in Salsomaggiore, the only hotel in which they'd been able to get accommodation.

A small man with hair that looked like it was destined to become the world's next alternative fuel source ventured forth from the office at the back. A television shouted loudly and excitedly after him.

'*Si?*'

'Armstrong,' announced Morph, wisely deciding to avoid intricate personal exchanges. Ali was certainly in no fit state to translate, having put back a good three-quarters of a whisky bottle during their journey down, and he didn't have the energy to employ his usual semaphoric skills. He only hoped the receptionist, who had booked them the room from the other hotel, had explained the situation clearly enough.

'*Arrmastrronga. Si. Due camere. Passaporti.*'

Morph and Chris handed their passports over and the clerk, who was probably also the hotel proprietor, tried to place them into a small drawer under the desk with some others. They didn't fit. He grumbled something to himself about British egos and then slipped them on to the shelf below. He gave them their room keys and pointed up the stairs. '*Cinque,*' he said, holding up the four and a half fingers of his left hand.

'I think he means fifth floor,' said Morph, confirming his

suspicions by eyeing the number on the wooden key ring. 502.
'Lift?' he asked, miming with his hands a box that moved
upwards.

'No, no.' The man shook his index finger at them.

'Can we leave him here while we take the luggage up to the
rooms?' asked Chris, politely placing Ali on to a wooden chair by
the reception desk. 'We'll come down for him later. He's too
pissed up to make it by himself.'

The man briefly observed the woozy, bloodshot eyes of the
swaying Arab and shrugged uncaringly. He turned and vanished
into the back office where the television was still shouting loudly
and excitedly.

Morph and Chris bent over, picked up their luggage, and
initiated their trudge up the first flight of stairs. Another dodgy-
looking landing, another flight of steps.

'What floor are we on?' asked Morph, sweaty and red in the
face with his efforts. His luggage was much heavier than that of
his companion who only sported two small suitcases. Admittedly,
Chris hadn't started with that much, and the other bag was Ali's,
who believed in travelling very light. He was beginning to regret
packing the obligatory sweater and the extra pair of shoes and all
the other things that he'd brought, just in case. And he wished
he'd let Sharon, his secretary, go ahead and book all his rooms
from Bournemouth. If he had done so, he certainly wouldn't have
been forced to stay in this dung hole.

His usual technique was to get the hotel receptionist where he
was staying to choose a hotel, phone up for him and book a room
in advance. That way he could deal with any unforeseen events or
delays in his otherwise tight schedules. It also guaranteed him a
good room and no language hassles; after all, if the natives in the
trade didn't know the best hotels at the most reasonable prices,
who did? Well, that had been the case up until now.
Salsomaggiore, it seemed, was all full up for the holidays. He
hadn't known that it was a tourist town, famous for its natural
thermic waters and miracle cures until the hotel receptionist had
bored him with a good half hour's worth of it, together with the
fascinating fact that his auntie lived there as well. And after all
that, the only available decent room, he'd been informed, was in a

five-star luxury hotel where film stars, pop stars, and even plumbers might feel a little disconcerted by the prices. Therefore, on his far more modest travel budget – well, beggars can't be choosers, as they say.

So now he was stuck with a scrubby little *pensione*, a sort of very cheap bed and breakfast without the breakfast. Only by a stroke of luck had he managed to avoid having to share a room with Ali and Chris – that would have been pushing it too far. He seemed to get into enough trouble just by going out with those two in the evening, let alone if they'd had to share the same living space.

He had to hold his breath as they reached another landing and were rudely confronted by the communal toilet. The thick odour that issued forth had obviously managed to develop on a completely different evolutionary scale to any previously known hotel bacteria; germs that would have given even industrial-strength disinfectant not only a run for its money, but most probably would have flipped it on its back and held its shoulders down for a count of ten and a complete submission.

'Oh, wow!' exclaimed Chris, horrified. He hadn't smelt anything quite so nauseous since visiting the Portaloos at last year's Glastonbury pop festival. 'Phoowee! This smell brings back memories. Now that's what I call truly wicked.'

Nostalgically curious for a closer whiff, he popped his head inside the door and disappeared into the disquieting blackness. There was silence for a few seconds and then a blood-curdling scream ripped through the stench-filled obscurity.

'Aaaaaaaah!' it went.

Morph dropped his bags where he stood and raced in after his friend.

Click!

The light came on, momentarily dazzling the intrepid would-be saviour. Hands shielding his eyes, he backed off defensively into the corner. Considering the amount of primordial matter that covered it, the one naked light bulb performed its function miraculously well. Even the bare, copper wire it hung from had seen better days, probably before the start of the Second World War.

Morph blinked at the grinning face of the goat-bearded hippy before him, framed by a backdrop of yellowish-brown wallpaper that managed to cling on, it seemed, only by decades of habit. The tasteful decor also included the obligatory, very dark and suspect patches, creatively and abundantly splattered around the walls, floor and even the ceiling. All the stops had been pulled out on this one, Morph thought, no expense spared.

'Hey, guy! Cheer up! Can't you take a joke? Or did you really think that the sewer blob had got me?'

'You've got to be joking. I only came in to give it some support. Besides, odds are no self-respecting sewer monster would want you for its lunch.'

'Eh? Why not?'

'It's much more likely to take you for another of its species and make an attempt at procreation.'

The light bulb began to flash and fizz in a most menacing manner.

'Oh man, I think she's gonna blow!'

'And take the whole damn electrical system with it!'

They dived out of the room, finishing in a pile on the landing floor.

FIZZZZZA... PHUT... BANG!

Fragments of glass tinkled to the toilet floor.

'Far out! That was a close one, man.'

Morph shook his head and climbed to his feet. He spotted the room number on the door before him and sighed.

'This is our floor, which means', he pointed towards the black void they'd just escaped from, 'that is our communal bog.'

'Oh, heavy bummer!' moaned Chris. 'I forgot to check if there was any bog paper inside, man.'

Having inspected their respective rooms and frightened the resident cockroaches back down the drainpipes, Ali was dutifully helped upstairs and placed on his bed next to Chris's. Then the unpacking began.

Well, it couldn't really be called unpacking as such. Unpacking is what happens after you've been shipped like cattle from coach to plane to coach again by some viciously inhumane package holiday company; after you've entertained the sprogs for hours and finally resorted to lacing their milk to keep them quiet during the interminable and inevitable delay at the airport departure lounge; after you've maintained your composure with the officious little man with the huge, bushy moustache at the other end who managed to find some non-existent discrepancy with your visa admission; after you've endured that unendurable wait for your luggage to be unloaded off the plane, never knowing until the last second if it's been sent instead to the furthest reaches of Outer Mongolia, or if the suspicious-looking character in the child-molester sunglasses is going to make a grab for it as soon as it rolls on to the conveyor belt, or, worse still, discovering that you can't remember what your luggage looks like anyway and grabbing the cases of the suspicious-looking man with the child-molester glasses by mistake; and finally, after arriving at your hotel destination, you rip away the custom's security tape from around your suitcase only to discover that it was binding everything together (an old customs trick if they happen to break your bag during a search) and watch helplessly as your vacuum-packed possessions explode all over the room, thus forcing you to spend a further agonising thirty minutes of your creeping catatonic state picking everything up and putting it away. Now that's unpacking!

What Chris was doing, on the other hand, was peering inside the small red rucksack he'd bought at the Swiss supermarket and wondering if there was anything in there that merited its liberation or transfer to one of the few drawers in the sparsely furnished room. It was the first time he'd opened the bag since they'd left Geneva.

One thing of which he was almost sure, there wasn't that much reason to fear any miscalculations in his laundry – although you never knew. Normally he had very subtle sub-divisions of dirty clothing, ranging from the highly toxic to the 'worn less than twenty-four hours and still good for a while yet' classification. But all his new underwear was still in the plastic packets he'd bought them in – he really hadn't felt the need to change – and he had no socks to bother with because, except in winter, he never wore them anyway. Besides, in the heat and humidity of the climate they now found themselves in, the flip-flops he'd borrowed from Ali were the perfect commodity.

After one or two rather timid initial pokes and prods, he gathered the courage to empty everything out on to the bed. It's amazing where all the bits of fluff come from, he thought, as he rummaged through the pile. It was a new bag when he'd bought it, everything that went into it was new, but still big lumps of fluff had managed to miraculously conglomerate inside.

He counted the items he had managed to accumulate in the brief space of time since his emergence from Morph's car boot. Three special offer compact discs entitled *Hits from the Sixties*. He scratched his head a little puzzled; they had seemed like such good buys at the time. He noticed that the fluff had already firmly wedged itself in between the edges of the plastic casings. Three T-shirts with various humorous anecdotes on them – although he couldn't remember what they were – still in plastic wrapping. Two pairs of flowery summer shorts and a pair of long, light cotton trousers for the occasional breezy day – on Ali's advice. All still as yet unremoved from their wrappings. Toothbrush, with obligatory fluff on the bristles, and paste. Razor, still unused. He wondered why he'd bought that too. Hairbrush, likewise. A packet of half-eaten mints with the inevitable fluff on the top one. And finally, of course, the traveller's essential plastic, imitation Rayban sunglasses. He put them aside, they'd be useful, they would. Satisfied with his itinerary check, everything, except the mints and the glasses, then got bunged back in the bag. It would save time not having to pack when they left.

He glanced over at Ali, flat out on the single bed next to his. His eyes were open and staring at the ceiling. He must be nearly conscious and probably in need of some kind of sustenance, he reasoned, and kindly offered him the fluffy mint.

'Thank you,' Ali croaked back. Unseeingly, he reached over with a trembling hand and took it. His mouth felt as dry and rancid as a sunburnt camel's scrotum and the gritty, sandy bits that the mint deposited only succeeded in enhancing the sensation.

A loud thumping arose from the room next to theirs, and Ali put his hands over his ears, grimacing with pain.

'Is that my head?' he groaned.

'No, I think it's just Morph next door in the shower

explaining who has the tenancy rights for the next twenty-four hours or so.'

'Huh?'

'He's on a cockroach extermination binge.'

Chris cupped his hands round his mouth and shouted out so that Morph could hear through the wall. 'Live and let live, I say! They've got just as much right to life as you or me, man!'

The answer came back pretty swiftly.

'In your case, hippy, you're more than right.'

Chapter Thirty-Four

Jacqueline King, board member of the Italian chess league, FSI, and the international chess federation, FIDE, stood up and smoothed her skirt back down again to her stockinged knees. She tapped the microphone and spoke:

'The organisers and sponsors of today's event, the Italian Open Chess Championship and myself would like to thank all of you for coming today, all one hundred and twenty-four competitors. It's a marvellous sight to see all of you here, honouring this noble and time-honoured game. Thanks also to the sponsors of today's event; Mr Signori of the Italian publishers, Mursia, and Mr Harper of the international publishers, Batsford.'

A restrained applause filled the spacious, centuries-old hall once owned by a family whose power and influence had rivalled that of the mighty Borgias.

Two of the five gentlemen sitting next to her rose briefly, and the one to her left whispered something in her ear. She smiled into the microphone. 'Oh, and Mr Signori reminds me that stalls selling both publishers' ranges of books can be found just outside in the main corridor.'

A little good-humoured murmur resounded around the flaking white walls, amplified by the arched, frescoed ceiling and the cool, flagstone floor.

'I would also like to propose a special vote of thanks and appreciation to our surprise sponsors, MEGA Industries, whose financial assistance in this tournament enabled us to raise the prize money considerably, and also its level of international attention, thereby attracting some quite notorious competitors (she nodded over at one or two faces immersed among the sea of tables and chessboards outstretched in front of her) and promising a high quality of entertainment for this weekend.

'Are we to believe that you too are a follower of Caissa's, Mr Andersson?' She turned towards a sturdy-looking figure at the end of the table.

Andersson rose smartly, gave a brief nod, smiled and reseated himself. A unanimous cheer of appreciation and clapping arose, and, as an afterthought, he held up his hand in a kind of presidential acknowledgement. He nodded his regards to the speaker, and made a mental note to ask Menti if he knew who the bloody hell this Caissa was, and what political or financial circles she was active in.

A smile crept across Max's face. If only Andersson knew who the speaker really was. Jacqueline King was a strange name for a goddess to choose as an alias – he would have to ask her about that one day – although the need to keep her real identity a secret required no great intellectual effort, and her active participation in events like this was all too obvious. The building had temporarily become a place of worship – her temple and her followers. Here she was at her most powerful, and it was here that her destiny would be played out. Another irony.

He watched her turn from Andersson back to the competitors. Max's eyes feasted themselves on the sinewy compact body and wondered if all wood nymphs were made that way. He couldn't help it, she was just so hot. Even the microphone seemed to think so. It had spat and hissed aggressively at the FSI official slumped next to her, but once held between those enticingly delicate fingers... well, it behaved most responsively.

Despite the sheltered cool of the huge hall, Max was beginning to get a little hot under the collar. He tried to clear his mind; he needed blood pumping round his brain and not anywhere else at that moment in time. He gave himself a sharp pinch on the thigh; since schooldays it had usually proved effective in taking his mind off such things.

Was the attraction he felt for her some form of idolisation, perhaps? Was it quite natural for a chess player to desire and idolise the game's deity? In fact, taking the thought to its logical conclusion... He grinned to himself as he tried to guess just how many others in that room were probably, right at that moment, entertaining thoughts that they'd be most reluctant to reveal to their good wives and girlfriends at home. Well, if nothing else, she was unwittingly helping to take their minds off their pre-tournament nerves.

'Okay,' Caissa continued in a soft, good-humoured tone – she was obviously enjoying every second – 'that's nearly all the formalities over with. As you all probably already know, of the thirty thousand dollars, or one hundred and twenty million lira, prize money, fifteen thousand will go to the winner, the rest will be divided up between the top four runners-up, and not according to the usual category classifications. The tournament follows strict FSI/FIDE regulations. The maximum time allowed for each competitor is ninety minutes a game. The tournament lasts the entire weekend, best of six games, beginning with three today, and tomorrow with another three, one in the morning and two after lunch. A copy of the timetable is here on the desk for those who don't already have one. The organisers have appointed twenty volunteer referees who are wearing the FSI armbands. In case of a dispute, their decision is final, and any refusal to accept this will result in immediate expulsion and disqualification. Placings of consequent games are decided by computer and will be posted before the start of every round on the boards situated around the room. You may begin. Thank you and all the best.'

Hands reached over boards and shook, and the austere atmosphere of the grand hall echoed with the strange staccato clicking of dozens of chess stopclocks suddenly being activated.

He'd won two straight games and, after sizing up the rest of the competition, Grandmaster Vassily Myslovič went over and seated himself at table seven, a contented man. The ratings said it all. On paper at least, he was bound to collect a fair share of the winnings even if he didn't win outright.

Ever since his emigration from the old Yugoslavia to Italy over ten years back, there had been little in the way of lucrative competition close to home. Most of the decent prizes required travelling abroad and that meant investing his precious savings without a sure guarantee of breaking even.

The competition on the international circuit had been getting tougher and tougher, and his job as a bricklayer didn't help him that much. He had considered a change of profession and had heard that plumbing was a good line, but it was so difficult finding someone to train you.

This weekend would help him out a lot. Most of the super grandmasters were mixing it in China right now, sticking the boot into each other for the right to have a go at the world championship in February the following year. And that left fine pickings. These open tournaments were generally nice little earners because anyone, despite their age or category, could enter. Most of the weaker players did it just for the experience, or to try their luck and gain a few extra rating points if they succeeded in beating someone pretty good, but the fact remained that it was usually the highest rated players who walked away with the cash.

He perused the sparring sheet and smiled. The computer had selected him a non-classified as his third opponent. A non-classified that had got lucky by the look of it. It wouldn't be much of a challenge, that was for sure. He took a deep breath and sighed. He preferred a good challenging game when at all possible. How much easier it would be to let all the lower rated players battle it out among themselves first of all, and then let the emerging winners face the cream like himself.

His opponent came over and sat himself down opposite. Vassily reached over and offered his hand for his bearded adversary to shake.

'Mysloviç,' he announced, but his opponent ignored him, preferring to stare down at the chequered board with its pieces neatly set up in front of him, as if spellbound by some mysterious force.

Mysloviç smiled to himself again. This one was obviously a little awestruck at the thought of playing against someone of his calibre. He could understand that; he remembered how he had felt at the tender age of eight in his first international tournament against the bigger boys. He smiled in sympathy and held out his hand for the second time.

'Mysloviç,' he repeated with greater compassion.

Very slowly his opponent raised his head. Two cold, black holes, magnified unnaturally by the glasses he was wearing, penetrated through to Vassily's soul, and a shiver ran down through his spine when finally they spoke.

'Yesss... Mysloviç ... Vassily. International grandmaster. ELO rating 2640. Born Ljubljana, Yugoslavia, in the year nineteen hundred and sixty-two, April thirtieth. A Monday. First international competition…' The recitation continued for a further minute in the same emotionless, flat drone, recounting the most important successes and failures of the Slav's career with concise clinical detail.

Vassily twisted uncomfortably in his seat, his gaping jaw giving evidence of the third world dentistry which, along with so many other things, had finally led to his decision to emigrate. He'd never heard his life's history so briefly and accurately summarised before. Actually he'd never heard it before, period, especially over a chessboard, and especially from someone who bore no small resemblance to the man who used to extract his teeth as a child.

Belvois reached over the table towards the stopclock, ignoring Vassily whose hand was still hovering in mid-air.

'I eat grandmasters for breakfast,' he growled menacingly, his voice retaining that unnerving and unworldly quality of before.

Belvois hit the button which started Vassily's clock.

'Play and prepare for annihilation, grandmaster Mysloviç.'

Max had never played so well in his life. True, he had a huge advantage in that, unlike the others, he was not pressed for time. Freeing himself from his body to aid his concentration, he could hover over the table in a lotus position, and spend as much time as he wanted contemplating a position before returning to make his move. The cross-legged lotus position was a nice little touch, he'd thought, seeing as normally, when bound by ordinary physical laws, it hurt like hell. Outside his body, though, he was not bound by anything, not pain, not time itself.

To be honest, however, he was beginning to feel a little guilty about it all. It was a bit like cheating, but he was here to win, for the honour of the game and for Caissa as well. And up until now, he had managed to restrain himself from slipping out into the car park where he'd left a selection of excellent reference books on the back seat of his car. It would be absolutely no hassle whatsoever just to immerse his immaterial face among the pages and read the appropriate lines. Sure, if it came to a showdown between him and Belvois, he would most certainly do so, if only to even out the odds a little. Most probably Belvois already had all the opening moves along with their latest updates programmed in his memory. It takes a cheat to take a cheat, he reasoned.

All three of his opponents had fallen relatively quickly. Two first category players and then a candidate master like himself had gone down to a neat little combination on the twenty-third move of his favourite Leningrad-Dutch defence. He had no more to go that day. A straight three points would put him up on the top ten tables against the toughest opposition.

He wandered over to the little bar and knocked back a quick black coffee pick-me-up. He'd wait for the final placings to be announced for the next day, then he'd go home to Maria and dinner. As the thick, sweet liquid oozed through his system and kick-started his mind, he glanced around the room at the players who were still finishing off their games. Little groups gathered curiously around those still in action, and Max managed to catch a glimpse of the bearded Belvois on board seven. Having come in as non-classified, he'd had to fight his way up through the ranks. He went over to the scoreboard which consisted of a computer printout sheet pinned to a cork board.

Not surprisingly, Belvois also had two clear wins. Who was his opponent now? He looked down one of the adjacent sheets. Myslovič! Well, it remained to be seen. Maybe the top-rated Slav would do it, as long as he hadn't underestimated his opponent, which actually was highly possible as no one had warned him that he was about to face a state-of-the-art mishmash of human and computer intellect.

A thought suddenly occurred to him. Why hadn't Caissa bothered to inform others as she had done with himself? Wouldn't it have made sense to place all the top players on their guard against him?

'I couldn't,' came a discreet female voice from beside him. 'Even *I* have to follow certain rules. There's a limit to the amount of direct interference I can make.'

'What?' cried Max in surprise. 'Have you started reading my mind now as well?'

'Nothing of the sort. You were talking to yourself while I was coming over to greet you.'

'Oh, was I?'

'Besides,' continued Caissa, ignoring Max's obvious disconcertion, 'what would you have me say to them that would be convincing enough without revealing too many things best kept secret? And even then, how could I still guarantee their sanity afterwards?'

'I'm still sane,' said Max, defensively. 'Well, more or less.'

'That doubt in itself, dear boy, is a sign of mental well-being. My friend Sigmund once informed me of that.' She laughed good-humouredly, and then inhaled deeply as if filling her lungs with fresh air that didn't exist. In fact, the air inside the musty hall was by now decidedly stale and sweaty, and getting more so with every minute that passed. 'Pure energy! Can't you feel it?'

Max shook his head. 'No, but the effect it's having on you is quite obvious.' Her ethereal presence seemed to be pulsing with light.

'I love these events,' she exclaimed ecstatically, 'they make me feel sooo good.' A smile seemed to be eternally present on her features. 'Anyway, I came over to compliment you on your successes here today.'

'I hope it continues,' said Max, 'even if I do feel like I'm cheating a little on the time side of things.'

She clasped his hand and squeezed it warmly. 'The end justifies the means. You keep up the good work. Everybody has their own particular ability, and it's right to exploit these things to their full.' She took another exhilarated breath. Her eyes sparkled with hidden energy. 'Ahh, when I feel like this, no one can stop me. See ya later, alligator!'

Max watched amused as the goddess went over to table sixteen where a game was in its final throes. There was a spring in her step and joy in her movements that reminded him of an adolescent girl.

A ruckus rose up from the other side of the hall and all eyes turned to watch Myslović who, pushing his chair angrily backwards, got up and stormed out of the hall.

Chapter Thirty-Five

There was nothing left for her here but defeat and humiliation. She felt betrayed by her colleagues and, more importantly, the man she'd thought she was in love with. Cathy finished sorting through some of the things she would need for her coming flight and stay in Scotland.

Aunt Mary and Uncle John had been surprised and delighted to hear from her over the phone, and had been very happy to have her visit them. As a young girl, she had stayed with them for several summers while her father had been conducting some research at Edinburgh University. Memories of that little cottage near Stirling and their jovial and kindly company brought a smile briefly to her face.

Certainly, she couldn't face going back to Washington, the lab, their home, and all the memories of Robert. She had tried to build herself a new life here, hoped to build one, but instead... Perhaps a bit of time among her relatives would help clear her ideas and enable her to discover what she wanted to do with her life. 'Friends are all very well, but the family is always there for you when you need them.' Her father's words. How she missed both him and Robert.

Tears welled up again in her bloodshot eyes and trickled down the side of her face. They ran down to her lips and she tasted their saltiness.

Perhaps running out now was not the answer, but that cold look in Pierre's eyes had terrified her, as if nothing had passed between them except a clinical exchange of bodily juices. That horrid empty, emotionless way in which he had regarded her in the laboratory that morning. He remembered everything perfectly, that was obvious, but seemed to feel nothing for her any more.

During the few moments they had been alone in the laboratory, she had gone up to him, embraced him warmly and kissed him on the lips. Up until then she had hoped that he had been putting on an act for the benefit of Andersson and Menti. Instead, he had spoken her name as if it had been just a label attached to a piece of machinery, a method of identification to distinguish it from the others in the room. He had thanked her for her 'professional diligence and concern that had gone above and beyond her duty', and said that now he felt there really was little need for any of her services. He had disentangled himself from her arms, politely assuring her that he felt in perfect condition, both mentally and physically, and that he was eager to prove it to everyone by successful completion of his final task.

Perhaps he was still ill and her reaction had been too quick, too irrational and too emotional, but she couldn't have faced him any longer. She had turned and ran out of the room, almost knocking Menti over as they had passed in the corridor and had come back to her apartment. She didn't even know if she'd run or driven back. She was in turmoil. What had they done to him? Just so that bastard Andersson...

Anger and frustration rose up inside her. She had to clear her mind and think. She took a deep breath and, getting up from the bed, walked over to her bedroom mirror where she began to dab at the run mascara around her eyes with some tissue. She shouldn't have left so quickly, it had been playing into their hands. She threw the blackened paper into the basket beside her dressing table and passed a brush through her hair, flicking the long, blonde, wavy locks backwards, away from her face. There! Now she bore less of a resemblance to one of the undead.

She shoved some of her more essential items in her suitcase and sat back down on the bed again. Even though he had changed, surely it wasn't his fault. Andersson and Menti were responsible for his present condition, and she equally so. She had been so sure of herself, so confident in her own genius. Now, what was she doing? Pierre needed her help and here she was about to run out on him altogether. If she still loved him, how could she abandon him without a fight?

She sprang up from the bed, her mind made up. She would go to Salsomaggiore, find the hotel they were staying in and then... well, she'd think of something.

Suitcase and car keys in hand, the shrill call of her phone interrupted everything and froze her in the doorway - a classic demonstration of the proverbial perfect timing.

Chapter Thirty-Six

Ignoring the protests, Chris rolled some of Ali's herbal tea in a Rizzla paper and lit up. He then reached down from his bed to where the copy of 'What's On Italia' was lying, picked it up, and lay back on the hard feather pillow.

'Well?' asked Ali expectantly. 'Is it marijuana?'

'No, man. But it sure tastes better than those French cigarettes I've got.'

'Oh,' said Ali, and went back to reading some tourist brochures he'd found at the reception desk. 'Did you know that this town was founded by the ancient Romans and used as a holiday resort, and that the thermal waters here are said to have miraculous healing qualities?'

'Wowwww! Far out and fuckin' freaky, man!'

'Er, actually, as much as I appreciate your rather surprising enthusiasm, I do find it just a little exaggerated. After all, there are a lot of these places scattered around the country and in southern Europe in general and many claim to…'

'No, man. The photo of the chick in my dreams. You know, the one who was supposed to be presenting a draughts game or something like that?'

'Uh, yes?'

'Well, do you remember how she was dressed before?'

'Rather elegantly if I remember correctly, as would be befitting the occasion and the fashions of today.'

'Yeah, right. Well, check this out, then!' Chris sat up and thrust the magazine picture into Ali's view. Dutifully, he squinted at it, and then raised his eyebrows slightly.

'I must have been mistaken, or maybe it is another picture,' he speculated. The girl was dressed casually in jeans and a T-shirt and she was smiling at the camera. He wasn't even sure if it was the same girl. They all seemed to look so alike, these western girls in magazines.

'No, no, it's the same picture. Look!' Chris pointed at the article underneath that Ali had translated the other day over cappuccino in the café bar.

Ali nodded. 'Maybe you have just picked up an earlier edition by accident.' He went back to perusing the tourist bumpf. It was another hour before they would go out to eat and he was getting very hungry.

Chris shook his head and threw himself back down on the bed, continuing to stare at the page. Apart from the unbelievable sexiness of the babe in question, and her continual reappearance in his dreams, there was something about the photo that didn't strike him as quite right. Was it really just the way she was dressed? Or maybe her smile? Suddenly his eyes bulged wider.

'Oh, wowoaah! Oh, man! Now she's waving at me!'

'I believe if you stop smoking that "cigarette" there, she will soon stop,' commented Ali, dryly.

He'd got a point. Chris eyed suspiciously the smoking roll-up between his fingers, shrugged, and then turned back to the page. The chick was still waving, but now she seemed to be signalling him to go into the bar behind her. Strange, he'd never even noticed what was in the background of the photo before, but he could have sworn…

'It's not the joint, man. Er, she's inviting me into a bar.'

'What?'

'She's gone in, man. This is fuckin' cosmic!'

'What?'

'I said she's gone in the bar, man, and this is… oh, fuckin' freaky far out, man!'

'My!' exclaimed Morph as he entered the room. 'What a gifted and comprehensive variety of adjectival expletives! And all linked together with such admirable alliteration!' He closed the door behind them and added, 'How they hangin', hippy?'

'The sexy chick in the photo, man. You remember the one I showed you?'

'Yeah?'

'Well, she's just upped and gone.'

'What?'

'Aw no! Not you as well!'

'What?'

Chris looked despairingly from one companion to the other. 'Are you both in league and trying to do my head in? All either of you has said for the last two minutes is "What?"'

'What?' cried Morph beginning to feel a creeping sensation of disorientation, his original outburst of eloquence now reduced to monosyllables.

'It is true,' confessed Ali. 'We do keep saying "What?"'

'Oh, jeez!' moaned Chris, almost forgetting the photo. 'What I'm trying to say is…'

'Ha! There you see, it is catching! Now you too are doing it,' interrupted Ali, in a victorious tone.

'Wha?' cried Chris. 'When?'

'Just then,' jumped in Morph, his wits quickly returning, 'when you said, "What I'm trying to say is…"'

Tactics. Disorientate before being disorientated. Fight back. Flummox first, question later. Get the hippy before he gets you.

'Noo!' cried the hippy. He put his roll-up out in the ashtray by his bed and looked very sad indeed.

Ah, the joys of hippy taunting, Morph thought. And how easy it is too. He would certainly have to do this more often.

'Please, look at the picture.' Chris held the magazine page up at the two of them with outstretched arms.

The plea was so pathetic that both Morph and Ali had no choice but to oblige.

'It does look like the same page and magazine,' agreed Morph. 'But I don't recognise the photo at all. I mean, it's just a picture of a bar…'

'Which has very little in common with the article on the chess competition below it,' Ali reasoned.

'Unless that's where they all go to get rat-arsed after,' Morph suggested, helpfully.

'Most mysterious. And you're sure you have not got hold of a different edition?'

'I swear, guys. She just waved for me to follow her and disappeared into that bar. It's the weirdest thing I've ever seen.'

'And it has nothing to do with that thing you've just smoked?' Morph pointed at the roach in the ashtray. 'It smells very strange.'

'Naww, that stuff's just regular herbal tea. I should know, I've smoked loads of the stuff when there's been nothing else to get, when there's been a heavy drought period, you know. Herbal tea doesn't get you high, doesn't do anything, just smells good.'

Ali stroked his chin in thought. Suddenly he got up from the bed and, grabbing the magazine from Morph's paws, ran out of the room.

'I have got an idea,' he shouted as he disappeared down the hotel stairs. 'I shall be back in two shakes of the tail of a camel.'

When he returned – presumably in the time it takes for a camel to shake its tail twice – he was a little red in the face and panting from the effort of climbing back up the five flights of stairs. 'Ma Chérie!' he exclaimed, excitedly.

'Oui, mon cher?' responded Morph in his finest French accent, which was about as good an argument as any for the English never to attempt it.

'Wha?' said Chris, slightly bewildered.

'Don't start!' Morph pointed a warning finger at him. 'You can't handle the pace.'

'The name of the place in the picture is the Ma Chérie – a type of nightclub. I asked the man in reception. It opens tonight at nine.'

Chapter Thirty-Seven

Bellies full of pizza once again, Morph, Chris and Ali sat in the club Ma Chérie waiting expectantly for something to happen and, in the meantime, swelling their guts pleasantly with cold beer.

The other two watched while Morph demonstrated just one of the many essential and interesting social skills it is possible to pick up while drinking with friends in a low-action pub.

'Hoopla!' The half-soggy beer mat span its way up into the air and, in complete accordance with the laws of gravity, span its way back down again, barely missing the top of Morph's glass.

'And it is supposed to land on the top and remain there, is it?' asked Ali with forced interest.

'Well, yes, of course it is.'

'May I ask why?'

'Eh?'

'Why should you spend all that time trying to make it land on top of the glass when you have to remove it again after if you want to continue drinking?'

'Well, it's part of the skill, that's all. It's not easy to do. It's the achievement that counts, like climbing a mountain, but not quite as dangerous.'

'I see. It also seems to be rather unhygienic, as that beer mat was not the cleanest of things I had ever seen before you began, and now, counting the number of times it has fallen to the floor and bounced off Chris's head, I would probably have to add that it is even less so.'

'My head's not so dirty, man!'

'Your uncle's right, hippy. You're hair would never pass government sanitary approval. However, I must admit that bouncing it off your noggin does increase its entertainment value.'

Before the hippy could react, Morph flicked the soggy mat again. It arched beautifully through the air, promising to make direct contact with the nose of its intended victim. But, at the last second, Chris ducked, and it landed instead with a wet 'Flap!' on the nape of an unsuspecting customer sitting behind.

A hand lashed out and caught the mat before it had a chance to begin its downward flight to the floor, and a blonde, crew-cut head turned slowly to face his assailant.

'I believe this is yours.' The intonation was perfect, but the accent held traces of Germanic origin. The blonde giant held out his hand and politely offered Morph his beer mat back.

Morph took it timidly, thanking him and apologising profusely at the same time. He placed the mat gingerly down on the table before him and swallowed hard. Taking into account the awesome physical dimensions of the Mr Universe in front of him, he wondered how the hell he'd failed to notice him before.

The big German grinned and the others smiled back at him in relief. At least he was good-humoured and seemed to have taken it all quite well. But then, twisting on the stool back round to his own table, he grabbed his full glass, drained its contents, and thumped it down empty before them.

'C... C... Can I offer you a drink?' Morph stammered a little nervously.

'That's really very kind.' He reached over and, with a hand that almost completely enveloped the litre glass, emptied Morph's beer down his throat in one mighty slug.

A look of extreme dismay passed over Morph's features as he watched in helpless silence. Then, in turn, both Chris's and Ali's followed similar fates.

Indignantly, and with a fearlessness that did him proud – or, on the other hand, demonstrated a wondrous misconception of the laws of self-preservation – Chris rose to his feet. 'Hey!' he shouted, 'That was mine!'

The behemoth followed suit, knocking over the table with his ample beer belly as he stood. Despite the fact that his bowels were beginning to sink rapidly, taking refuge down where his knees should have been, Morph couldn't help but be slightly puzzled at the sudden appearance of the huge stomach. He could have sworn that, up until a few seconds ago, the man had had the physique of a Greek god.

'ROARRR!' roared Blitzkrieg, throwing his arms up in the air.

Ali reached up and pulled Chris back down to his seat. 'Do not intimidate him.'

'ROOAARRR!' roared Blitzkrieg again. Stalactites of saliva dangled from the roof of his open mouth.

For the second time that day, Morph's bowels dropped completely. The three of them sat petrified by the spectacle that now confronted them.

It was like a special effects scene from a horror film. The metamorphosis was alarmingly rapid. His stomach continued to bloat and the crew-cut head of hair began receding from off his forehead and, as if in compensation, grew out long and unkempt at the sides. The clean-shaven jaw suddenly developed a five o'clock shadow, which fast became a 'late ten in the evening' shadow, and a couple of extra undulating chins just kind of popped out of nowhere.

'Allah in heaven!' exclaimed Ali, under his breath.

Even his clothes seemed to have taken on a transformation of their own. The white shirt he was wearing now had the cuffs rolled up to the elbows, revealing two small heart-like tattoos on both of his hairy forearms. His well-fitting jeans suddenly became grossly baggy – despite his massive increase in bulk – and the back sagged down, partly exposing his naked posterior. A classic case of 'workman's bum'.

'Er… Time to go, guys!' advised Morph, finding his voice but not his feet.

'H HU HUL HULK?' stuttered Chris, likewise rooted.

Of course, what the intrepid trio did not know was that the monster before them was not a creation from the Marvel comic empire, but simply the beer god, Blitzkrieg, and, like most beer gods, was afflicted by something modern science, if they ever got to know about it, would probably term 'Deitus Intoxicus Blobum'. One drop of the amber nectar and he transformed into a rampaging, unstoppable monster, a change which was not only physical but also mental.

Blitzkrieg began to rave. He was suddenly in possession of a delightfully wide range of colourful vocal obscenities. They started from his gut in a kind of uncontrollable rumble, 'Yuuuuuuuuh…' and then passed along his windpipe,

'YuuuuuuuUUUUUH…' finally exploding in an ecstasy of reckless abandon from out of his dribbling mouth, 'YUUU… YOU FUCKIN' WHAT? WHAT THE FUCKIN'…?'

It really was a most creative and commendable performance, rendered even more so by the fact that every word he slurred, every offensive oath and curse and insult he threw, was instantly understood by everyone in earshot as if it had been said in their own native tongues – just one of the countless advantages of being a beer god at full polyglot strength.

Ali was quite upset. Despite his understandable fear and trepidation at the monstrosity before him, family honour demanded satisfaction. It had been a long time since someone had sworn to do that to his mother. It was unpardonable, even if she had been dead for over twenty years. Not bearing to look, he closed his eyes and rose bravely to meet his fate.

Both Chris and Morph grabbed him and pulled him back down again. But it wasn't necessary. Blitzkrieg had already forgotten them, distracted by a far greater task: he was on a mission.

'You sons of fuckin' bitchin' bastar…'

He was whirling around the tables in the bar, draining every glass of beer that caught his eye and burping uncontrollably. He was also remarkably agile and swift for a man of his bulk.

'Yur gunna get yur fuckin' heads kicked in,' he chanted merrily at the three athletic types who, backed by an angry-looking bouncer, were moving in on him.

Mercifully it was all over in a matter of seconds.

'Ha haaargh!' jeered Blitzkrieg in triumph, while simultaneously attempting and failing to balance an empty glass on his head. He drained another and then looked through the base at its distorted image of the club. It was then that he saw… the bar! He bulldozed over towards it, gulping down the beers of innocent customers as he passed, oblivious of the unconscious bouncer that he was still holding effortlessly in his left hand.

'Stop! Halt!' boomed an authoritative voice from the other side of the club. Everyone – everyone except Blitzkrieg, of course – turned to look at the off-duty policeman who was brandishing a standard issue Beretta handgun.

Why me? Luigi Quagliaroli was thinking. He'd only recently graduated from traffic school and hadn't the foggiest idea of how to handle this situation and the behemoth at the bar. He certainly wasn't going to make an attempt at tackling it physically, especially after the way it had dealt with those other four guys, and he couldn't start shooting in a crowded public place. He fixed the monster, who was sat farting, burping and blaspheming at the far end of the club, with his best death stare. Well, if there was one thing all those evening card games at the academy had taught him: if in doubt, bluff it!

'Halt!' he shouted again. Speak slowly and clearly, show no fear – he was in command of the situation. 'Put... the... beer glass... down and...'

And then the empty glass bullseyed his forehead, the lights went out and he fell to the floor.

'One huunndred and eighty!' shouted a delighted Blitzkrieg, imitating the tones of a Saturday night darts match commentator and, rolling over to the other side of the bar, stuck his head under the beer taps, pulled back a pump handle, and began some serious guzzling.

'Hello, boys!' The voice was light and airy, filled with pleasant humour, and in total contrast to the atmosphere of pure unadulterated terror which was hanging over the club like a spectre of doom at that present time. 'I'm glad you got my message. I'm sorry I'm a little late for our rendezvous. A woman's prerogative, however.'

She stopped as she saw the expression on their pale, bloodless faces. Chris looked up and tried to speak, but failed, and just gaped from her back to the burp-and-fart monster over at the bar. Caissa glanced around her, looking slightly disconcerted. Then she caught sight of Blitzkrieg and tutted. 'Oh, dear! Has he been on the tipple again?' She shook her head in disapproval. 'Really, it's so embarrassing. He promised me he wouldn't touch a drop tonight!'

She started over towards the hunched blob. The terrified bar staff were huddled together in the far corner, trying to look as inconspicuous as possible.

'No, lady! Do not go over there!' Ali beseeched her in horror.

'It is very, very dangerous.'

'And why on earth not?'

Ali, Morph and Chris all gestured wordlessly at the strewn bodies, upturned tables and chairs, and smashed glasses.

'Blitzy!' Her tone had changed to one of severe reprimand. 'Stop it at once!'

From the other side of the bar, bleary, bloodshot eyes peered at the slinky, black, feminine form that was fast approaching.

'Phwor! Orwight babe? Giz us a kiss, go on!' And turning to the trembling employees bunched up near the dishwasher he announced, 'That's my babe! Bit of all right, eh?'

They all nodded eagerly in unison.

'I really am most terribly sorry,' apologised Caissa in her sincerest tones. 'He really doesn't want to hurt anyone and if he does, he's always so embarrassed in the morning.' She placed a little bundle of banknotes on the table. 'I truly hope this is sufficient to pay for the damages.'

She shook her head once more at him and tutted reproachfully. Then, as if from nowhere, she produced a plate of food and placed it on the bar under his nose.

'Here, dear, eat this!' she commanded.

Blitzkrieg couldn't resist it. It was that smell again. 'Munchies! Grub! Yum yum!' he announced and got stuck straight in.

'Use this and don't be an animal!' cried Caissa, and gave him a fork.

The effect was almost as rapid as the initial transformation.

'Oooh, my head!' moaned Blitzkrieg almost immediately after gulping down the last mouthful on the plate.

'Poor boy.' Caissa sympathetically stroked the blonde hair that was beginning to grow back over his receded, bald patch. 'C'mon,' she continued gently. 'We really should be going now and leave these poor people to clear up the mess you've caused.' She took him by the hand and led him towards the exit, his massive bulk diminishing visibly with every step.

'Oow!' he groaned again.

Incredulous eyes watched as their source of terror was led puppy dog-like out of the club.

As she passed, she turned to Morph, Ali and Chris and said,

'Would you gentlemen be so kind as to help a lady in distress? I've got to get him back to the hotel before he collapses on me.'

Outside the Majestic Hotel, they helped Blitzkrieg, who was by now delirious with hangover, out of the back of the big, black BMW that Caissa had just driven them up in.

She got out and handed the keys to the waiting valet.

'I won't be needing it for the rest of the evening,' she said. And then, turning to the trio who were struggling to hold Blitzkrieg's loose form upright, added with obviously practised nonchalance, 'Just plonk him on the baggage trolley over there. It'll make things a lot easier.'

They struggled over and gratefully released their burden. Blitzkrieg flopped down like a puppet whose strings had been cut.

'There, that's much more manageable!' remarked Caissa. She sounded quite pleased. She went over to the trolley and gave it a tentative push to check its mobility before starting off with it towards the hotel entrance.

The doorman bowed to her as she approached.

'Does madam require any help with her baggage this evening?'

'No, no, thank you. I believe I have the situation quite under control.'

The doorman nodded in acknowledgement of her wishes and held the door for her instead.

Caissa turned to the three waiting expectantly behind her. 'Anyone for cocktails and explanations?'

'It's a bit better than our digs,' Chris said a little grimly, taking in the cushioned luxury and marble grandeur of an executive class hotel room, the likes of which he'd only seen in movies.

'And the toilet's better, too,' commented Morph, as he exited the bathroom. 'No roaches in there.'

Caissa came over from the cocktail cabinet in the corner of the spacious suite carrying a tray of drinks. She placed it down on the table in front of them.

Ali sipped at the thick, sweet liquid and worried slightly at the way he'd been abusing his liver in the past few days. 'Excellent. Not what I was expecting at all. I do not think I have ever tried this before. Very good.'

'Oh, thank you. It's made with nocino, a local drink distilled from nuts, with, of course, some of the more commoner elements of a cocktail. An old friend gave me the recipe last cent... er... years ago.'

Morph slurped, enjoying the warm burning sensation down the back of his throat while Chris knocked his straight back and began to cough violently.

'He's not really used to alcohol,' Morph explained, as he slapped the hippy punishingly hard on the back. 'Everything else, it seems, but not strong alcohol.'

'So, how is your friend?' Ali asked. He was curious to get some answers and did not want to beat about the bush any longer. The whole thing was much too interesting.

'Oh, he'll get over it. He always does.'

There was a crash and a splinter of broken glass from inside the bedroom where they'd put Blitzkrieg.

'There goes the crystal decanter. Sounds like he's coming round.'

Chris threw an anxious glance over at his other two comrades. Caissa caught it.

'Oh, don't worry. I admit that he has a bit of a drinking problem. But he'll be quite docile and sorry now. You'll see.'

'And what about that freaky change?' asked Chris, not completely convinced, but anxious to believe anyway and just as curious as the others to get to the bottom of it all.

'Let's just say it's a type of allergic reaction.'

'An allergic reaction?' all three exclaimed together.

'Yes, sort of.'

'And what was it you gave him to eat that made him change back?' Ali began to feel a certain empathy for the afflicted Blitzkrieg. So he wasn't the only one with ridiculous allergy problems. 'It was quite potent and immediate.' Maybe he'd finally found someone who had an answer, someone who could help him with his own problem.

'A hot vindaloo curry.' She turned to Chris and Morph. 'I believe in your country it has become something of a national remedy for those that have indulged in excessive levels of alcohol abuse on a Friday and Saturday night, right?'

Morph nodded. 'I always prefer a prawn madras, personally.'

'Mmmm!' agreed Chris.

'Excellent! And Ali? What would you like?' Caissa picked up the phone. 'We can get it brought up. One of the chefs in the hotel is native Indian. It's one of the reasons we came here.'

Twenty minutes later they were all sat around the dining table.

'I must admit', munched Morph, 'to feeling very peckish, even though I've already had pizza tonight.'

'That was hours ago, man.'

'We should have ordered more popadoms. There are never enough.' Ali was beginning to regret his choice of a mild rogan josh which had left him feeling a little on the unadventurous side.

Caissa wiped her lips with a hot towel and shifted forward in her seat. A glimpse of naked cleavage nearly caused Chris to make the fatal error of sticking his nan bread dipped in curry sauce straight in his eye. He missed and jabbed the end of his nose instead. Close one that, though! Hot curry sauce in the optic department is not something to be taken lightly.

'Okay, boys,' Caissa began, 'I guess you've been wondering, for example, why the car we arrived in didn't break down under Ali's influence?'

All three glanced at each other. How did she know?

'Well, listen up, because I've got a very interesting proposition to make you...'

Chapter Thirty-Eight

For a plan that had come straight from the mind of such a beautiful woman, Morph couldn't help thinking that it was just a little toilety. Simple, but toilety.

It seemed to him that they'd been waiting in the basement washrooms for most of the morning, three hours and twenty-two minutes to be exact, from when they'd first arrived. Above them, in a huge hall they'd caught a glimpse of before going down the steps, an important chess tournament was going on and their mission was to stop a dirty cheat.

At least there was no real element of danger involved, and no real crime to commit either. All they had to do was hang out in the toilet cubicles and wait for this person who looked almost exactly like him – Morph hoped there was only one up there – and work it so that Ali could brush up against him. It wasn't even being dishonest because, as far as they had understood, this fellow was sporting some kind of computer device which gave him all the answers. Well, one touch from Ali would soon put an end to that. And then his own part was even more fun. In the case that his victim should leave the tournament to avoid any possible exposure or embarrassment, then it would be Morph who would substitute him by going upstairs, and losing the next few games. Something which certainly wouldn't be too difficult to do!

He glanced down at the cheap digital watch he'd been forced to use, and pined for his precious family heirloom, inherited along with the family business when his father had retired. 'It'll bring you luck, as it did me,' his father had said, as he had handed it to him with pride, one of the earliest examples of an electronic watch. 'And it hasn't lost a second in over twenty-five years.' If Ali could send such a faithful mechanism awry, well, he reckoned that this guy's computer thingy wouldn't stand a hope in hell's chance.

That was if this guy was human, he thought. It seemed the rest of the participants in the hall had responded to nature's call, some two or three times, and because of their permanent presence there that morning he was now on polite nodding terms with one or two. Everyone had paid a visit, everyone, that is, except the man they wanted.

And, unbeknownst to Morph, the man they wanted had been creating quite a controversy upstairs amongst players and organisers alike. A lot of the top players were pushing for Belvois' disqualification on the grounds of a lack of good sportsmanship and unnecessary rudeness from an uncategorised upstart. They said that he was using a psychological ploy to put them off and that it was most unnerving to play against someone who had not only taken the trouble to memorise your entire career, but retold it to you before beginning play. They complained that he showed no respect for the honourable traditions of the game. 'He refuses to shake hands, declares his intent to massacre you, and then, worst of all, at the end he says, "I told you so," and jeers in your face!'

But disqualification was, of course, out of the question, as Andersson pointed out by simply threatening to place the presentation cheque back inside his jacket pocket and calling them sore losers. So the disgruntled players had to be satisfied with an FSI official politely asking Belvois not to be so rude to the other contestants in the future.

It was Max's turn to sit and listen to his life's story. He couldn't help but notice its remarkable brevity.

'There's more to it than that, Belvois.'

'Nothing of importance, Cugini.'

There was a remarkable difference in him from the last time they had spoken and played together, Max observed. Or perhaps he was like that even then; maybe with the problems he himself had been having at the time, he hadn't noticed the change. Whatever the case, this was not the mild-mannered, inoffensive guy who he had got to know at work. Whatever they'd stuck inside his head, it had obviously had a negative effect on his personality.

Uncertainly, Max offered his hand over the board, and then withdrew it again very quickly when it got snarled at savagely.

Belvois leaned over the table towards him, a small quantity of saliva frothing up in the corners of his mouth and on his whiskers.

'Here,' he growled, tapping the side of his head with his left index finger, 'here is total recall.'

'I liked that film.' Max grinned. He wasn't going to play Belvois' game.

'Every position, every good or bad move ever recorded in the history of master play is imprinted on my memory and, even better, I understand why they were made. You don't stand a chance, *candidate master*.' He spat the last two words out like they tasted bad.

'But I have the advantage of the white pieces,' retorted Max. Then, on reflection, he decided it was a pretty weak threat and added, 'And anyway, I'm the good guy.'

Just for a moment Max thought he caught a glimpse of confusion flitter across Belvois' bearded features, but it vanished again just as quickly, and he started Max's clock with a thump.

'A word of advice?'

Caissa's voice fluttered at his ears, and Max floated up out of his body and joined her where she was sat cross-legged above the table.

'Please feel free.'

'Have you got a plan?'

'Well, yes. I was hoping to distract him for a couple of seconds and, while he wasn't looking, swap all the pieces around in my favour.'

'You're up against a computer.' She ignored his attempt at sarcasm.

'I'd gathered,' replied Max, 'and I doubt I'm any match for him. He's just wasted most of the championship favourites like they were novices. It's somewhat unnerving, if not downright scary. He seems more machine than human.'

'I had noticed,' Caissa answered grimly, 'and there lies your advantage.'

'How?' Max shrugged his ethereal shoulders.

'Well, how do you go about beating your home computer? It has similar advantages to him, doesn't it?' She nodded downwards at Belvois' immobile form.

'Unplug it?' Max offered meekly.

'No, silly. Take it out of its opening book. Do something which probably hasn't been recorded in master play!'

'It's risky, but it's worth a try, I suppose.' He raised his eyebrows at her. 'What do you suggest?'

'Maybe pawn to queen's rook three for starters?'

Max floated back down, re-entered his body and made his first move. The response was more or less immediate:

1. a3 e5

A good answer, theoretically sound, typically aggressive, and deserving of a completely unexpected response.

2.d4

That stunned him! Belvois sat back in his chair, stared at the board and frowned.

Meanwhile, down in the toilets, the natives were getting restless. The smell of disinfected urine wiped and smeared across all surfaces with a damp mop hung in the air, swinging from nostril hair to nostril hair in gay abandon. Chris was beginning to feel a creeping nausea and his head was beginning to spin.

'Uh! Hey, man, come on! It's my turn to lurk outside,' he whined. He checked his watch for the twentieth time that minute. It was strange, but the numbers didn't seem to be changing at all.

'Shut up, hippy! We all agreed at the beginning to forty-minute turns each. One outside the toilet on watch, and two in the cubicles. That way nobody gets suspicious of the same three men hanging out in the johns all morning. Everyone gets their turn outside, and right now it's mine, and then Ali's.'

'Yeah, well, my eyes and nose are stinging, man, and my legs and arms are covered in strange itchy, red lumps. And I've gone right off my leftovers from last night's curry. Does anyone else want to finish it?'

It's funny how time can practically stop when you really want it to get a move on. For Chris at that moment it was probably the most obstinate and contrary thing in the whole of existence, except for, maybe, his sister.

His old history teacher, Mr Green, a tall, gawky man with cruel, thin lips and an immensely skiable forehead, suddenly flashed into his mind. Must be the effects of the disinfectant fumes, Chris suddenly thought; it was flashback time again. Green had despised him like he had despised all his students. Actually, Green had despised everyone, including his fellow teachers.

'Time waits for no man,' he would quote at him when he arrived a little late for his afternoon lessons, 'and neither does history. May one enquire as to the reason for your retarded arrival? Perhaps another excessively over-eager attempt to break the already formidable record that this school's students have set for bad punctuality?'

'Er... I went home for lunch and my watch must have stopped, sir.'

'And why would it want to do that, small boy? Tired of its useless and unobserved existence at the end of your arm, perhaps?' He had a remarkable propensity to communicate almost exclusively in interrogatives and to disregard any answers as superfluous.

'Sorry, sir,' he had mumbled resignedly at his boots. It was pointless; everybody knew that the 'UFO flying over the roof and stopping all the clocks' excuse only worked on the religious education teacher, Mr Payne. He knew what was coming next, they all did. First the 'time' speech...

'So you're sorry, are you? Well, you know what's going to happen now, don't you? Good timing is so very important. Do you realise that time is the very basis of our existence and rationality? Without it everything would disintegrate. There'd be chaos! You're just going to have to learn to respect time and what our precious allegiance to it means. Have you any idea what life would be like if deprived of it? Deprived of our modern concept of hours and minutes? No, I didn't think so.' He gestured towards a blue door at the back of the classroom. 'Well, in you go laddie, and give me your watch.' The tone was always so matter-of-fact.

Chris remembered that door. It was exactly the same colour as the one facing him now. A door that opened up to an empty store cupboard, a world of dark mustiness, of undefined dimensions, and one or two cardboard boxes. There was no electric light bulb. Once inside you were enveloped by a thick, all-encompassing blackness. Not even the light from the classroom could penetrate. Many were the tales of supernatural horror employed to frighten first-formers that had that cupboard as its setting.

After fumbling around in the darkness for his usual cardboard box to sit on, the normal procedure would be to sit very quietly and listen for sounds in the enforced darkness. There was always something else shuffling in there, and a ritual presentation had to be followed.

'Who lurks there?' It was standard cupboard speak.

'Tis I, Chris, the late one.'

'Greetings to thee, o late one!'

'Oh, hiya, Jamie! Been here long?'

'Dunno. Preggy's here too somewhere, and Rufus the Brown, I think.'

'Hi, man.'

'Yoh, couscous features!'

Chris unlocked the cubicle door and stuck his head out. 'I've been cramped in here with Ali for way over forty minutes now.'

'Rubbish! Ten, maximum.'

'Yeah? Well, I wouldn't know 'cos I've just realised the watch I bought early this morning doesn't work any more. It doesn't tick. I think Ali must have got to it.'

'Of course it doesn't tick, feeble-minded hippy. It's digital.'

'Yeah? Well, it's stopped anyway – at about half twelve – and now I've got no idea of the time whatsoever, and also I need to use the other cubicle for genuine reasons.'

It was true that there was another cubicle, but they had decided it would be wiser always to leave the other free for the function it had been originally destined for.

'Okay,' said Morph. 'Seeing as it's a genuine excuse, but then straight back in the other one with Ali, your time's not up yet.' He was bluffing, of course, because his watch wasn't working either. Perhaps it was something to do with Ali's aura expanding when he was nervous. Whatever, now none of them had any idea of the time.

Chris popped out and slipped into the next cubicle, leaving Ali alone and sitting on the toilet, a copy of *Le Monde* in his hands. Quite sensibly, he'd bought that particular paper before they had embarked upon their mission that morning for more than one reason:

1. To pass the time – obviously.

2. Because the others wouldn't want it, or be able to read it, as it was in French.

3. In the eventuality that he should succumb to the call of nature and find the public conveniences lacking in certain vital supplies. He always preferred a quality paper.

Chapter Thirty-Nine

Caissa studied the marble chessboard, her fine black eyebrows arching slightly in concentration, trying to ignore the constant rustling and crunching in the background.

'That's not a very comfortable position,' she commented to herself. While she watched, the white queen moved forward to take up a central position on the d4 square. 'Uh-oh, looks like I may just lose control of the central squares.'

The rustling and crunching rose in intensity.

At last, sufficiently irritated, she turned round and squealed. 'Will you stop making all that flaming racket when I'm trying to concentrate!'

Blitzkrieg lifted his eyes dolefully at her. 'It's okay, I've nearly finished.' His gaze dropped again briefly as he scooped out the rest of the crumbs from the bottom of a packet of salt 'n' vinegar crisps and shovelled them into his mouth.

The crunching started up again.

She glared.

'Sorry, babe,' said Blitzkrieg, his mouth still full of crisps, but managing nonetheless to convey an apologetic expression.

She sighed and went back to the board, only to turn once more in his direction. He'd opened another packet.

'Well, can't you at least pour them into a dish or something, thereby minimising the noise?'

Blitzkrieg threw her an 'it's not my fault' look and then added, 'I'm sorry, babe. It's not my fault. It's just that they seem to lose all their flavour like that. They taste much better straight from the packet.'

'You know,' said Caissa, suddenly losing interest in his discourse, 'I do believe it's time to launch a surprise flank attack.'

Chapter Forty

'Does anyone want this curry?' Chris asked again. 'I've only eaten about half.'

'Budge up a bit!' came Morph's voice from inside the same cubicle. He hadn't had lunch, but he had no appetite either.

'No! You and your fat ass have already got more than half the toilet seat,' Chris retaliated.

There then ensued some rather heavy shuffling and grunting, which caused the cubicle and the one next to it to shake violently. The door of the adjacent cubicle suddenly shot open, and a very worried French chess master headed quickly for the washbasins, nervously washed his hands, wetted down his hair and walked over to the hand-drier, all the time maintaining a wary eye on the rattling cubicles.

Suddenly silence fell and, apart from the four feet, visible quite plainly below the toilet door, there was nothing else unusual to be seen or heard. A voice from behind the Frenchman made him start.

'It does not work any more, I am afraid,' Ali explained apologetically.

Joel Montaud stared, eyes wide and aghast, at the smiling, white-robed Arab before him, a tightly rolled and torn copy of his country's favourite national newspaper, *Le Monde*, in his left hand.

'S... S... Sorry?' he stammered.

Ali repeated himself and added that he was sorry too. However, if he wanted, he'd managed to find some paper towels in a cupboard in the corridor. Eyes assuming snooker ball dimensions, the Frenchman shook his head quickly and backed up to the entrance. 'Non, non, it will not be at all necessary. You see, my hands are already dry. Look.' He held up his palms as proof and made good his escape up the stairs.

'Oh, dear!' said Ali, biting his lip, 'I do hope this other gentleman turns up soon. The situation appears to be getting a little awkward.'

Fresh squabbling erupted from inside the furthest cubicle, and one of the two pairs of feet abruptly vanished from sight.

'What the hell are we doing here anyway?' moaned Morph, bitterly. 'I mean, we've been lying in wait in this hellhole for... for God knows how long now. We've seen and heard more calls of nature than an ornithologist in a wildlife nature reserve, and the one animal we want doesn't seem to share the same needs as the rest of mankind.'

He paused and sat down on the now completely unoccupied toilet seat. 'And what's more, I'm not even sure why we agreed to do this.'

'You... did it for... money, man.' Chris's voice was small and had a strange, choking quality about it. 'She... offered you some sort of... really heavy hospital deal, yeah? Some hospitals... that really urgently need loads of plastic... signs. Whereas I did it for... a much more... noble reason.'

'And what was that, hippy?'

'She's really... sexy, man. And... she promised to... teach me how to do all that astral... dream-travel... stuff. Far out.'

'And I agreed to do it because she says she knows how to help me with my little problem,' said Ali.

'And you believed her?' asked Morph.

'Yes, I think she really does know something. You saw her extraordinary power over that monster. She must be some sort of mystic as well because of all that stuff with the photo and Chris's dreams.'

'Probably all just hippy hallucinations and coincidence.'

'And she knew all about us and my problem. Something that not many people know.'

'Okay, so she was particularly convincing. I believed her too. But if this guy doesn't turn up soon, I'm getting out of here. I can't take the smell or the confinement any longer.'

Ali decided that perhaps it would be a good idea to block the main toilet door open so as to improve the air circulation. He went over to the exit, opened the door, and then closed it again just as quickly. 'He is coming!' he whispered sharply to the other two. 'Quick!'

Calmly and efficiently Morph reached up and unhooked the hippy from the metal coat peg on the inside of the cubicle door. Some more shuffling and frantic scuffling ensued before the lock would open up to let them out. The duo stumbled forward out of the box that had been their shared home for a good deal of the morning.

Morph lost his footing slightly as they came out and the sudden jerk caused his glasses to fall from his nose. They bounced lightly and resiliently off the damp, stone floor. He stooped, picked them up, and wiped them on his Lacoste shirt. Then, replacing them firmly on his nose again, he peered out in the direction of the exit just in time to see the heavy door fly off its hinges with a deafening crack of splintered wood and flatten Ali to the ground beneath it.

Belvois lifted his eyes from the board for the first time since the start of the game and smiled in triumph. It wasn't a very nice smile. 'Told you so,' he growled at Max, and got up and left the table without any further ado. It was time to relieve certain bodily needs that had been plaguing him. He was sure that they had affected his playing and that was why it had taken up to the forty-first move to defeat this particular opponent. There remained one more game to play, one more opponent to demolish, and that would be it. Total victory! And then he'd be free, free from his contract, free to do what he wanted, free to…?

He paused briefly for a moment, somewhat confused. What exactly was it he'd planned to do after? Something about Cathy, but he couldn't think why he would have wanted to spend his time with her. She was a good scientist. He owed all he had become to her, and they had spent an entertaining afternoon together satisfying the natural needs of their bodies, but there was no reason to repeat the experience with the same female – he already remembered every single detail of that encounter. And then there was something else, something about his music and the guitar he'd learned to play. For some reason he had given great importance to it, and there again, he couldn't see why. He'd learned to play it just like the master musician he had studied, but now he'd done so, surely there was no point in continuing.

Perhaps he should learn something else? It all seemed such nonsense. Yet, all the same, there was something inside him telling him that he was missing out on an important detail, something that wasn't registered in his memory data banks. Certainly, he would have to ponder further on this.

He was heading down the steps to the basement toilet when he saw him. The image of a boogying, white-robed Arab falling on you in a club and hurting your mind is not something easily forgotten. Especially not when it had happened just the night before, and especially not by someone in possession of a computer-powered, photographic memory!

It took a split second to calculate the situation: the probability of meeting the same person twice in two different buildings and in two different cities. It was a trap! No, an ambush! His sensitive hearing had picked up whispers and other voices down below. Muscles and reflexes were suddenly pumped with adrenalin, and his aggressiveness factor rose with clean, computer-calculated efficiency.

Best strategy: a surprise counter-attack. He charged down the stairs, a blur of movement, and the bathroom door exploded off its hinges.

'He's splatted Ali!' cried Chris, paralysed by mixed feelings of awe and fear. It didn't matter much anyway because, an instant later, he felt nothing whatsoever, victim of a vicious backhand that sent him back to the black void of Mr Green's store cupboard.

Even as the longhaired youth was still falling to the ground, Belvois had already swung round to face his final opponent. However, what he saw next stopped him, suddenly and unexpectedly, dead in his tracks. And this is what he saw:

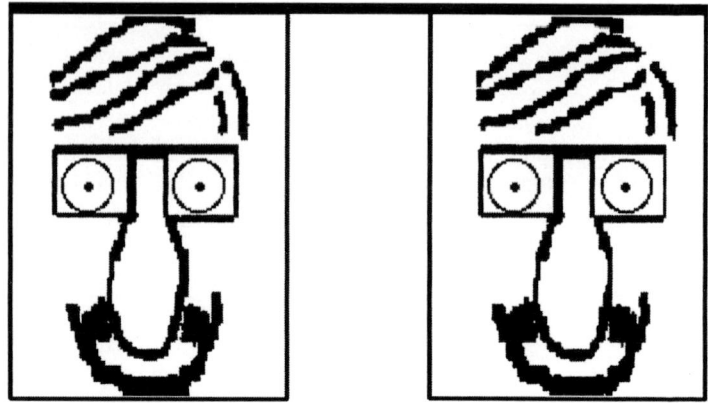

'Check!' exclaimed Caissa's opponent, as he appeared in a dramatic puff of smoke in the armchair on the other side of the marble chess set. Red eyes glared triumphant and his sharply chiselled features seemed almost serpentine as he laughed, a demonic laugh that displayed two rows of pearly white teeth.

'Your combination has failed,' he sneered at her, 'and to the victor the spoils, as they say, no?'

Caissa remained seemingly unruffled by the unwanted intrusion. The smile on his lips faded, and he fixed her with his best intense stare.

'So, how do want to pay, baby?' He was relishing every moment. 'All in karma or...' he licked his lips and eyed her up and down, '...or part in nature?' He erupted once more into diabolical laughter.

Behind her the figure of Blitzkrieg rose ominously up from the sofa where he'd been lying. He placed his hands on the back of the armchair, and Caissa, without turning, patted one of them calmingly.

'I'm glad to see you're enjoying our little game, Belfagor. I must compliment you on both the way you have played up until now, most commendable, and on your taste in dress – the military general's uniform is very becoming, a nice touch. But I fear your claim to victory is a little too anticipated. The game is far from over.' That had stopped his bravado a little, she thought, and so she added, 'I would also appreciate you knocking on the door like everyone else before entering. The smell of brimstone is really a most offensive odour and extremely difficult to get rid of.'

Belfagor seemed a little taken aback by the last reprimand and removed his general's cap, sniffing the air around him.

'Aww!' he said, sounding a little hurt, 'It's not as bad as that other guy's. After all, I'm only the Prince of Mischief, not Darkness.' He looked from her to Blitzkrieg and back. 'And soon to be your prince, milady.'

Blitzkrieg started forward, but Caissa maintained her hold on his hand, gripping it firmer.

'As I have already informed you, Prince Belfagor,' – she pronounced his name and title in that belittling tone in which women excel so well – 'the game is not over until the final move has been made.'

Fear manifested itself in the form of saliva and dribbled down from the corner of Morph's mouth. Ali lay unconscious or worse under the big, wooden door, and Chris was moaning deliriously in a sea of curry sauce all around him. It was most gruesome, and now it was his turn, and he was very, very scared.

He was stood face to face with the beardomorph version of Terminator and any resistance would be useless. He considered moving, but he knew his legs had turned to jelly beneath him and were only keeping him upright at that moment out of pure force of habit. He tried screaming but, failing to emit even the tiniest of audible noises, closed his mouth again. There was nothing left but to close his eyes and await the inevitable.

Just a minute! Wait! That was it! Why hadn't the doomsday man finished him off? Why had he stopped and was staring goggle-eyed at him? It was the Morph effect; it had to be!

It was certainly most uncanny; even he was surprised at their similarity. They were even dressed the same: same Lacoste, same jeans, same everything! An old Marx Brothers movie flashed through his mind: the scene from *Duck Soup* where Harpo dresses up as Groucho and then tries to convince the other that he's looking in a mirror. An absurd idea entered his head. It was a long shot but worth a stab. Flummox first, question later!

Belvois stared. He'd heard stories of things like doppelgängers, he'd even seen people in the street that looked a lot like him, but this one… this one was identical, even dressed the same.

He looked down at his shoes.

Simultaneously, Morph did likewise.

He fingered the crocodile emblem on his T-shirt.

So did Morph.

He adjusted his glasses on his nose.

So did Morph.

He pulled up his jeans slightly, revealing his white socks.

So did Morph.

He scratched his head, bewildered.

So did Morph.

He took one step forward.

So did Morph.

He reached out and grabbed Morph by the neck.

Morph didn't do anything.

He pulled him forcefully close up and headbutted him hard in the face. He released his grip, and Morph sank to the ground like a discarded rag doll.

'That'll teach you to take the piss, fuckface,' growled Belvois at the limp form at his feet, and, unzipping his flies, he walked over to the urinals on the wall.

'Ha ha! The game is mine! You can't possibly win now!' roared Belfagor. 'And you'll soon owe me more than you can afford to pay.' The horns on his head seemed to be growing visibly and, with a wave of his hand, he gestured aside the chess table that separated them. He then got up from the armchair and lunged at Caissa, effortlessly picking her up from where she had been sitting, and pressed her lithe form next to his.

On contact, Caissa realised that it wasn't just the horns on his head that were rapidly increasing in size.

'Blitzy…' she squeaked. He was holding her so tight it was difficult to get a lungful of air.

Blitzkrieg exploded into action. With a howl and a mighty leap he launched himself over the armchair between them, clearing it by a good six inches, and came into hard contact with the back of Belfagor's one free hand.

His head spinning, Blitzkrieg tried to sit up. He groaned. He hadn't taken a belting like that for quite some time. He groaned again and rubbed his numbing jaw. The blow had knocked him right across the other side of the room.

'Grr!' he grrrrd, and charged again, only to find himself unceremoniously seated once more at the far end of the room, the swelling on the side of his face growing quickly.

'Okay, big boy,' sighed Caissa, ceasing to struggle in the powerful arms. 'I've never been able to resist the charm of a man in uniform.'

He relaxed his grip, and she slid a little closer up against him, fingering the shiny brass buttons of his jacket.

'Especially when I know that there's a real beast deep down inside, just waiting to get out.'

'Ha ha!' He was triumphant. 'This is more like it. You're not going to regret, or forget, anything of this, sweet thing.' He held her tight once more and kissed her passionately on the lips. 'Once a nymph, always a nymph, eh?'

'Our boy's on top form, wouldn't you say?' beamed Andersson from behind his bushy moustache. 'And he's just given that other office boy, er, what's his name? Cugini, a hammering. Quite a convincing performance.'

Menti wondered how his boss's top lip could stand all that extra heat and humidity during the summer months. 'Uh, yes,' he replied a little uncertain. 'Although I strongly urge that we run him through some severe tests when we get back to the lab. He seems to be showing unnecessarily high levels of aggression, and he has taken to wearing glasses again, even though he doesn't need them.'

'Oh, nonsense! The glasses thing is just a psychological trick. He told me so himself, says it makes him look more inoffensive to the other players and therefore of greater psychological shock value when he actually gets nasty. You should have realised that yourself, being a shrink.'

'Uh, yes. But then, he's also been pretty rude to everyone else as well, not only the other players, but the waiters and waitresses in the hotel last night, the officials here at the tournament. Me. Everyone. All really nice people as well.'

'Naah! A little extra aggression is just what the General ordered. The boy's just mentally psyched up for the tournament, wants to win, you see.' Andersson eyed one of the score sheets that gave Belvois five straight wins, no losses, and smiled. 'Everything's going great. The money and contracts are as good as in the bag.' He paused and glanced around the hall. 'By the way, have you seen the General? He seems to have wandered off.'

'No,' Menti answered thoughtfully. 'Perhaps he has gone to have a quick chat in private with Belvois.' A look of concern then passed over his face. 'Oh, dear! I do hope he doesn't say anything out of place! I mean, it wouldn't be very good if Belvois started insulting the General, would it?'

Andersson frowned as he realised the potential gravity of the situation.

'Where's Belvois?' he demanded with urgency.

'I think he went to the toilet.'

'And where are the toilets?'

Having paid several visits himself that day, Menti had no difficulties at all in responding to that particular question.

'You'd have thought they'd have put some little plastic WC signs up, though,' grumbled Andersson to himself as he headed off, trying to remember if Menti had said to turn left or right at the end of the hall.

Chapter Forty-One

Max stared at the board and realised the situation was hopeless. He'd just lost to Belvois once again. This time there were no excuses; he'd done his darndest and it hadn't been good enough. Nevertheless, he felt kind of relieved. He began to feel as if a great weight had been removed from his shoulders; his part in it was over, even though he'd failed.

Caissa should have chosen someone really good to play this machine-man, someone who would have had a chance against him. From what she had told him before, he wasn't the only basket in which she'd placed her eggs, and he hoped for her sake that they were sturdier containers than he had proved to be.

He looked around the room. There were still some class players whom Belvois had not yet beaten. The French guy, Montaud, he'd been playing very well. He hadn't lost a game either and only one draw. So the sixth and final match was probably going to be a showdown between him and Belvois. Good luck, Montaud!

He got up, walked out of the hall and along the corridor that led to the fresh air outside. Actually, it wasn't so fresh any more. By now, the mid-afternoon sun had replaced that morning freshness with its usual sweaty humidity. Still, if he didn't want to, he didn't have to suffer it.

There was a little park just across the road and he decided to plonk his body down in the shade under a tree and then get out of it.

'Well? How did it go?'

Max looked up to where the voice was coming from. Maria was sitting on a branch above him. He gave her the thumbs down.

'Oh, well,' she shrugged. 'Come up here and play with me for a while.'

Max stepped out of his body and leapt up to her. He landed lightly beside her and together they floated up among the treetops, laughing and giggling, leaping from one branch to another, playing some ghostly version of tag.

Of course, none of the other park strollers paid even the slightest attention to this rather curious spectacle. They were, after all, invisible to the eyes of most of the human race. Most, but not all.

A little girl of five stopped playing with her doll for a moment to smile at the antics of Max and Maria high above her head. After, she would tell her mother about the 'funny flying people' and receive an extra big hug for having such an active imagination; either that or be sent to a child psychologist.

'It's certainly much more fun now you can do this too,' said Max, while performing a triple backflip somersault on to a branch below.

'Catch!' cried Maria, as she jumped from a leafy twig at the very top of an old oak and into his waiting arms. She looked up at his face. 'I've always been a quick learner, you know.'

It was true. Max had found the technique a little difficult to explain at first, but he'd found the right words in the end and she'd taken to it quite naturally. All it needed was to catch the right moment between the passing from consciousness into deep concentration, and then just step right out of your body. The trick was to realise when it was happening, the point that every human mind passes through when he or she falls into deep thought. That median between the world of physical reality and the timelessness of pure concentration, the world of intellect and spirit. At precisely that instant, the weights that anchor the mind to the body get released.

'I think the problem is,' Max had theorised to her, 'that a part of the spirit remains trapped in the body, the more earthly part, the emotions and things, and they act like a kind of anchor, an invisible umbilical chord if you like. So the only way out of the world of pure thought is the way you came in, and then, of course, the weights are instantly reattached. But, if you can catch the right point, the bridge between the two worlds, you can just jump off it, step right out, freeing the mind and spirit together, simultaneously.

'You remember when you've been really involved in

something, I don't know, a good book or something, and you suddenly realise that an enormous amount of time has elapsed? Well, during those moments, you were totally oblivious to what was happening around you because your thoughts weren't where your body was. Where do you think your mind had wandered off to for all that time? You have to get out just before you enter that world, taking all of you as a whole, that's all. It's a matter of timing.'

The means of reaching the required moment of concentration were far from limited, almost anything would do: reading, watching TV (only if there was anything good on, of course), knitting, trainspotting, the list could go on and on.

So she had tried it. She'd picked up a book, and Max had waited for her outside his body, ready to try and help, to sort of pluck her out when she was about to pass over. A couple of goes was all it had taken. She'd been a little frightened at first, and her initial reaction had been one of panic, like his had been. But then she seemed to get used to the odd, bodiless sensation and they'd gone for a quick flight down the street and back.

And now she was here to see him! Her body somewhere in Piacenza, another city, but her essence here. She'd learnt how to do it completely and independently. It was the final proof that 'outsiding', as they had decided to call it, could be taught to others.

They bounced off branches, leapt as high as they wanted, and floated like feathers down to the ground again. They flew through the outstretched arms of the trees in the little park, abandoning themselves to the pure delight of corporeal liberation, of being together, the joy of the moment. Tumbling and somersaulting, twisting and spinning. Every instant was precious and it seemed it could last as long – or almost as long – as they wanted.

'You know,' said Maria, as she missed Max's arms and passed through a couple of branches before flying back up to where he was standing, 'you're right about the fact that it's easier to think when outside. No distractions and all that. And I've come up with an advanced theory…'

Max eyed her cautiously. Even here? Even now? Last time had cost him a few pairs of his favourite socks. 'Are any of my socks involved again?'

'Er, yes, in a way,' she answered in a mysterious tone.

Max's face sank a little, but brightened up when she added, 'But only indirectly.'

He sat down on the branch he'd been balancing on and braced himself. Well, he wasn't really sitting on the branch because he was intangible, more like suspended in the air a minuscule distance above it. He peered out at the horizon and sighed. He was ready; resigned, but ready. Okay, he thought, roll the ugliness!

'Have you ever thought about why, every now and again, you see a shoe just lying there on the ground? Never two shoes together, just one, all lonely and abandoned?'

'No,' Max responded bluntly. It wasn't true though. He had pondered the mystery once or twice himself, but without arriving at any solid conclusions.

Maria ignored him and continued.

'Well, I was reasoning that it's most unlikely that people lose a shoe while out walking, right? Because they'd notice. I mean, all of a sudden your foot would get cold, bits of dirt and gravel would stick in your skin and you'd probably begin to hobble. Don't you agree?'

'Yes.' The answer was automatic, and he already had an inkling as to what was coming next.

'And that people, in general, do not go around with shoes just dangling precariously out of their bags ready to fall to the ground and be lost at any moment because people aren't that careless. Shoes are expensive, right?'

'Uh-huh.' He was trying to think about nice things, like all the people he could help by teaching them outsiding, the money he'd won at the casino, the seaside, chess, anything.

'Well, you know the theory that everything has a spirit, a soul, even the most menial of objects?'

Max nodded. After all he'd been through in the last week, he sure wasn't going to bet against it.

'And so I got to thinking that maybe it's not because people lose their shoes, but maybe it's the shoes who lose their people!'

'Oh?' This was going to be a tough one, he just knew it.

'So last night...'

Here we go.

'...I couldn't sleep. I guess I was just too excited about having learned to outside. So I decided instead to test my new theory...'

Here's the crunch.

'And I placed one of your shoes out on the lip of the balcony wall, in a position where it couldn't fall off, but could easily get confused by the isolation and vast expanse it was suddenly confronted with.'

'Which one?'

'The bedroom balcony.'

'No. Which shoe?'

'A shiny, red one.'

She was mad.

'And guess what?'

He didn't need to.

'This morning when I woke up – you'd already left for Salsomaggiore by then, of course, it was about tennish – I went out to the balcony and it had vanished!'

Max shifted a little on the branch he was sitting on and sighed quietly to himself again. What had she got against his clothing anyway? Why was it always *his* stuff she picked on? It took ages to wear in a good pair of shoes so that they were just the right shape to fit your foot.

'So it had completely vanished? No trace below the balcony?'

'No, absolutely none.' She sounded so pleased with herself.

'So what do you think happened?'

'Well, either it panicked and got lost...'

'Shoe panic?'

'Exactly! Suddenly finding itself out in the open like that, it got disorientated, or even frightened by the vastness before it, panicked and simply wandered off like a child who'd lost his mother in a supermarket.'

'Or maybe it was simply carried off by a cat or something,' Max suggested sadly.

Silence.

'Yes,' she said thoughtfully. 'I had considered that as a possible alternative explanation. Yes. Shoe-napping cats. Cats that prey on frightened, isolated and defenceless shoes and drag them off, abandoning them to their fate at the sides of roads and in parks and things.'

'I find the first theory slightly more feasible,' announced Max, after a decent and respectful period of mourning.

Chapter Forty-Two

Andersson cautiously stepped over the broken door and the body lying underneath it. He edged past a semi-conscious hippy covered in a strange, suspicious-looking brown substance, and then he spotted him.

'Belvois! My God, man! What have they done to you?'

He rushed over to the immobile, bearded form on the ground, but, as he did so, a hand grabbed him firmly on the shoulder, restraining him from advancing further. Andersson reeled wildly.

'Industrial espionage, I can only assume,' said Belvois calmly, zipping up his flies with the other free hand.

'Ah, Belvois! My boy! I knew nothing could have happened to you!' Andersson was genuinely relieved. His merchandise was in one piece.

'Yes, sir. Probably the Arabs.' He nodded towards the unconscious form dressed in a white, Arabic gown under the door.

'But you sorted them out magnificently.' Andersson laughed and patted Belvois on the back. 'You'll have to give me a full report after you've won the tournament. One more game, my boy, and we've bagged the lot.'

He pulled his mobile phone from out of his light, cotton sports jacket and added, 'You go back upstairs and finish the action there. I'll make a quick call to security and see to these clowns, whoever they are.'

Obediently, and without even a glance backwards, Belvois started up the stairs to the tournament hall.

'By the way,' Andersson called up after him, 'have you seen the General?'

'No,' came the reply, sharp and simple.

'Hello, police?' While talking, he searched the clothing of the unconscious Arab at his feet. Maybe he could find some clue as to who these people were. 'Fzzz… puff…' responded his state-of-the-art communication device. Andersson's brow knitted. Perhaps there was a problem with reception from down in the basement. He tried again. 'Hello, police?'

'Fzzz... puff... wheeee... bang!' said his super-small two hundred dollar phone. Flames exploded from the back of the gadget, and instinctively he let it go. It fell to the ground and shattered into six or seven interesting and rather artistic shapes which continued to burn and spark with great zeal.

Shocked and somewhat dismayed, Andersson took one step back, placed his foot unseeingly in some of the scattered remains of Chris's curry, and slipped, falling head over heels backwards. His head hit the solid stone floor with a very loud and echoey crack.

And then there were four...

His senses began to return. Through blurred vision, Blitzkrieg could make out Caissa's form over by the drinks cabinet. She was serving that devil, Belfagor, with a drink, and the bastard was over the other side, lording it with his feet up on the sofa.

'A little Beaujolais would be nice,' he was saying.

Blitzkrieg groaned and rubbed his throbbing jaw.

'What about you, Blitzy, dear? Do you need anything?'

'Aspirin.' The word grated up his throat, but it came out intelligibly enough anyway.

'Aww, let him be!' said Belfagor. 'Self-pity is his best medicine. Come over here and bring me that drink you promised.'

Drink! Of course, that was it! That was what she meant!

'A beer,' he croaked. 'Give me a beer.'

'Here, catch!' shouted Caissa, and deftly launched a can at him.

'Whaaaa!' cried Belfagor in surprise, because 'Whaa!' was in fact the only reaction he had a chance to make. In the time it had taken him to complete the final diphthong, honed reflexes had caught, opened, downed the contents, and crushed and thrown the can dead-centre into a paper basket in the corner of the room. Small marks of chipped wall paint just above the basket gave previous evidence of such remarkable marksmanship. The fastest ring pull in the western hemisphere – maybe even the fastest in existence – was once more in action.

'NNAAARRRG!'

'Oh, goody!' said Caissa, clapping her hands. The transformation was usually something she regarded as rather vulgar, but she'd learnt to live with it. After all, a beer god has to do what a beer god has to do, she reasoned. All the same, Saturday night piss-ups with his mates around her place were not and would never be permitted.

'Yurr!' yurred Blitzkrieg in delight. 'Extra strong special brew!'

His hair receded, the biceps and pot-belly quadrupled, the tattoos reappeared on his forearms and his jeans once again dropped down just far enough to expose a good clean section of workman's bum. Quite exemplary, Caissa thought. Although she'd never quite fathomed how the jeans managed to do what they did.

Belfagor stood up, aware that events could be taking a turn for the serious. He'd heard tales about the vulgarities of the hop gods – he'd always been a grape man himself – but he'd never really had any direct experience with one. A bit like dogs for cats, hop drinkers generally made for uncouth and unpleasant company for him and his ilk.

He stared, a little taken aback as, in the blink of an eye, the growling, raving blob consumed another three cans, basketing all three one after the other.

With the back of his hand, Blitzkrieg wiped the froth from his mouth and turned to face Caissa. For some reason he was real mad but he'd be damned if he could remember why.

'Slaaag!' he roared at her, and the drinks cabinet trembled.

Caissa raised her hands in a gesture of innocence. 'Not me, dear,' she exclaimed, a hint of amusement in her voice. 'Him!' She turned and pointed at Belfagor.

'You fuckin' what?' Blitzkrieg suddenly half remembered why he was feeling so narked.

For the first time in his devilish career, Belfagor began to feel a strong churning in his stomach. Well, no, actually, not exactly the *first* time. There had been that terrifying confrontation with the other guy, the one who stank really badly of brimstone, the one who was holding all those karma debtors until their trials came up – 'Judgement Day' had been the slang terminology for a fair few centuries. So, for the *second* time in his devilish career of manipulation, cheating, adultery and other such fiendish acts, Prince Belfagor was a bit scared.

'You're gunna get your fuckin' head kicked in!' It was chanting at him while approaching much too rapidly for his liking.

Belfagor took a wild swing at the charging blob, but a giant hand caught his fist and a crushing hammer blow landed squarely between the horns on the top of his head.

It was Prince Belfagor's turn to feel his legs crumble beneath him and sink humiliatingly to the ground.

How could this vulgar hop-consumer be so immensely strong? Then it occurred to him, as all the little stars completed their final orbit around his head, that the rise in popularity of beer over recent centuries probably had something to do with it. Possibly more people now worshipped beer than they did wine. Whatever the case, that had really hurt.

The initial terror, however, had passed. Now he was peeved. He sprang nimbly to his feet, facing his assailant, and gave a blood-curdling roar, the same roar he had used many times and to great effect on angry farmers who had banded together to avenge the wounded honour of village girls.

Fire and brimstone exploded around him, burning away the blue military uniform to reveal a huge, hairy, well-muscled chest and strong, powerful, goat-like legs. He was feeling mean and he roared again, beating his naked chest with his fists.

Modestly, Caissa averted her gaze, but then curiosity got the best of her and, despite herself, she glanced down between his legs and swallowed hard. So it wasn't just a sensation she'd had before when he had pressed her tightly up against him. The legends really were true.

The human facade now completely burnt away, Prince Belfagor stood in all his natural glory. Facing his adversary, he opened his mouth wide to issue another spine-chilling roar. However, before he could utter a sound, a cruel but nevertheless highly pertinent crystal decanter flew at him, smashing and shattering its way through millennium-old teeth. And so Prince

Belfagor bit the carpet rug once more.

But gods of mischief are made of sturdier stuff, and that was the last straw. Staggering to his feet, eyes red, nostrils snorting blue flames, he spat the remaining loose teeth from his mouth. As his vision cleared, he blinked in disbelief at what he saw. That intolerable piece of malt and hop vulgarity, that styleless, uneducated, ignorant slob had made his final arrogant and most fatal mistake. He was back at the drinks cabinet, one arm around the girl, as she helped him guzzle down a six-pack of lager.

He leapt forward, a huge leap of supernatural distance and force that would have taken him right through the wall on the other side of the room if he hadn't intended to use the blob as a cushioning bumper.

Caissa just had time to issue a warning squeak before Belfagor completed his devastating attack, smashing his face with a sickening snapping sound on to Blitzkrieg's idly outstretched fist that still happened to be gripping a half-full can of lager.

The air finally cleared itself of beer and blood, and Blitzkrieg slowly turned to look down at the crumpled pile of limbs at his feet. He gave it a disdainful kick, and it rolled harmlessly away to the back of the sofa.

Caissa decided it was time to prepare a good hot curry, but, before going into the kitchen, she walked over to the other door that led to the games room and popped her head inside.

'You boys all right? I hope the noise didn't disturb you too much.'

The Frenchman and the American both raised their heads from the game and looked a little puzzled. 'What noise?' they asked in unison.

Satisfied that her guests were not wanting for anything, Caissa headed for the kitchen, stopping only to glance and smile at the favourable end-game position on the marble chessboard that had remained miraculously untouched through the carnage of beer froth, blood and broken furniture around it.

Chapter Forty-Three

After the break, there was a small but curious disturbance when four people, one of them a major tournament sponsor, were discovered unconscious in the basement toilets and taken to hospital.

Initially, Andersson's identification had caused an understandable sense of apprehension, until someone pointed out that the presentation cheques were all signed and valid; then things went back to normal and players began to seat themselves at their newly designated tables.

Belvois seemed unstoppable. At the end of the fifth game, only Joel Montaud, the French international master with four and a half points, was capable of stopping him. Max, on the other hand, due to his one loss, was now sitting at table five while, at the number one board, the ominous figure of Belvois awaited the arrival of his final victim.

'Ooh, my lucky number!' exclaimed the Frenchman, as he came up to the table, dabbed at his mouth with a white handkerchief to remove any remains of the coffee he'd just knocked back, and sat down opposite his opponent.

Max cringed in anticipation at what he knew was coming.

Belvois scowled across the board at the Frenchman as he offered his hand.

'Luck?' He stabbed Montaud's choice of word and left it lying bleeding in the gutter. 'Luck is something you need when playing children's games such as Monopoly or Snakes and Ladders. In this game there exists only varying levels of incompetence, the winner being the one who demonstrates himself to be the least incapable of the two.'

Montaud retracted his hand, pursed his lips thoughtfully and nodded amiably at the theory.

Max, eavesdropping intently along with all the other players in earshot, raised his eyebrows. It was obvious that he had decided to change psychological tactics for the last game.

Belvois went on. 'It remains to be seen then, if your level of incompetence is lower than mine.' He paused for effect. 'But I doubt it greatly.'

It was Montaud's turn to scowl. He made the first move, 1.e4, and hit the clock angrily, forcing Belvois to play his. 1. _ g5. And it was just then that the unspeakable happened.

They hadn't been seen on the tournament circuit for a long time, ever since certain FSI officials had laid a trap for them and succeeded in locking the group inside an empty tournament hall for the whole weekend last winter. But now, inexplicably, they had returned once more to terrorise the entire chess community. In front of the hundreds of eyes in that tournament hall – players, press, organisers and sponsors alike – the chess world was to be stricken once again by the hit-and-run tactics of the Chess Cheerleaders Club. Yes, the CCC was back.

Everyone stopped what they were doing and stared. Yet again, they'd managed to infiltrate security measures. Yet again, they'd succeeded in slipping past the professional staff on the door. (Well, to tell the truth, the professional staff was called Gino and happened to be a cousin of one of the organisers, and on a normal day loaded and unloaded furniture in a warehouse, but that's beside the point.) Yet again, they'd managed to disrupt an austere and dramatic moment in chess history.

Nobody knew exactly when and where they would strike next, but when they did the effect could only be described as one of pure and utter devastation. Nobody even knew from whence they came (or for that matter, where they legged it to afterwards), or why, in fact, they did it at all. Some blamed it on the IBF (the International Bridge Federation), others on the KGB, saying that they were getting revenge for the mass desertion by quality Russian players to the west and that it was an attempt to lower the tone of European chess. Others said that it was merely genuine, but tragically misplaced, admiration for the players themselves.

Nevertheless, the fact remained that there, before the good, respectable and distinguished people in that hall, now stood three of the most scantily clad nubiles the chess world had ever seen.

'One, two, three...' they began, wildly waving multicoloured pompoms about in the air.

Veteran tournament-goers exchanged wary looks. If a sure-fire method of instant character assassination existed, this was it. They were all wondering who would be the 'chosen one', whose chess career would be on the line this time.

Certainly their last victim, Sergei Livstick, had never fully recovered. It was well known that since that fateful hit he'd never been able to enter a tournament hall again without being the source of anonymous sniggers and muffled chants of 'Go, Sergei, go!' Finally paranoia had got the better of him, his concentration shot, and his consequent retirement from tournament activity left the chess world mourning the loss of one of its most creative talents.

'He's the best there is, yeah! He's the one who knows his biz, yeah!'

The obvious question is: why on earth didn't they just place warning descriptions of these girls in the hands of door security, thereby preventing their entrance and putting a stop to this horror once and for all?

'He's the one that's at the top, yeah!'

The discorded chanting was, of course, interspersed by equally bad-timed and choreographed high kicking and pompom waving.

'He's gonna win the cup cup cup. Yeah!'

Ouch!

Returning quickly to the original question of door security, the problem was quite simple. The vast majority at chess tournaments are men, and, as such, when faced with long, naked limbs and low-cut cleavages, no one had ever paid that much attention to the particular idiosyncrasies of their facial features.

The tension among the players was rising, the very air seemed taut with it.

'Go Belvois…'

The relief was almost tangible.

'…Belvois go!'

Joel Montaud leant forward over the table and whispered his condolences.

'Oh, bad luck, monsieur!'

Belvois just stared at the girls. No emotion could be read into the lines on his face.

But they had by no means finished yet.

The brunette in the middle turned around and bent over to pick something up from the floor behind them, displaying as she did so a pair of beautiful, white, frilly panties underneath her yellow miniskirt.

An ooh! of appreciation passed around the hall and the blonde to her left winked at her friend.

Yes, they were warmed up, the wink said. And ready for the *pièce de résistance*, the final onslaught.

The brunette straightened herself and turned around to reveal – a gasp of horror rose up from the hapless, captive audience – an acoustic guitar!

Belvois' eyes opened wide. Something missing, something that had been balancing precariously on the tip of his mind's tongue for the last few days suddenly got washed off by a torrent of cerebral saliva. The music! The girls! The panties! The guitar!

Convent-educated for a brief period, the brunette had learnt her guitar technique from one of the nuns and had been much sought after during church services.

'I'd like to teach the world to sing,' she began.

Her two 'comrades-in-pompoms' shot her a bewildered look – it was almost too much even for them.

'I know it's not the most appropriate song,' she explained by way of apology, 'but it's the only one I can remember.'

The other two just continued to stare at her.

'I said I could play a little, not that I was Eddie fuckin' van Halen.' At that, the others shrugged their shoulders resignedly and turned back to the job at hand, the recipient of which, having twisted his chair around to face them, was sitting astute and attentive.

So the song continued, punctuated in appropriate places by shouts of 'Yeah!', wild pompom waving, and, of course, the mandatory high kicking.

'Oh, mais c'est trop!' complained the Frenchman despairingly. 'How can one continue to play in such circumstances?'

'No, no, it's wonderful!' Belvois suddenly exclaimed. 'Now I remember. It's all just rock 'n' roll.'

'I beg to differ on that point,' Montaud began, but his words fell on unhearing ears.

'Three chords will do it! Three chords will get you to heaven!' he shouted with joy. 'I remember now! I'm me again!' He threw his hands up in the air, rushed over to where the girls were and hugged them one after the other.

Dumbfounded, they stopped and let themselves be embraced; nobody had ever shown such enthusiasm for their work before.

That smell! He recognised that perfume. Belvois turned back to the brunette and, with a swift movement of his hand, whisked away the wig she was wearing. Blonde hair tumbled out from underneath in great ringlets.

'Cathy!' he exclaimed with joy. 'Is it really you? Oh, I've missed you!' His voice held no trace of the cold, emotionless tones of moments before. He was like a man waking up from a long nightmare. With Cathy still in his embrace, he glanced around the hall at all the surprised faces.

'Oh, Belvois!' Cathy nearly sobbed with relief. 'You're back again. Tell me it's true!'

'It's true.'

She grasped his face between her hands. 'I thought they'd damaged your mind, destroyed you. I felt so awful, so desperate, I thought I'd lost you for ever.'

They kissed passionately.

'Bravo, bravo!' Heartfelt cheers and applause broke out from the spellbound spectators.

'Best goddamned value for money tournament I've ever been to,' announced a sincere American voice from the crowd.

The other blonde CCC member approached Cathy and whispered, 'Can we go now, then?'

Cathy twisted inside Belvois' embrace and signalled with a nod to the affirmative. 'Yeah, thanks a lot. And thanks for the loan of the guitar.'

So, while the attention was safely centred on the kissing couple, the two girls swiftly packed up the guitar and snuck quietly off.

'C'mon!' said Belvois. 'We've got a lot to talk about.' They were about to walk out of the hall together when she looked up into his eyes.

'And the tournament?'

Belvois halted. The tournament, of course! Well, what did he give a damn? He was himself again and he'd got Cathy back. And anyway, after the way Andersson had treated the both of them, his debt was paid. He had no intention of wasting another second and turned back to where he had been sitting. The game hadn't progressed very far.

1.e4 g5.

2.d4.

Belvois winked at his opponent and made his move.

2. _ f5.

Montaud frowned for a split second, and then his face shone with happiness. 'Merci, monsieur,' he exclaimed with joy.

3.Qh5 mate.

'Queen to h5, mate,' nodded Belvois, and grinned. 'Looks as if you were right and luck truly is on your side today.' He toppled his own king over on the board. 'You win,' he announced happily, and gave a little bow to the other players around him.

'Au contraire,' said the little French master as Belvois turned to leave, 'the lady luck eez with you today.'

Belvois placed his arm around Cathy and led her out of the hall. 'Until the next time,' he called back suddenly, 'ha ha ha ha!'

'That was a good sinister laugh you got in at the end there,' commented Cathy in genuine admiration as they walked interlocked down the corridor and past the bookstalls. 'Superb gothic resonance.'

'Thanks,' replied Belvois, sounding pleased. 'The hall acoustics helped a lot, and it made a nice little finishing touch, didn't it?'

And the two walked out of the cool mustiness of the tournament building into the slowly setting sun.

Chapter Forty-Four

When he came round, Chris still had the smell of disinfectant in his nostrils and, with it, all the visions of the nightmarish event came flooding back.

'Aaah!' he screamed and sat up straight, only to find that he was no longer in that terrible toilet place, but in some kind of luxury hotel room. Plants and flowers bloomed outside their window and a colour television near the ceiling was giving the latest cricket scores in English. Ali and Morph lay in separate beds next to his.

'So, the hippy wakes.' Morph's voice rose up from out of the pages of a magazine.

'Morph! Ali! We're still alive!'

'Yes,' replied Ali, 'and we seem to be in some kind of very expensive private hospital ward.'

A look of panic swept across Chris's features. 'Oh, jeez! Am I still in one piece?' He started frantically checking all his limbs. 'Oh, doh! My doze. He beat me up and broke my doze.'

'You're all just fine,' came a woman's voice from the doorway.

Their heads turned to see Caissa smiling at them.

'A few bruises, but no broken bones. Nothing serious.'

She looked from one to the other sympathetically. Chris and Morph both sported splendid, bandaged noses, and, outdoing them both, Ali had a bandaged nose, chest and also hands, after holding them up instinctively to protect himself from the falling door.

'Poor boys!' she pouted, feeling somewhat guilty.

'Jacqueline!' exclaimed Chris. 'I'm sorry we didn't succeed with the plan.'

Morph rolled his eyes in despair. Stupid lovesick hippy. 'Well, I think we've suffered enough as it is. I don't think it's us who have to apologise. All morning in that awful place and then getting beaten up for it afterwards!'

'No, you're quite right,' Caissa responded sincerely. 'But we won anyway.'

'Really? How?' asked Ali incredulously.

'Oh, that, I'll explain another time. Suffice it to say that one of the bad guys had a change of heart, so to speak. And Chris managed to take out the big bad boss.'

'I did?'

'Yes, dear. Indirectly. He slipped on your curry sauce and is now in another wing of this hospital suffering from amnesia.'

Chris suddenly looked very pleased with himself.

'So we didn't need Ali to ruin his secret computer or anything – just spill some of Chris's leftover curry,' concluded Morph, shaking his head at the irony of the situation.

'Oh, and that's something I wanted to talk to you about,' Caissa added, turning to Ali. 'I have something for you that will help alleviate your er... allergy.'

Ali tried to straighten up a little in bed. Caissa handed him some herbs in a packet.

'More herbs!' he exclaimed, more than a little disappointed. He wasn't really sure what he had been hoping for, but somehow herbs... Chris was already looking interested.

'Oh, but I assure you this stuff really works.'

'So you *are* some kind of witch, then!' Ali declared knowingly.

'Well, yes, in a way. But this I got from an old friend who really knows a thing or two about herbal remedies, trust me.' She handed him the packet. 'He told me that you should roll it up and smoke it, and that your problem will not return. It's a permanent cure.'

'Smoke it? Far out, man!'

'Best keep it away from him,' Morph advised, throwing a disapproving look at the hippy.

Ali held the packet up and inspected it. 'You know,' he suddenly announced with a strange sigh, 'for so many years I have been plagued by this allergy that machines have to me, and it is only now when I feel I can cure the problem once and for all that I am not sure that I want to.'

'Uh?' grunted Morph and Chris in unison.

'Well, you see,' he went on, 'I have just realised that it is not so much a problem, but something that makes me special. Something that makes me stand out from the crowd.'

'The beardomorph finally got to you, did he?' interrupted Chris.

'So, thank you very much and I accept this with gratitude, but I do not think I will be smoking it just yet.'

Caissa smiled at him. 'It's yours to do with as you wish.'

She went over to Chris and kissed him on the cheek. 'Here,' she said, 'take this, it'll bring you luck.' She handed him a little ankh-shaped talisman. 'Wear it round your neck and never remove it.'

'Far out!' said Chris, studying its wooden simplicity. He placed it over his neck. 'And the astral travelling?'

She winked at him. 'Oh, for that I'll be seeing you in your dreams.'

She turned to Morph and kissed him too on the cheek. 'Thanks for your patience and all your help. I'd like to be able to explain everything, but I'm afraid it wouldn't be right.'

She went over to the door. 'Oh, by the way. This is a private clinic and your stay and room is all paid up until you're ready to leave. Be seeing you, boys.'

She was turning to leave when Chris shouted after her, 'But what about Morph? Doesn't he get anything?'

Caissa smiled, pointed to Morph's mobile phone by the side of his bed and winked. It burst into life, and Morph picked it up. 'Hello?'

The momentary distraction was enough. When their eyes returned to the doorway she was gone.

A minute later Morph terminated the call and shook his head in astonishment. 'How did she do that?'

'Well? Who was it? Did what?' asked Chris, impatiently.

'It was the office phoning to say we've just received a massive order from several private hospitals and clinics in the Bournemouth area that are in desperate need of all sorts of plastic signs and room numbers!'

'Is everything all right?' asked one of the ship's waiters as he passed them with a trolley of sweets destined for the perusal of the family of five the next table on.

'Absolutely fine,' responded Belvois, and he took another sip of his grappa liquor.

'The captain would like to know if sir will be playing with the band again this evening. Your performance yesterday was truly superlative and most appreciated by all.'

'Please inform the captain that a little later on I'll be very happy to do so, yes.'

'Splendid,' the waiter replied, and then gave the thumbs up to the captain at the other end of the boat. 'Oh, and tomorrow evening the captain also requests the pleasure of your company at his table for dinner.'

Belvois looked over the table at the elegant, blonde beauty sitting opposite and raised his eyebrows. She laughed.

'Please tell him we'll be honoured to accept his invitation. Thank you very much,' said Cathy.

The waiter nodded courteously and left, pushing his trolley over to the three drooling children in the family behind them.

Belvois and Cathy got up and strolled out of the dining room and through the doors which led out to the open port-side deck of the ship. The huge Mediterranean moon lit the sea with a thousand twinkling lights and Cathy slipped her arm around Belvois' waist and sighed. 'It's so beautiful. A cruise ship to the Orient was such a good idea. I only wish it could go on for ever.'

'It can,' replied Belvois simply. 'With the money I've got saved in the Swiss bank account, and with some cunning investments, the interest rate alone would pay for…'

'That's not what I meant,' she interrupted. 'Besides, there's the matter of my research to continue. The little gizmo that you've got installed there could help cure a lot of other people's problems too. Just look what it's done for your sight. I was wrong to have let Andersson convince me otherwise. No more super soldiers. And then there's your rock 'n' roll pilgrimage tour to be considered. "Three Chords Away From Heaven" and all that.'

Almost without thinking she brushed his hair back to check the implant behind his ear. Belvois winced away.

'I wish you'd stop doing that!' he reprimanded her, more sharply than he had intended. 'There's absolutely no need.'

'Sorry. Force of habit.'

'And I'm not sure about the rock tour. Anyway, you'll be needing an assistant in all this, and who better than...'

'A know-it-all like yourself?' she teased.

Belvois grinned at her. 'There are some things that I still find hard to comprehend, like your involvement in that weird chess hit-and-run terrorist group, the CCC. I think I must be missing something there."

Cathy shook her head, placed her hands on the ship's railings and gazed out at the calm sea.

'No, you're not missing anything. They were all in cahoots with a woman called Jacqueline King who is one of the members of the Italian chess federation, itself part of some national sports organisation, UEFA or FIFA or something...'

'The FSI and FIDE,' Belvois corrected her.

'Anyway, it's just as much a mystery to me as it is to you. I was just about to leave my apartment to come to see if I could help you when I got a call from her. Apparently, she seemed to know almost everything and wanted to find a way of getting you out of the tournament legally without losing the sponsorship which could damage the organisation's reputation for future events.'

'Indeed. The FSI doesn't have the funds to pay out that kind of money without sponsorship. It could have been very embarrassing for them.'

'Exactly. And if you were expelled from the match, Andersson would have withdrawn everything. However, if you were to lose the last game, Andersson would be legally obliged to pay up anyway. And she said that I was probably the only one who might have a chance of convincing you to do so.'

'She was right.'

'But to do so you had to be the Pierre that I had known before and not the cold monster that you'd become. She said she'd had a long chat with a very eminent psychologist who seemed to think that there was a strong possibility that some form of shock might bring you back to your normal self, but that there was no time to waste. She had a plan, but it also required my full cooperation.'

'So you used the three things that were closest to my heart to shock me back to normality.'

'Yup,' she answered, jovially. 'Music, the sight of the guitar, and...'

'You.' He kissed the nape of her neck. 'And the brown wig was so that Andersson or Menti wouldn't recognise you until too late. But what if I had refused to lose or quit the tournament? All said and done, it was the last game. What would you have done then?'

She punched him playfully in the side. 'After all I'd gone through?' She pushed her lithe form up against him and wiggled a finger between the buttons on his shirt, rubbing a patch of bare skin on his chest. 'Besides, I knew that if I succeeded in getting you back to your normal self, there'd be nothing you could refuse me.'

Belvois nodded in willing acquiescence. She was dead right there. He took her by the arm and began to lead her back inside the dining hall where the band was just starting up. 'And the motivation behind the CCC girls? Why do they do it?'

'That's part of the mystery. Not even Jacqueline King knew that. But she said that for every good thing there was a bad side and vice versa. Even though they are not too appreciated by the players, or at least by their victims, the crowd and press love them, and some turn up in the hope of getting a snapshot just of them. They bring a lot of publicity and outside interest to the tournaments so they have always been secretly tolerated by the highest levels of her organisation. A kind of necessary evil if you like.'

'And for this one time, they managed to come to some reciprocal agreement?'

'Yes. Although Jacqueline said she'd had to coax them out of retirement. Apparently, about six months ago, some of the less-informed members of the FSI organisation had succeeded in tricking the girls into attending a false tournament and had locked them up for an entire weekend in an empty hall all alone.'

'All's fair in love and war, I suppose.'

'Yes, but the poor things were so shocked by their experience – it was such a very cold winter and they'd had hardly any clothes on and nothing to eat – they had sworn never to do it again.'

'But this woman got them to change their minds?'

'All except one.'

'Well, who knows! After their unmitigated success this time, with any luck, they might decide to make a comeback,' said Belvois.

'Oh, I really do hope so. Such nice girls!'

They walked up to the bar where the one barman was already under siege. The band were still tuning up.

'Just promise me one thing,' said Belvois, turning his attention from the stage, 'that you'll accept a few guitar lessons before ever performing in public again!'

Epilogue

'Oh, go on. The B-one-one-twelves. The black bombers, you know, the amphetamine antidepressants.'

'No.'

'Well, how 'bout some of the reds you gave the guy that was in the room next to mine. He told me they were dynamite, had him trippin' out for hours.'

'No.'

'A couple of barbs, then? Barbiturates?'

'No.'

'Not even a couple of blue F-thirty-ones?'

'No. And anyway there's no such thing.'

'Just teasing. Well, how 'bout a valium?'

Huffily, Nurse Ryder finished tucking in the bed sheets and carried the tray with the remains of her patient's breakfast out of the door and disappeared down the corridor. She was used to male in-patients bugging her for something other than her access to the drug cabinet.

Chris lay in the hospital bed and sighed. Briefly, he toyed with the idea of smoking some more of Ali's herbal remedy, but then decided against it – he was on too much of a downer. Here he was, back in the same Bournemouth clinic that he'd originally been abducted from three weeks before, back where it had all started. 'Some good luck that thing brought me,' he moaned in self-pity. He hoisted the amulet which still hung around his neck and examined it for the thousandth time. Maybe she'd lied to him. Maybe Morph was right and he was just a lovesick hippy. It all seemed so unfair. Morph had got a magnificent contract of work, Ali his cure, well, most of it anyway. And himself...? Well, she hadn't even bothered to visit him in his dreams, let alone teach him how to astral-travel.

'Poisoned again by probably the only bad burger still in circulation.' He rolled over on to his side and stared out the window of his private room. Rain was pelting down outside. 'It could have been worse,' they'd said. 'The burger could have been contaminated with mad cow disease,' they'd said. 'You're a very lucky young man,' they'd said. He glared at the amulet, feeling somewhat betrayed.

The summer was over and he'd spent most of it in and out of hospitals.

'You haven't changed anything!' he accused the wooden ankh.

He was just on the verge of disposing of it once and for all when there was a polite tap on the door.

'Yeah?'

The door opened, and a tall, skinny, pinstriped suit with matching pointy nose and chin stood framed in the doorway. 'I'm awfully sorry to disturb but I'm looking for a Mr Hasi. I was informed that this was his temporary abode.'

'You what?'

'Mr Hasi?'

'Yeah?'

'Mr Christopher Hasi?'

'That's me, man.'

'Oh, good! I do apologise for it taking me so long to find you. I've been here just over...' he glanced at his watch, '...two hours. You see, I couldn't find your room; had to keep asking directions from nurses and people. No numbers on the doors, you see. And the few corridor and ward indications that are around are all scribbled in the most terrible handwriting on sheets of paper that have been stuck as temporary signs to walls, quite illegible. Strange case that, though.'

'What?'

'Well, apparently, a short time ago, someone stole all the signs and room numbers off the doors and walls. Most mysterious. Oh, but I'm forgetting myself. May I come in?'

'Uh, yeah, sure, man,' answered Chris, a little surprised that someone had actually asked his permission to enter the room; he'd got so used to people just barging in and out, checking his pulse rate, his temperature, and not giving him any decent pills.

The man reached inside his jacket pocket and handed him a business card.

'Arthur Wicket Junior of Wicket and Wicket Insurance,' he announced, perhaps a little too over-dramatically.

Chris read the card which informed him of more or less the same thing, apart from a couple of phone numbers and a fax.

'We've been authorised by our client Meat and Things, to offer you a small compensation for your er...' he looked at Chris in the hospital bed while trying to find the right adjective, 'discomfort.'

'Oh, yeah?' He glanced down at his amulet dubiously. A lifetime's supply of beefies, maybe?

'In return for your absolute discretion in this matter, of course, and by signing this document here which protects our client from all legal responsibility for your present condition.' He rustled a sheet of paper in Chris's direction.

'Huh?'

'You're not to breathe a word of what has happened to the press or anyone like that. And, in return for your absolute silence, goodwill and complete cooperation in this matter, I have been authorised to offer you the following sum of monies.'

He handed Chris a cheque and the words 'For fifty thousand pounds' floated once around the room on the mystical musical strains of a genuine Indian sitar and then flew out of the window and got lost somewhere in a field of marijuana and sunshine.

Max was sitting working at the computer in his apartment the next time he saw Caissa.

'And here's me thinking you'd be lolling it up on some tropical island with Maria.'

'Book first, tropical island later,' he said, getting up and greeting her with a kiss on both sides of the face – some Latin ways do have certain advantages. 'I've got to try to do my little bit for mankind before doing my bit for myself.'

Caissa raised her eyebrows at him. 'Most commendable.' She tried to peer over his shoulder, but he blocked her view.

'For that you can wait until it's published.'

'Well, the least you could do is tell me what it's called.'

'*Outsiding: What it's about and how to do it*,' he answered. 'What do you think?'

She looked at him thoughtfully for a minute and replied, 'I hope you haven't said anything about me in it. That could destroy its credibility completely.'

Max nodded. 'No. It's just a straight fact guide, more or less, and a list of some of its potential advantages. The other stuff, that casino and everything, that's all best left for those who wish to make the discovery on their own. Anyway, I'm not sure even *I* believe it and I've been there.'

'Good. Otherwise you'd be declared as loopy as all the others.'

'What others?'

'Hmm. Let's forget it.' She looked around her. 'Where's Maria?'

'Working.'

Caissa looked surprised. 'Why? Didn't you take enough money from the place in San Remo?'

'Yes, and to be honest, when we need some more, I'll be quite happy to repeat things. But the bar where she works is owned by her parents and she has to look after it until they get back from holiday in another week – family commitments.'

Caissa glanced around the room and wondered casually for a moment at the one, red and shiny man's shoe in the bin. 'Well, anyway I just popped by to thank you for your help.'

'Oh,' said Max, looking a little downcast. 'I didn't do very well on that score. It was Belvois himself who decided on that.'

'I know. But you did your best. And it takes many parts to make a whole, and a game can't be won without all a side's pieces cooperating in harmony. We won in the end, didn't we?'

Max smiled. 'Well, it may interest you to know that I didn't make it to master status, after all, because I lost to Belvois, an unclassified player, but at least I got a share of the winnings and another little trophy for coming fourth.' He pointed over to the top shelf of his bookcase which displayed a number of different shaped cups and other types of trophies, some having lost their shine and lustre over the years.

'I know that too. I'm just sorry I couldn't be there for the final presentations.'

'And now it's my turn to thank you for all your help and guidance. I'm totally indebted. Without your explanation and advice I'm sure I would have gone truly loopy, as you put it.'

'Paid in full,' answered Caissa, airily. 'And now I've got to fly. There are a lot of major and minor tournaments over the next few months to be attended.'

'I'll be seeing you at one or two of them, then,' said Max, kissing her on both cheeks – some Latin ways *really* do have certain advantages. 'Oh, by the way, there is one more thing I'd like to ask you before you take off.'

'Shoot!'

'Do you remember the washing machine episode?'

'Oh, yes,' she laughed. 'An idea of Blitzkrieg's I'm afraid. You're not still upset about that little joke, are you?'

'No, no. It's just that I'd like to know...'

'Yes?'

'That is, if you do know...'

'Yes?'

'What happened to my socks?'